WHERE Hope STARTS

ANGELA D. MEYER

CrossRiver

WHERE HOPE STARTS
Copyright © 2013 Angela D. Meyer

ISBN: 978-1936501-151

All rights reserved. No part of this publication may be reproduced or transmitted in any form or by any means, electronic, mechanical, photocopying, recording or otherwise, without written permission of the publisher. Published by CrossRiver Media Group, PO Box 187, Brewster, KS 67732, www.crossrivermedia.com

All Scripture quotations in this publication are from THE MESSAGE. Copyright © by Eugene H. Peterson 1993, 1994, 1995, 1996, 2000, 2001, 2002. Used by permission of NavPress Publishing Group.

This book is a work of fiction. Names, places, characters and incidents are either products of the author's imagination or used fictitiously. Any similarity to actual people, organizations or events is coincidental.

For more information on Angela D. Meyer, please visit — www.AngelaDMeyer.com

Editor: Debra L. Butterfield
Proofreader: Alice McVicker
Printed in the United States of America

To my family.
You made it possible for me to
pursue my dreams. I love you!

Acknowledgments

*A*lmost five years ago I penned the first words to *Where Hope Starts*. Since then, I've had a lot of help bringing it to publication.

To *God*, thank you for opening a door when I least expected it and most needed it, giving me a nudge to pursue my dream.

To my husband, thank you *Kevin* for walking this journey with me.

To my kids, thank you *Elizabeth and Matt* for your patience during the many hours of writing, editing and marketing when I had to delay our times together.

To my publisher, thank you for believing in my story and being with me every step of the way with advice, education, and support.

To my dear friend *Sharon Miller*, thank you for dreaming with me, being a sounding board for all my plans and ideas, getting excited about the process with me, crying and laughing with me and praying for me. You are indeed a faithful and cherished friend.

To my *beta readers*, thank you for faithfully reading my manuscript and giving me valuable feedback.

To *Ryan Crosby*, thank you for giving your time, energy and expertise to make my book trailer a reality.

To *Andrea , Luke and Matt*, thank you for volunteering your time to portray the characters in my story for the book trailer.

To Omaha City police officer, *Kim Woolery*, thank you for providing me with background on police work and the jail system.

1

Come home.

Karen Marino choked back a cry as she stared at the words scribbled on the front of the envelope. She slid her fingernail under the flap and gaped at the plane ticket nestled inside a letter. *Why now?* She gritted her teeth. Heat flushed from her neck to the top of her head as she remembered the look of disgust on her father's face.

The clash of pans in the restaurant kitchen startled her back to the present. "What the...?"

She glanced at her watch. *Almost eleven.* She slid the ticket and letter back inside the envelope and tucked it into her purse. She took a deep breath before stepping out of her office.

"Steve, how does the schedule look?" Karen hired him straight out of culinary school. His lack of experience paled next to his talent, and within a year his specialties had drawn in customers from all over New York City's five boroughs, earning the restaurant a five-star reputation.

"Perfect, my love." He crossed his arms and smiled. "Now, when are you going to marry me?"

She laughed. "Your mother would be disappointed. I have more red hair than Irish blood." She enjoyed the attention her hair brought in The City, where she no longer stood out like an apple on an orange tree.

"My ma would love you anyway." Steve placed his hand over his heart.

She shook her head and waved him back to work, then strode through the kitchen inspecting the line cooks as they prepped for the noon rush. "Be sure and clean up as you go....No, not that dish. Use the glass one. And keep a towel nearby....How long have you worked here?...Don't wipe your hands on your apron."

She stopped. "Jimmy," she yelled above the din of the kitchen. Her voice carried to the break room where the young man sauntered out with a donut in one hand and a coffee cup in the other.

"Yeah?"

She glared at him. "What's with all these dirty pots and pans?"

The guy shrugged. "Had somewhere to be last night, so I saved them."

"Get rid of that donut now and finish your job in the next half hour, or you're fired, no matter who your cousin is."

He threw the donut and coffee in the trash can and plodded off to his station.

"Karen."

"What!"

"You okay?" Her assistant manager, Cathy, raised an eyebrow.

"Sorry, didn't mean to snap." Karen took a deep breath. "Is the dining room ready?"

"No problems there. But…" Cathy glanced over her shoulder. "Barry's at the bar."

"Not with the new owner coming in." Karen clenched her fists. If she talked to her husband now she would lose her cool. "Did you tell him I was busy?"

"Yes. But, he's got that look."

Karen rolled her eyes. That meant another of Barry's money-making ideas. Ideas didn't pay the rent. "I better go talk to him."

Barry grinned as she approached and she paused at the sight of his dark wavy hair and strong jaw line. If life were a photo, he would take her breath away. But once you added sound and action, that fantasy vanished.

She bit her lip. A part of her longed for what they used to have. *How does a man change so much?* He used to lead people. Now he controlled them, like the other night. Karen shuddered, then closed the gap between them. "We're about to open. You need to go. We can talk tonight."

"Like all those other times? Please." He leaned against the bar.

"I said, we'll talk."

Barry slid off the bar stool. Although he stood only a few inches taller than her five foot seven frame and didn't work out enough to have an impressive build, he carried himself with a bravado that demanded attention. "We'll talk now. You'll like this idea. It's a chance to get in on the ground floor of a start-up company."

Karen caught a whiff of liquor on his breath. "A little early to be drinking, don't you think?"

"Don't change the subject." He banged his fist on the bar.

She jumped. His eyes grew dark. She backed away, her eyes frozen on his hands. "You need to leave. Now."

"Why?" Barry's voice grew louder.

"So I won't lose my job." The new owner was a powerful man. Barry could blow it for her.

"Miss Indispensable? Lose her job?" His empty laugh bounced around the deserted room.

"Please." Karen reigned in her hostility.

"I will do as I please." He took a step toward her.

"If you hope to get your hands on my money, try honey not vinegar." She crossed her arms and stared at him.

"What are you talking about?"

"This approach will not get you what you want."

He looked behind her and backed away. "Yeah, maybe we should talk tonight."

Karen wrinkled her brow. *What's got into him now?* She turned. The new owner walked toward her. He reminded her of Danny Devito. Short, stout, and balding. Add a bit of swagger to his walk and you would have her new boss. She groaned. Glancing Barry's direction she saw him leave through the kitchen. *I hope he didn't just cost me my job.*

She turned to face the man. She mustered a smile and extended her hand. "Karen Marino. You must be Mr. Simon."

The man stared at her. "You're fired." He smiled like a kid who just lifted a trinket from the store and got away with it.

"You can't do that." Her throat closed up. *Breathe.*

"I own this place, I can and will clean house as I see fit."

His reputation was well earned. She forced herself to unclench her hands. "I built this restaurant into what it is today."

"There's no place in any of my restaurants for what I just witnessed. Home stays at home."

"You'd get rid of me for one incident?"

"It's not just one incident."

She bit her tongue and glared at the man. *Who talked?*

"Leave now. Come back and clear out your desk after lunch."

"Fine, I don't need you or your restaurant. I have my reputation." She regretted the words as soon as she said them.

"When I'm done, you won't have a reputation."

She turned and fled to her office. A man that powerful didn't make idle threats. She grabbed her purse, squared her shoulders, and marched through the kitchen. She would not be shamed out of here. She did nothing wrong.

Her assistant manager barked orders at the staff. The new owner smiled while he watched. *So Cathy betrayed me.* An old pain grabbed at Karen's heart. *Why do people turn on me?*

Letting the door slam on her way out, she rushed into the flow of human traffic. The wall of buildings hid the breadth of the sky and pressed in around her. Exhaust fumes mingled with the aroma of pizza from a nearby kiosk. She jumped when a taxi blared its horn. Two people shoved each other to get in, arguing over appointments. She picked up her pace, needing to escape the surroundings that for the last fifteen years had made her feel so alive. An image of the family orchard in Missouri filled her heart.

Her past caught up to her present and the old emotions, released from their prison, pinballed around inside her. She ducked into a nearby alley and leaned against the wall. Pressing her hands against the wall, she took several calming breaths against the tears welling up in her chest. She needed to think, not cry.

She pressed her fingertips against her eyes. *I don't want to go back to the apartment yet, and I don't have an office anymore. Where can I go?* She fought the desire to throw things and stomp her feet. She would not lose control.

Something brushed against her elbow and she jerked away. A pungent odor assaulted her nose as a man in a tattered jacket stepped closer.

"Some money for food?" He reached out his hands.

She pushed the man away and tucked her purse close to her body as she stumbled out of the alley and hurried away. Her thoughts latched onto her husband and the impossibility of the situation. Lost in a daze she walked several blocks before her stomach growled, reminding her of the time. She paused and looked around. Carnegie Deli looked like a good choice. Crossing the street, she stood in line for her turn, anxious for the line to move, yet longing for a slower pace.

Pressure built up in her right eye and tension grew between her shoulders. She dug through her purse for some pain reliever and popped two in her mouth.

"Next."

She looked up at the man behind the counter. "Uh, I'm not sure, what—"

"I'll take a Woody Allen and a coffee." A construction worker shouldered his way past Karen, slapping some bills on the counter.

Karen glared at him, then raised her voice above the next person trying to steal her place in line. "Give me a Woody Allen, too."

Within minutes her order sat next to the construction worker's sandwich. She grabbed her plate and cup of coffee, and turned to find a seat in the crowded dining room. From across the room, she saw two women get up from their table. She rushed to grab one of the empty chair.

She settled in to her seat and thought of the first time she came here. She was on a blind date, and he wanted to share his favorite place to eat. Crowded elbow to elbow with strangers at the shared table, it was not exactly romantic, but the food was delicious and plentiful. Her sandwich was piled so high with meat she ate for several days off of the leftovers.

Now, the deli gave her the anonymity she needed.

Cradling the coffee mug in her hands, she allowed the heat to calm her nerves. The day had not gone the way she planned. Lately, not much had. She rubbed her temples then scooted her plate forward to make room for her note pad. Avoiding the glares of her table mates, she pulled out a pen and began to list her options.

Find a job. *In this economy? Right.*

Barry find a job. She laughed.

Dip into her savings. She ripped the paper off the pad and wadded it up. Not again. That money was for the future.

Her head pounded as she fought back the tears. Barry's scheme might be all they had. *Maybe not.*

She reached into her purse and pulled out the letter. Karen remembered how special it felt to be a daughter of Charles and Annibel Hannigan. They were well respected in the community and at church, and then everything changed.

What's so important that they want me to come home now? She laid the ticket aside and unfolded the letter.

Dear Karen,

Please come home. Your mother is dying and she needs to see you. She needs to know you understand. You need to hear what she has to say.
We are both sorry for the past and ask your forgiveness. I've enclosed a plane ticket. Change the date to what works best.

Love, Dad

Her hands trembled as she held the letter. *Mom's dying?*

She laid the letter down and leaned her head onto her hands. She lost their favor with no explanation, and now they offered it to her again on a silver platter. It felt fake. What had she done to lose their favor in the first place? She wiped at tears she couldn't stop. Did they think an apology could make up for everything?

"Hey lady, if you're done, why don't you move on. There's folks waiting for a seat."

Looking the bus boy directly in the eye, she reached for her sandwich and took a bite. He waved at her in dismissal and went back to work.

She glanced out the window as a mother bent down to look her child in the eye. She pointed at a large bulldozer across the street. The little boy smiled, looked back at her and nodded. They hugged. She grabbed his hand and continued walking.

She and her mother used to have a relationship like that. Carrying on like they were the only two people in the world. She looked away. Maybe going home wasn't a viable option either.

She bit her lip. *Am I supposed to just forgive them?* How could they ask that of her? She hit the table with her fist and the coffee mug jumped, spilling onto the letter.

"Hey, watch it!" The man next to her grabbed his paper and picked it up ahead of the offending liquid.

"Sorry." She grabbed some napkins and sopped up the mess. Blowing out a hard breath and tapping her fingers on the table, she checked her phone for the time before dialing her best friend.

Megan and Robert Fletcher reserved a table every Tuesday night at the restaurant Karen managed. Over time she became friends with Megan despite her penchant for religion. She always listened and gave good feedback.

And she's the only person I trust.

Karen wouldn't get the same attentive ear once Megan and Robert had their baby. The call went straight to voice mail, so she left a message. Megan must be at the women's shelter she managed.

Karen picked up the letter and airline ticket and stuffed them in her purse. A walk might help her think better. Catching the waitress' attention, she asked for a to-go bag.

Back on the street, her mind quickly turned to what her lack of employment meant for her life. Stay in New York and try to find another job without a reference. Give Barry's scheme a chance. Or go home.

She cringed at all of those options. Like it or not, she had to consider them or maybe...her steps faltered as she did some quick mental calculations.

It would be risky and Barry wouldn't like it, but she didn't care. She quickened her step. She needed to stop by the bank.

2

"Out of service."

Karen stared at the sign on the elevator. "Ugh." She shifted her box of belongings to the other hip and pushed open the stairwell door. She didn't need this.

Her visit to the bank proved fruitless. A decent investment portfolio and a well-funded savings account aside — no job or no business plan meant no loan. The only property she could buy was in Lake Woebegone or some other hick town where used-up restaurants could be bought for a dime.

If she used her savings on daily living, her dream of owning her own restaurant would go the way of her job.

Before life soured with her parents, her mother taught her the ins and outs of entertaining. She used to set up her dolls around the table and pretend to be the waitress serving food. A degree in restaurant and hotel management was an obvious choice. Her next step in reaching her dream had been to manage a restaurant in the Big Apple.

When she arrived in Manhattan looking for a management position, most establishments didn't want to hire someone fresh out of school. But she found a place with great potential and proved herself. Running a five-star restaurant came as natural as breathing.

Stopping to catch her breath, she rested the box on the railing. No need to dwell on the impossible. Looking up the stairwell, she shook her head and resumed her upward trek. An apartment on the sixth floor sounded great when the elevator worked — one month out of the year.

At just 500 square feet, their apartment wasn't the Ritz, but it worked. A window in every room but the bathroom sold her on the corner apartment. She loved to throw back the curtains and fill the space with light, pushing away some of the darkness that filled her marriage.

After the wedding, Barry promised they would buy a place of their own. Something bigger. In the meantime, he moved into her apartment. They found they enjoyed the coziness and spent more time making memories than searching for the elusive perfect condo. Six years later when he lost his job and things started spiraling downward, she was thankful for monthly rent instead of a hefty mortgage.

The injustice of the day boiled over as she huffed past the fourth floor, ignoring the pounding in her head. How could Barry be so stupid? She asked him over and over not to come to the restaurant.

In all likelihood his plan held more promise than substance. Since his real estate career tanked, these new opportunities popped up on a regular basis in between his part-time and temporary jobs. Mostly she listened and nodded her head until he lost interest. The last one he mentioned was some multilevel marketing scheme he bought into with a credit card to the tune of $5000. He never actively pursued it that she could tell and had let it fade like many of their dreams.

Then there was his gambling.

The last time she bailed him out of his debts it nearly drained her savings and she warned him if he ever put them at risk of losing everything again, she would leave.

She just wanted him to follow through on his promises.

Karen reached her apartment, dug in her purse for the keys, and opened the door. After entering, she kicked the door shut behind her.

"Barry?"

No answer. She dropped the box on the couch and tossed her sweater over the arm chair. She peeked into the bedroom to be sure he wasn't asleep, but he wasn't there either.

"What are you doing home?"

Karen jumped. The door must not have latched or she would have heard him come in. She paused. Barry would hit the roof if he found out she'd been fired. Even if it was his fault. She chewed on her lip and turned to face him.

"Well? I'm waiting for an answer."

"I took the night off." She skirted past him to the kitchen.

He grabbed her shoulder and spun her around. The smell of liquor on his breath was stronger than at the restaurant. She turned away and closed her eyes.

"Don't think I'm good enough for you? Maybe this'll change your mind." He yanked her into his arms.

"Please, not like this." She struggled to break free.

"I was good enough for you last week."

"You hadn't been drinking. And that was before you hit me." She glared at him. The bruise was gone from her face, but she still felt it in her heart and she dared him to face the truth.

Instead, his anger exploded. "I'm your husband. You'll do as I say." He grabbed her wrists and dragged her toward the bedroom.

"No." She twisted, trying to break free.

Entangling his fingers in her hair with one hand, he wrapped the other around her waist and jerked her tight against his torso. He kissed her, twisting their lips together in some unnatural dance of feigned affection.

Karen grimaced and pushed against his chest, breaking contact. Their eyes locked. He curled his lip but she refused to back down. He let go of her waist and raised his hand, as if ready to hit her. She flinched and couldn't stop the tears.

"How did we get here?" She didn't realize she spoke the thought out loud until she saw his eyes soften. He held her gaze for a long moment then dropped his hands.

"I wasn't going to hit you."

"I don't know that." She held her breath. A look of sadness filled his eyes and she felt a slight stirring of hope.

"Karen?" The intruding voice ended the silent truce. The hardness in his eyes returned and he pushed his words through gritted teeth. "We're not done."

She stumbled back as he pushed her away from him. "We're here, Megan. Come on in." She followed Barry to the front door and threw her best friend a grateful look.

"The front door was cracked and I wanted to be sure no one had broken in." Megan faced Barry. "You guys okay?"

"Peachy." Barry grabbed his keys from the coffee table.

Megan wrinkled her brow in question. Karen shook her head.

"Don't expect me till late." He tramped past Megan and out the apartment, slamming the door as he left.

Karen locked the door behind him and leaned against it squeezing her eyes against the tears. She jerked when her friend touched her arm and the dam broke. She crumpled to the floor and cried.

Megan sat down and hugged Karen while she emptied herself of the fear. "What's going on?"

"The abbreviated version?" She didn't want to get into the whole story right now. She sniffled and sat up.

"Sure. Let's move to the couch." Megan found a spot to sit, then pulled her long pony tail around, brushing her fingers through the chocolaty colored tresses while she waited.

Karen followed and sat cross-legged facing her friend. She never really understood why Megan wanted to be her friend. They were different in every way. Megan's brown hair to her red. Megan's calm to her unrest. Megan's faith to her apathy. Somewhere between the differences, they were drawn together. And here they sat. Megan ready to listen to recent events that would change Karen's life forever.

She took a deep breath and recounted the events of the day. "He probably would have hit me again if you hadn't come..."

"Whoa, whoa. Wait." Megan leaned forward and held up her hands. "He hit you? When was this? And why didn't you tell me?"

"The other night. He was drunk then, too. I didn't tell you, I guess, because...I don't know." Karen sighed and swiped a tear. "I hoped it was a one-time thing. Talking about it makes it real, you know?"

"It's real all right."

Karen nodded. "There's more."

"That man." Megan crossed her arms. "I need to get Robert over here."

Karen held up a hand to stop Megan's tirade. "It's not Barry. I got a letter from my dad."

"You've never talked about your family."

"There's a reason."

"I guess there must be. What did he want?"

"My mom is dying." Karen exhaled a pent up breath.

"I'm so sorry."

"Don't be. I'm…not." Karen clenched her fist. A sob broke loose from deep inside her and tears streamed down her face again. She covered her face with her hands. "I miss my mama."

Megan hugged her and let her cry.

"I don't want to feel this way." Karen pulled back.

"She's your mom." Megan reached for the tissue box and handed it to Karen.

"Not after I turned thirteen."

"What happened?"

"I'm not sure. She just seemed to give up. It was the same day Dad suddenly turned on me. I don't know what changed. He won't tell me. He says I have to talk to mom." Karen shifted on the couch.

"That doesn't make sense. He should tell you."

"You think?" Karen wiped the tears off her face.

"So, are you going back?"

"I don't want to, but with everything else going on, I guess so." Karen closed her eyes and leaned her head back on the couch.

"You're smart to get some space and force this issue with Barry before it gets worse. Many of the women at the shelter wait until irreparable damage has been done before they get help."

"Not me. Anger is one thing, but when it gets physical? I'm not sticking around." When Karen left home, she vowed she would never let anyone do that to her again.

"Do you want to stay with us a while before you leave?"

"Thanks." Karen smiled. It would be nice, but she needed to face the past once and for all. And with her mom ill, now seemed to be the time. "Somehow I think with your baby coming I would just be in the way."

"You've got about six months before you have to compete with baby space. Besides, even then, I think Robert would be happy to let you wash the diapers. So if you need somewhere to go when you get back…"

"No thanks. I'm not changing diapers." Karen got up and walked over to the computer. She had to make an online bank transfer for the trip.

"When do you plan to leave?"

"Today, if I can find a flight." Karen sat down at the desk. "That's odd. Barry never leaves the computer on." She moved the mouse and gasped as an image of a naked woman filled the screen. Her stomach churned and she gasped for air. Covering her mouth, she took a few deep breaths.

Is this what Barry does with his day? She opened up the browser's history and stared at the list of sites with women's names included. She pushed back from the desk and stood up, fists balled.

Megan came up beside her and choked back a cry. "He's a jerk. I'm so sorry you have to deal with this, too. You okay?"

"What do you think?" Karen yanked the plug out of the wall then swore when she realized she hadn't made the bank transfer. She plugged the computer back in and waited for it to boot up, pacing between the couch and kitchen counter. "Barry's yelled at me, hit me, and now cheated on me. For all I know, he's out with some woman right now. I should divorce him."

"You have every right to."

Karen stopped pacing and looked at her. "You agree with me?"

"I agree you have every right and I would certainly understand if you did. But…" Megan sat on the arm of the couch. "I know you don't want to hear this right now…"

"Not if you're going to start a bunch of religious mumbo jumbo and tell me some pie-in-the-sky ending to all of this is possible."

"It's not pie-in-the-sky, but it is possible to save your marriage."

Karen narrowed her eyes at Megan. It was the same old thing. "Thanks for the platitudes, but no thanks. I'm not sure I want to save my marriage." She walked toward the kitchen.

Megan placed a hand on Karen's arm. "It's not platitudes. It's a lot of hard work." Megan dropped her hand. "I've never told you much about my early years with Robert, have I?"

"No. What's it got to do with this?"

"We've dealt with pornography, too."

"Robert?"

Megan nodded. "It doesn't matter how successful someone is. Anyone can fall prey to sexual addiction."

Karen rolled her eyes. "I don't like it, but it's just pornography, not some addiction."

"I saw those sites on your history. And the frequency. It's more than a passing thing or an accidental pop up. He's hooked."

Karen paced the small kitchen. She wanted to confront Barry, to scream and bang on the wall and throw things, but she feared turning her rage loose. "How could he do this to me?"

"The addiction removes all logic from the equation. Somewhere inside he probably still loves you, but the chemicals in his brain from the high of sexual pleasure block it out and keep him locked in his own prison."

"That sounds like a defense." Karen glared at her friend.

"I would never defend what he's done, but you need to understand you're not to blame. It's not because you aren't enough. This thing usually goes way back to wounds from long ago."

"It still sounds like a defense."

"I'm trying to help you understand it," Megan persisted.

"I don't want to understand it right now. I want to…to…" Karen let out a guttural cry between gritted teeth. "I have to keep this under control."

"Why?"

"Because anger destroys things." Karen turned her back on Megan.

"This addiction needs to be destroyed, so don't let anyone tell you not to get mad. You have to be angry enough to say no more. But you do need to forgive Barry or you won't be free."

Karen picked up a nearby vase and threw it across the room, shattering it against a wall. Silence settled in the room. Finally, she spoke. "Forgiveness is not part of my vocabulary right now."

"The process of forgiveness takes time, but you can do it with God's help." Megan's face reflected the grief Karen felt.

"I'm glad God helped you guys out, but He hasn't been in the business of helping me lately."

"Have you asked?"

Karen walked to the sink and stared out the small window. "I've never admitted it to you, but I used to be into God. Salvation. All of that religious stuff. But I haven't talked to God since I turned thirteen. Especially, not to ask for help."

"Maybe you should try again."

Karen felt a flutter of hope. *Would He help me?* She quickly squashed the thought. When her dad and mom turned their backs on her, she turned her back on their God. Surely He wasn't interested in her life.

"It's not just the pornography. I've got to take care of myself. And I don't think God cares to hear from me. Besides, if He did decide to help me out, it would take a miracle."

"Well, I'll be praying for one."

"I'm not sure that's what I want. Barry's just lucky I don't have time to stop by a divorce lawyer on the way out of town. Figuring out what I want to do will have to wait."

Megan nodded and gave her a hug. "I can understand that."

"Thanks." Karen reached for a tissue.

"Want me to hang around while you get ready to go?"

Karen shook her head. "Once I make my bank transfer, I just need to change the date on my ticket and reserve a seat before I pack and head to the airport."

"And you'll be flying where?"

"Missouri. But don't tell Barry—at least not yet."

"No problem." Megan walked toward the door. "Promise you'll call?"

"You know I will." Karen fought back tears as she hugged her friend. Megan had always been there for her. "I'm going to miss you."

Megan stepped into the hallway. "We'll keep in touch." She waved and headed towards the stairwell.

For a moment, she played with the idea of asking God for help. She shrugged. God wasn't interested in helping her.

Call on me and I will answer.

The words echoed in her mind, but where did they come from? Megan. She was always spouting off stuff like that.

Karen turned away from the door and looked around the apartment. She and Barry made a lot of good memories here. If only there was a way to erase the bad ones. She spied the photo album tucked in the bookshelf. She reached over and picked it up. No matter what happened she wanted to remember the good times.

She went into the bedroom and changed into her favorite pair of jeans and cowboy boots, then dragged a duffle bag out from under the bed. It was heavier than it looked.

"What's in this thing?"

She heaved it onto the bed, plopping it down next to the pillows. She unzipped the top and gasped as dozens of porn magazines spilled out across the bed.

We made love here! Was he thinking of me or these? She dumped out the bag, not caring if he knew she discovered his secret.

Bile rose in her throat and she ran for the bathroom. She rinsed her mouth and ran a cool wash rag over her face, then stared into the mirror. "I gotta get out of here."

She tossed her toiletries, a fresh change of clothes, and her photo album into the bag. Whatever else she needed she would buy when she got there.

She glanced around the room to make sure she didn't forget anything. *The ticket.* She spied the letter from her dad on the dresser next to her journal. She put them both in her bag, then paused. He mentioned the other letters, maybe she should take them, too.

As Karen scoured the closet she came across one of Barry's sweaters, her gift to him their first Christmas together. She held it against her face breathing in his musky scent. She smiled, remembering their first Christmas scavenger hunt. She hadn't had a real tree since leaving home, and Barry's efforts that first Christmas together was still one of her favorite memories.

Every year, they set out to hunt down the best tree in New York. The surprises he arranged along the way were different each year. Hot chocolate in Central Park, skating at Rockefeller Center, some outdoor concert in the snow, or some other holiday delight. But it always culminated in the discovery of a bona fide live Christmas tree. Her eyes moistened.

Then two years ago everything began to fall apart. *I will not go there.* She thrust his sweater back into the closet and climbed up on a step stool to check the top shelf. The bundle of letters tumbled out from their hiding spot, scattering all over the closet floor. She glanced through the pile as she gathered them up, most were from her mom and dad, and several from her siblings, Joanna, Albert, Elinor and Blake. She chuckled as she spotted one from her old boyfriend, David. After finishing college, she had moved to New York and made a new life. She ignored the letters from home, refusing to open the letters, although she couldn't bring herself to throw any away.

I wonder what they wrote.

She sighed, added her dad's newest letter to the stack, secured them with a rubber band and placed them in the duffle bag.

Good, or maybe not so good, reading for the trip.

3

*B*arry tromped onto the southbound Fifth Avenue bus, then dipped his Metro Card into the fare box before he muscled his way to the back of the bus.

He couldn't believe Megan waltzed right into their apartment thinking someone had broken in. *Yeah right.* He did not like people dancing all over his private affairs. He sucked in a breath. Would he have hit Karen if Megan hadn't interrupted?

How did we get here? Karen's question echoed through his head. She shouldn't have to ask. She threw his failures in his face at every turn. The size of the apartment, the shabby furniture. And no vacation since he lost his job two years ago. He snorted when he remembered the brochures she laid on their coffee table just last week. A cruise.

She probably even wanted a second home in the suburbs and a car in storage for Sunday drives. None of it was likely to happen any time soon unless she was willing to spend some of her precious savings. He gritted his teeth. *I should be the one providing those things for Karen. Like I used to.*

A woman boarded the bus with a baby in a backpack and a toddler holding her hand. Barry started to smile. A man should have kids to carry on the family name. Did she blame him for their inability to have kids? Heat flooded his face. He got off at the next stop and continued south on foot.

He lowered his head and plowed his way through the rush hour crowd. He itched to shove the slower pedestrians out of his way when someone bumped into him and knocked him to the side. He turned back with fists raised. "Hey, be more careful."

An elderly woman struggled to keep her balance in the crowd. He met her gaze, but instead saw Karen's face poised in fear at his raised hand. He backed away. A tiny dog yipped at his feet. He tried to sidestep the mutt and tripped. His hands smarted where he caught himself on the sidewalk. Fearful of being trampled, he raised his arm over his head and tried to see the edge of the crowd to make his escape.

"Son?" The sound of the voice rattled him.

"Dad?" Barry looked up into the kind eyes of an older gentleman who stood between him and the flow of human traffic. The resemblance between the man and his father twisted his gut.

"You'll get trampled down there. Come on, let's get you up." The man caught Barry's arm and he rose to his feet.

The crowd parted around them while he leaned down to brush off his pants, afraid to look the man in the eye, fearful his father actually found him. But when he looked up to thank the man, he was gone. Had he imagined him? Someone yelled at him to move along as the mass of bodies closed in on him and bumped him from every side. Everyone blocked his way. His anger, quieted for a moment, smoldered to life again. Oblivious to whom he might offend, he pushed his way through the crowd and crossed the street.

The face of the lady he almost cold cocked seemed to mock him. He looked at his fists and clenched his jaw. Continuing his journey south, he shoved his hands into his pockets as though by restricting them he could control his temper. All he wanted was a little respect, but he couldn't seem to do anything right.

He never was good enough. Not for his parents. Not for his wife. Not for his friends. Everyone wanted — no, expected — more. He spat on the sidewalk. He wasn't even good enough for himself.

Several blocks later, his breathing returned to normal and his thoughts were not consumed with the unfairness of judgments made against him. The noise of the city crept into his consciousness. He needed a drink. He crossed back over Fifth Avenue and boarded another bus heading toward his favorite bar in Soho.

Barry weaved through the tables at Jack's bar. The place reeked of cigarettes. A nasty habit he never cared to pick up. He pulled himself up on the bar stool and waited while Jack talked on the phone.

"You're in a little early, aren't you?"

Barry cringed at the sound of Anthony's voice behind him. Located near to Tribeca, Barry's favorite bar drew in many well-to-do clients like Anthony. A plus for Jack. A downfall for Barry. He owed Anthony a lot of money and doubted he would leave without at least a bloody nose.

He turned to face the loan shark. As a former wrestler, Anthony was an impressive sight. Even his gray hair didn't detract from his measure of intimidation. All but the most innocent wilted under his glare, whether his goons were tagging along or not. And Barry was far from innocent. It took more bravado than he felt to hold eye contact. "Had a fight with my woman. Needed some help to get through the day."

Anthony nodded and put his arm around Barry's shoulders like his dad used to do. Barry squirmed. Anthony was as rotten as his dad had been righteous.

"You got my money?"

"I'll have it soon." If Anthony knew Barry had no plan, he could kiss his health goodbye.

Anthony grabbed the back of Barry's neck and squeezed until he winced. "I know you will, after all, you're a smart guy…." Anthony squeezed a bit harder. "One week. Then the interest goes up."

"I'll get it." Barry met Anthony's stare.

Anthony released his hold and patted Barry on the back. He took a deep breath and turned around on the bar stool as though unperturbed by the presence of the man more in control of his life than he.

Anthony's footsteps faded toward the back exit.

Barry rubbed the back of his neck. *Karen pegged me right. Stupid.*

Of course, he couldn't recall if she ever actually said it. But he could tell she thought it. The way she rolled her eyes made him madder than a sacked quarterback whose fullback didn't defend him. If she ever found out about Anthony, she would be right when she finally said the words out loud.

Jack hung up the phone, grabbed a bottle and poured two drinks. "Mind if I drink with you?" He jerked his thumb toward the phone. "My wife's mad."

"To women." Barry held up his glass. "Can't live with 'em and can't live without 'em."

The two men emptied their shots and Jack began to pour another round, but Barry refused.

"On the house?"

"I guess one more won't hurt." Barry slid his glass over.

Jack lifted his chin toward the door. "Bad man to get tied up with."

"Don't I know it. Somehow I plan to be done with him once and for all…very soon."

"Be careful. Plans have a way of getting messed up when it comes to Anthony."

"Yeah, well, he's messed up my plans long enough." Barry slapped some money on the counter and headed out of the bar. "See ya later."

He hurried out and boarded the northbound bus. A red-headed artist type boarded the bus, and an image of Karen replaced the hipster in front of him. He shook his head as he imagined running his hands through Karen's hair. Their marriage had been a sweet ride. They made good plans. Until he got fired and life went downhill.

Barry never told her the truth about what happened because he couldn't stand the thought of her disappointment, but he ended up a disappointment anyway. He saw it in her eyes every time she looked at him. Every time he came home and told her he lost another job. He wanted her to look at him the way she used to. Why couldn't she just show him a little respect?

Just the other day, after he'd been out job hunting with no results, he stopped for a drink before going home. Karen started in on him the minute he walked through the door. He just wanted her to shut up so he could crash, but she kept on and finally he made her be quiet. It was just a slap and hardly left a bruise.

He ducked his head so no one on the bus would see the tears in his eyes. He knew he stepped over the line. The fear in her eyes when she grabbed her purse and headed out of the apartment rocked him to his soul. No matter what he thought of his parents and their religious views, they modeled a good marriage. You didn't get there by hitting the woman you were supposed to love.

Guilt and shame invaded his mind. *I'm a fool.* Barry hit the side of the bus and several of the passengers looked at him. He glared back. He didn't need their scrutiny. He needed to clear his debt. On his own. Like a man. He pushed the tape strip between the windows and disembarked several stops early. He could use the walk.

When the anger boiled over, he didn't know how to handle it. His parents were never able to help him. They tried to point him to God after they became Christians, but as a teenager, he fought against the idea — unlike his younger brother.

Two years younger than Barry, Chad always did the right thing. Around the dinner table every night, their parents applauded his brother's choices while Barry dug deeper into his life of rebellion. He wanted freedom to do what he wanted and told his parents so numerous times. He had the right to choose, but his choices backfired, and he left home immediately after his high school graduation.

Certain that his parents were relieved, he assumed they never wanted to see him again. Just as well. He could never make up for what he did. Too much was said on both sides and too much happened that could never be undone.

A car horn blared and a fellow pedestrian grabbed his shirt and pulled him back onto the sidewalk. He nodded a thanks to the stranger, then crossed the street when the light changed.

This mess started when Dennis fired him. It was all his fault. Barry sneered. *You owe me.* It was only right. He picked up his pace. It was dark when he arrived at the apartment.

"Karen?" He switched on the lights and looked around, spotting a note on the kitchen table. With a huff he sat down and turned the envelope over in his hands. He smelled the paper where the scent of Karen's perfume lingered. He opened the envelope and unfolded the note inside.

Barry,

I need some space, and we both need to think. Changes need to be made — I can't go on like this. I'll be in touch.

Karen

Barry dropped his head into his hands as the letter floated to the floor. All he ever wanted was to make her happy. He grabbed the letter off the floor, crumpled it and threw it across the room.

"It's not all my fault. You're the one always picking apart everything I do." He imagined Karen standing in front of him and he shook his fists in her face. "I can't do anything right according to you. Why didn't you leave sooner?"

He paced the apartment, nostrils flared, fists clenched. "You drove me to it." He banged his fists into the wall, then turned and kicked a chair. It flipped over and landed against the wall. "Just stay away for all I care."

A knock sounded on the door. "It's your landlord. Your neighbors complained. Shut up or I'll call the police."

Part of Barry wanted to keep shouting and end up in jail, but as much as he hated to admit it, Karen was right. Changes needed to be made. He just wouldn't be the only one to make them. He took several deep breaths.

Tomorrow he would visit Dennis. Let him do his part to make things right.

Barry stopped in front of the computer and images of women popped into his head. His body relaxed and he longed for the comfort of the pictures. He turned the power on.

I deserve some leisure time.

He headed to the bedroom to change while the computer booted up. The mess of porn magazines on the bed stopped him short. At least he didn't have to hide them anymore.

He changed and returned to his desk. Scrolling through his favorites list, he clicked on a link that led to another link and then another. Within minutes he was lost in labyrinth of fantasy, drowning in the endorphins his body produced. Numbed to any thought or consideration of his wife and her feelings.

4

"Excuse me, miss?" The cabbie's voice broke through Karen's thoughts. She watched the back of his bald head as he talked. "My dispatcher says there's an accident on the Queensboro Bridge. We may be awhile getting to the airport."

Karen looked out the window at the snail's pace traffic and groaned. She could think of better uses for her time.

"Would you like a sandwich?"

"What?"

He looked back at her through the rearview mirror as the car came to a standstill. Bruce Willis's double held up a small cooler bag. "Food?"

She covered her mouth and stifled a laugh. *I'm just trying to catch a flight to Kansas City, and Bruce here probably has plans to save the universe. At least I'll die hard laughing.* It felt good to laugh.

"My wife always packs something for me in case I get caught in rush hour. I thought you might be hungry."

His kindness fed her as much as the food he offered. Her stomach growled and she realized she hadn't eaten since breakfast. "I can't take it. You're probably hungry, too."

"My wife always packs extra. Never know when I'll get stuck." He laughed and handed her a wrapped sandwich.

Karen accepted the food. "Thank you."

The driver weaved through the traffic while she ate. Family aside, she enjoyed Kansas City. It would be much more laid back than New

York, and she needed a change of pace. As the sun warmed her through the window, her headache eased. She allowed her body to relax and drifted into a light sleep as the taxi snailed it's way through the jam.

"We're almost there. What time's your flight?" The cabby glanced at her in the rearview mirror.

"Six."

"Might be close, but you should make it. Where are you headed?"

"Home." She sighed and closed her eyes.

"Ahhh. Not a pleasant reunion I take it."

"You could say that."

"I'll pray for you."

"Why would you do that?"

He shrugged. "It's what I do. I pray for the people I carry around."

"Well, don't bother God about me. He's not interested." She sank deeper into her seat. God lost interest the day she lost interest in Him.

"That's where you're wrong."

"I don't think so." She rolled her eyes.

"Have you been looking?"

"Do you know Megan Fletcher?" She met his gaze in the rearview mirror. "You sound a lot like her."

The cabby let out a big laugh as he pulled the car to a stop. "Then God is at work." He hopped out and opened her door.

"How much do I owe you?" As she set her bag on the pavement and reached into her purse, she noticed his prosthesis. "I'm sorry for staring."

"Don't be. If it hadn't been for this, I wouldn't know God. I praise him for my new leg every day."

"How can you praise God for that?"

"You'll find the answers in your own story. Now, the cars are lined up behind us." He reached for her hands, gave them a gentle squeeze, then returned to his side of the car. "Don't stop watching. God will show up."

As Karen stood on the sidewalk watching the cabby drive away, she realized he never took the fare. First cabby she ever met who refused money. Or shared food. She shook her head. His faith seemed real, but God wouldn't show up for her.

A bump from a passerby jarred her out of her thoughts. She lifted her bag to her shoulder and hurried into the terminal. When she called the airlines to change the date on her ticket, she opted to stay in Boston one night before flying on to Missouri. It was worth the extra expense. She needed to clear her head before she arrived on her family's doorstep.

The bank of departure computer screens showed her flight was on time. It would be close. She would have to run.

The flight attendant greeted Karen at the door of the plane. "Another two minutes and you would have missed the flight."

Panting for breath, she showed her ticket.

"Your seat is about halfway back on the right side. Let me know if you need help with your bag."

Karen dug the letters and her journal out of her bag, then shoved it into the overhead bin. Settling into her window seat, she fought back tears as her emotions finally overtook her.

She was exhausted. A nap sounded heavenly, but her mind still raced. Sighing, she sorted the letters by date while the plane backed out of the gate and taxied to the runway. The flight attendant's voice interrupted her progress.

"Ladies and gentlemen, welcome aboard. The captain has turned on the fasten seat belt sign. Please stow your carry-on luggage underneath the seat in front of you or in an overhead bin…"

Karen pretended to listen while she reread the letter from her dad, then scrunched it in frustration. *Why can't you tell me the truth yourself? Why did you keep it from me at all?* The questions drew her home like a moth to light.

As the plane leveled off at cruising altitude, she smoothed out her dad's letter and slipped it along with the others into her purse, then opened her journal.

June 7. The day my life fell apart. Note to self: It's time to corner Dad and get an answer once and for all.

She shoved her journal into her purse and took some peanuts from the flight attendant, then stared out the window. This trip began as a way to escape from Barry, but now, something she had no control over pulled her forward. She leaned back to rest until the plane arrived in Boston, the last of her headache dissipating.

Grabbing her duffel bag from the overhead bin, she followed the rest of the passengers off the plane. She yearned for a hot shower and comfortable bed at the hotel. She confirmed her departure time for the next morning and hurried past the luggage carousel to catch a taxi.

Numb from emotional turmoil and ready for the day to end, she stared at the water on either side of the bridge. The loneliness she avoided the past several years threatened to drown her. Thoughts of Barry's betrayal filled her mind. *I can't cry. Not here.* She leaned forward and tapped the cabby on his shoulder. "How much longer?"

"We're at the exit now."

"Thanks." She sat back and breathed a sigh of relief as the hotel came into view.

After checking in, Karen dropped her bag in the room and plopped down on her bed. She couldn't stop the tears. Was it just this morning she opened the restaurant as usual? She deserved a medal after today.

As her tears slowed, her stomach growled. Other than the handful of peanuts on the plane, she hadn't eaten since the taxi ride to the airport. She sucked in several slow deep breaths, then splashed water on her face. A few eye drops and no one would suspect what her day entailed.

Smoothing out the wrinkles in her shirt, she headed to the lobby in search of a vending machine.

"Karen?"

She stopped and turned around. A bucketful of emotions washed over her as she recognized the man in front of her.

"David?" She gasped as he wrapped her in a bear hug.

5

Karen melted into David's embrace. How many years had it been? She expected hatred, not hugs.

She stepped back to examine the man before her. David Ellis' good looks were still intact. His sandy blond hair was cut short, capping his six foot frame. A few laugh lines now framed his mouth, but his blue eyes still seemed to penetrate her defenses. He looked grown up. She sighed. *What if I married him like we planned?*

"How are you?"

She shrugged her shoulders. "Fine. Busy."

"Too busy to write or visit?" The delight in his eyes faded.

"Yeah, that. I guess my departure left something to be desired."

"You think?"

"Look. I'm sorry if I hurt your feelings, but there were bigger issues at stake than your ego." She bit her lip and chided herself. She owed him more than excuses.

"Where did that come from?" David looked behind him. "Can we go somewhere else to talk?"

Karen glanced around the lobby. One man ducked his head behind a magazine. A couple turned to each other and whispered.

She shrugged. "Fine. But I don't have a car."

"I do. Come on."

She turned from the curious gazes and followed David to his rental. A silver Mustang. "You ever get the red one you wanted?"

"Yeah. But it doesn't feel like I imagined. You're not with me."

"I am tonight."

"True. Want to see how it feels?" David jingled the keys at her.

"Your rental?" Karen smiled as the warmth of their past camaraderie replaced the distance between them.

"I may not trust you with my feelings right now, but the car…that's a different story."

"Not sure if that's a compliment or an insult."

"It's a statement of fact."

She snickered. "I don't get to drive much in the City."

"Here." He tossed her the keys.

She settled into the driver's seat, then ran her hand along the smooth leather interior and adjusted the mirrors. She turned the ignition, savoring the roar of the engine as it came to life then settled into a gentle purr. She pulled out of the parking garage and followed the signs to the interstate. Moving into the far left lane, she shifted into high gear and accelerated past the other drivers. The thrill of speed took her mind off the impending conversation.

The summer after her family fell apart, David took her driving out in the fields in an old pickup his family owned. Perfect for driving in the fields and for a couple of friends to hang out in to watch for shooting stars. It was old, beaten up and in need of a coat of paint, but that pickup and his friendship saved her sanity. Until his parents grew tired of the rusted look and bought him a brand new Camero when he turned sixteen.

Karen shook her head. They drove several miles in the quietness of each other's company.

David broke the silence. "Want to stop and eat?"

"Sure. Where?"

"Next exit. One of these towns is bound to have a place to eat."

She pulled off the highway and turned into the parking lot of a small bar and grill. "This will have to do."

The door creaked as they walked in.

"What do you think? Should we head down the—who would have

known it?" David stared at the walls, the bar, the jukebox, then back at Karen. "This looks just like Chuck's."

"You took the words right out of my mouth."

"You two want to sit and order?" A waitress stood in front of them with her arms crossed.

Karen nodded. "Please."

They followed the waitress to a table and took their seats. Karen trailed her finger through the menu. "For a minute there I thought we stepped through some time portal."

David leaned his elbows on the table. "Remember the time—"

"We won Chuck's all night dance competition," she finished in unison. They laughed, drawing the attention of some of the customers. Awkward silence replaced the laughter. When her eyes met David's gaze, she glanced down at the table.

He reached over and took her hand. A shiver ran up her spine. When they had first started hanging out, it boggled her mind that David Ellis, catch of the school, chose her. He told her it was because she listened. But as they hung out and stood up for each other, shared secrets, pulled pranks and drove the fields in his truck, their friendship became necessary to each of them.

They fell in love under the stars and even without the words spoken as promises or a ring to show the world, she knew David wanted to marry her. And that was enough. Until the day she couldn't wait any longer.

"Nice ring," David rubbed his thumb across her wedding ring. "Is that why you disappeared without a word after college? Didn't want to tell me to my face?"

Karen held up her left hand. "This didn't come along until seven years later. And other than a few pictures, it's the only nice reminder I have from my marriage."

"I'm sorry." David dropped his gaze. "It's just that I always hoped you would come back to me once you finished school. It hurt when you didn't and never told me why."

"I wanted to get away, and you didn't believe me about my family. If I stayed I would have gone crazy."

"Even if we got married?"

Karen looked at David with a weak smile. "My parents would have never approved."

"Why not elope?"

"Would you have suggested it?"

He held her gaze for a few minutes then slumped his shoulders. "You're right."

The silence enveloped them and threatened to suffocate her, but she didn't know what to say.

David got up from his seat and walked to the jukebox. She watched him drop in a quarter and push a button. He still seemed to care for her, had he waited this long? He turned and looked at her. She blushed when "Endless Love" filled the restaurant.

"May I have this dance?"

Karen took his hand and joined him on the floor, thankful he didn't press for more information. Maybe she would tell him someday, but for now she enjoyed his attentions.

Their bodies moved to the rhythm of the familiar melody. David first played it for her on her fifteenth birthday. Hidden away at their favorite spot, the stars overhead seemed to dance with them. That night his kiss stirred something new in her. For the first time since they admitted their feelings, she was tempted to follow David's lead into a more intimate relationship.

He wanted to have sex, but after watching her sister Joanna throw herself at every guy possible, Karen decided to hold out for marriage. David was patient. He tested the waters every now and then, but didn't push and she always thought the day would come when she could give her body as well as her heart to him.

Tears on her cheeks brought her back to the present. He leaned toward her, eyes locked with hers. She longed for the feel of his lips and her heart beat faster as she closed her eyes and swayed closer.

How long has it been since my husband kissed me this way?

Her eyes flew open and she jerked away, holding her hand over her mouth. She rushed to the bathroom and leaned against the wall, steadying her breathing. It felt good to be in his arms. Even better than the flutters the near kiss stirred. But one thought of Barry brought it to a halt. Tears trickled down her cheeks.

She looked in the mirror. *What does Barry see when he looks at me?* Physically she hadn't changed much, but did he still find her attractive? David obviously did. And the things you couldn't see in a mirror? She remembered the web sites Barry visited. As tears stung her eyes, she was thankful no one else was in the bathroom.

Why shouldn't I let David show me some attention? She kicked the trash can and it fell over. "Because I'm married." That's what Megan would say. Karen didn't like the direction her thoughts were going. Away from David. She kicked the trash can again, strewing the contents across the floor. She had been hurt so much. Why not find a piece of happiness? Didn't she deserve that much?

She held on to the edge of the sink and took a deep breath. *I won't let the anger or the tears take over.* She splashed water on her face until the coolness brought relief from the heat of her emotions.

After a quick look in the mirror, she picked up the trash, washed her hands, and returned to the table. She expected David to be ready to bolt, but he acted as though nothing happened. *Good. I don't think I can talk about what just happened. Not yet.*

"The waitress brought our food. I went ahead and ordered you some tea as well. This soup is great."

Karen relaxed, and they spent the rest of the meal engaged in chit chat. Their conversation revealed they were on the same flight to Kansas City, and he insisted on giving her a ride to the airport the next day. By the time they left, she regained her composure.

Back in her room, she dumped her purse out on the bed and gathered all the letters. She found the one from David and ripped it open to see what her former love wrote to her all those years ago.

Dear Karen,

I miss you. Please come home. I'm not giving up on us.

I finally convinced your sister to give me your address in New York City. I promised not to come after you. To let you choose. If it's something I did, please tell me so I can tell you I'm sorry. I'll wait for you.

With all my love,
David

She looked at the postmark. Two years before she met Barry. Would it have made a difference? She curled up on her bed, remembering the good times with Barry — and the bad. She thought about David and the unspoken promises of two teenagers. She wondered about the days ahead, then cried herself to sleep.

The next morning Karen bought a small box at the hotel gift shop, packed her wedding ring in it, and addressed it to Barry.

No note. He would understand.

On her way out, she dropped it at the front desk to mail.

6

Barry marked the frame for the hinge placement, and held the cupboard door in place while he drilled in the screws.

He chuckled. Maybe he should go into construction. When his muscles worked his mind didn't wander into murky waters. Like they did last night. *Why don't I just walk away from that stuff?* At least he had a plan for the debt situation.

"Barry. What are you doing here?"

Startled by the voice behind him, he bumped his head on the cupboard frame as he spun around. "Megan."

His face grew hot. He had planned to do some work and vacate the place before she showed up. The shelter for abused women was the one place that gave his life purpose. Ironic that Karen probably thought she belonged in one of these places now. *I'll change it. Somehow.*

"Can we talk?" Megan pointed toward her office.

Barry followed her down the hall. He was sure Megan planned to chew him up one side and down the other. He deserved it. In the light of day he could see that.

"Look, we appreciate your work here, but I can't let you volunteer for awhile."

Barry tensed. "Why not?"

Megan sighed. "These women come here for safety. By all accounts, Karen could come here for sanctuary."

"She told you?" He paced the office like a wild animal in a trap.

"I walked in on you guys, remember?" She sighed. "You can't be here when you're anger is out of control. You need help, Barry. You need God."

All thoughts of making changes flew out the window. "Leave. God. Out of it. He's never helped me. I'm not good enough. Just like I'm not good enough for your precious shelter."

"That's not it. Barry—"

"Forget it. I have more important business to take care of." He pushed past her, pulling out his phone as he hurried out of the building. He punched in Karen's number, but it went through to voice mail.

No one wants me around.

Barry waited for Dennis in the foyer of his apartment and admired the evidence of wealth around him. A part of Barry still wanted what his old boss had. But the path there was not to his liking. He would never be able to provide for Karen the way he wanted. He took a deep breath and shifted to salesman mode. Dennis needed to see his perspective on their past differences.

Megan thought he needed God's help. Barry laughed. Maybe if he said a quick prayer, God would help him with the next hour. *That's probably not what she had in mind.*

The housekeeper showed him to the living room where he waited for Dennis to appear. Barry snorted. He used to respect the man. That all changed when he found out Dennis' life was an illusion. The property deals Barry made for Dennis were only fronts for illegal activities.

Barry looked at his watch. *An hour.* Dennis knew how to grab control of a situation.

"Haven't seen you in a while." A godfather wannabe, Dennis stood with his feet wide, arms at his side, clenching and unclenching his fists. His stare bore into Barry.

He swallowed. Dennis owed him, but faced with his opponent, Barry's mouth went dry. "I was in the neighborhood."

"Right." Dennis looked Barry over, then nodded. "Scotch?"

"Sure."

Dennis handed Barry a glass. "To old friends."

Old friends indeed. Barry drained his glass.

Dennis laughed. "I see you still know how to drink. You went downhill when you started liking alcohol too much." He sat down across from Barry and draped an arm over the back of the couch.

I drank to numb the guilt. "It's under control now."

"You know, even a powerful man admits when he needs help. Uncle Benny still goes to AA." Dennis snickered.

"I said it's under control." Barry took a gulp of his scotch. More than his throat burned at Dennis' words.

"If you say so. How's Karen?" Dennis set his glass down and pulled over his cigar case. "Cigar?"

Barry shook his head. He knew where those cigars came from and at what cost. "Karen always wins at what she does."

"She should have taken the job I offered at my restaurant."

"She's fine where she is."

"I heard she got fired."

Barry jerked his head up. "You must have heard wrong."

"A rumor then."

"I'm sure it was." Barry narrowed his eyes. Dennis knew everybody's business around here. Especially in the restaurant industry. *Why didn't Karen tell me?*

"You know, I still remember your wedding day. She was a beautiful bride. The sequins on the bodice were a perfect touch. I'm glad I recommended that to the designer."

The dressmaker told Karen she was inspired and designed it just for her. Perhaps there was some truth to the accusations Karen made against Dennis' intentions. "My bride was perfect."

"Don't get touchy. Can't a man admire a beautiful woman?"

"Make sure that's all you do." Barry cringed at the thought of how the man in front of him treated his women.

"Good to see a man speak up for his woman. Be sure you hang on to her. Or I can't make any promises."

Barry finished his drink and set down the glass. Strings were attached to all of Dennis' gifts. Maybe this wasn't such a good idea.

Dennis leaned forward and put his elbows on his knees. "Barry, why are you really here?"

Barry swallowed his pride. "I need a job."

"I'm sure you do. But after the bad deal you made for me, I'm sure you can understand why I'm not jumping to bring you back."

That deal was Barry's attempt to make up for all the criminal activity he'd been a part of. He shrugged. "It was charity. You got a good deduction out of it. Besides, I found you a lot of good deals while we worked together."

"I don't think —" Dennis' phone rang. He paused to look at the number. "Excuse me." He hurried out of the room.

Barry knew a brush off when he saw one. *Maybe I should have prayed.* He stood up as Dennis returned. "It's time for me to go."

Dennis clapped a hand on Barry's shoulder. "I've been thinking. I do have a little favor you can do for me."

"What did you have in mind?" Barry tensed. Dennis didn't change his mind without a reason.

"Heather, the daughter of one of my clients, is in town and he expects me to show her a good time. My girlfriend is the jealous type. So, I think you should take her out for me. At my expense, of course. Then we can talk about a job."

"One favor. Then we talk? I have your word?" Barry saw no other alternative.

"You have my word." Dennis stuck out his hand and they shook on it.

"Where and when?"

"Tomorrow night. You can use one of my limos to pick her up at the Plaza Hotel. Then take her to one of my usual spots. Put it on my tab and lighten up, have some fun man. What Karen doesn't know, won't hurt her." He winked at Barry. "And go buy a decent suit. On me." Dennis shoved a handful of bills into Barry's hand.

"I'll stop by the next day to talk about a job." Barry knew fish when he smelled it. He could only keep his eyes open.

"Of course. I'll look forward to it." Dennis walked Barry to the door and showed him out.

He leaned against the wall of the elevator and counted the bills. "I didn't even need your help, God."

Saks Fifth Avenue provided a wide selection of suits. Barry tried on several before he found one that fit him as well as it looked. The mirror and suit mocked him with hints of better days. The larger size of suit proved his apathy of late.

No wonder Karen didn't look at him the way she used to. At their wedding she watched him with the same hunger reflected in his eyes. He pictured her walking down the aisle. Her strawberry red hair framed her freckled face and made him catch his breath every time he looked at her.

He chose a tie, shirt and shoes to complete the look then headed to the check out. He watched the people standing in line around him. He used to drop a couple of thousand in one spot just because it gave him a rush. Or to impress a date. His friends hung around because of his generosity. But it wasn't enough.

He paid for his purchase and left the store. The pedestrian traffic slowed his pace as he passed Rockefeller Center. He and Karen skated on the pond every Christmas Eve. Except last year. They fought, then he stormed out and got drunk. He had no idea how Karen spent the night. They never talked about it. He pursed his lips and zigzagged his way through the crowd as though the memories chased him.

This little favor for Dennis was the first step to get his life back. He hoped it wasn't some plot to drive him further into the ground. *I gotta get my mind off this. I'll drive myself nuts.*

Come to me and rest.

Where did that come from? Barry stopped and shook his head. *I don't need rest.* His stomach growled. Right now, he needed food. He followed his nose to the closest street vendor. "I'll take a slice."

The man took his money and handed him a thick cheesy slice of pizza. Hanging onto his bags with one hand, Barry grabbed the folded slice and ate as he continued north by foot. Pizza had been one of his favorite things when he first landed in Manhattan almost fifteen years ago. And he and Karen had enjoyed more than their fair share on dates. Even when they could afford the fancy food, they always came back to the slice.

He chuckled. She would love this one. The crust was thicker and had some sort of seasoning in it that tempted him to go back and get a whole pie.

He took note of the vendor. *I'll bring Karen here when...* He cursed under his breath and tossed the used up napkin in a trash can. He fingered the remainder of Dennis' money in his pocket and decided he could afford to skip the bus.

Stepping out into the street he waved down a cab. He was not in the mood to mess with the crowds.

7

Karen passed through the security check at the airport ahead of David, found an empty chair near her gate, sat down, and dialed Megan.

She picked up on the first ring. "Hey girl. I'm glad you called. Hold on." Megan spoke to someone on her end, then, after a lot of background noise, came back on the line. "Sorry, it's hard to find a place to talk without interruptions around here. How are you?"

"Good. Glad to be out of there. Has Barry asked about me?"

"No, but I'm sure he will."

"Please don't tell him my plans."

"All I know is you headed home. Care to tell me more?"

Karen hesitated. "I don't want to think about it right now."

"When you're ready, I'm here. Are you doing okay?"

She noticed David walking through the security gate. "Gotta run. I'll call later." She hung up and walked to the end of the terminal, out of David's line of sight. She dialed Barry. Voice mail picked up on the fourth ring and she breathed a sigh of relief.

"Barry. I assume you found my note. I need time to think so don't try to call me. By the way, I sent you a package." She ended the call, slid her phone into her pocket and turned around, bumping into David.

"I just followed to make sure you were okay." He backed up a step. "What's the story?"

"How much did you hear?" She didn't want David to know the state of her marriage. As if her actions on the dance floor last night hadn't already clued him in. She sighed.

"Said you needed time. What did this guy do?"

"Too much. I don't want to talk about it."

"So why don't you divorce him?"

She took a long look at David and wondered that herself. "Are you still waiting for me?"

"Ever since you walked away without a word." His gaze taunted her. He turned around and headed to the gate.

Tears stung the back of her eyelids as she remembered the letter he penned before she met Barry. Was there any chance for them if she left Barry? She sucked in a ragged breath.

Hope tried to sprout in her heart, but guilt weeded it out. She looked at her now bare hand. Why did I send my ring to Barry? Her gaze found David, and she followed him toward their plane. "It would be so easy to let myself fall in love again. But I can't. Not right now."

"What did you say?"

"Huh?" She nearly collided with a fellow passenger. "Oh, sorry. Just talking to myself." She quickened her pace as a flight attendant made the final boarding call.

Karen stopped in the aisle. Her seat was next to David's. "Did you arrange this?"

"Believe me, I wish I had. Perhaps it's fate. Want me to scoot over?"

"I like the window."

He stepped aside and she slipped into her seat. Her hand felt bare and she tried to shield it from his view. He would read too much into it. For most of the flight she kept her hand hidden, but when the "fasten your seat belt" sign woke her, David held her hand, stroking it. She snatched it away.

"You took off your ring."

"I put it somewhere for safe keeping."

"Still. A man has to wonder."

"No, he doesn't." The plane approached the Kansas City area and she turned away from David. Searching the rolling hills below for Westfall, she spotted the old water tower at the edge of town.

She rolled her eyes. If she and her friends had wanted more entertainment than fly-catching, they headed into Kansas City. Westfall was the most boring place for a teenager to grow up. There was no Main Street, only four blocks of store fronts around the town square. Neighborhoods branched off like mazes resembling old cow paths.

The only thing interesting about Westfall was the man it was named after. A man shot down by an outlaw. Karen looked at the surrounding acreages with large houses and stables. Her parents' property included an orchard. The area disappeared from sight before she could determine which one belonged to her childhood memories.

Her homecoming would surprise her family as much as doing a sky dive down to her parents' property. She chuckled. That would be quite the entrance for the long-absent daughter.

When the plane rolled to a stop at the gate, David stepped aside to let her into the aisle. Several more passengers managed to edge out of their seats before he followed. She expected him to look for her once he entered the terminal, but instead he went straight into the arms of a beautiful woman with long blonde hair and a body like a model, dressed to show it off.

Karen turned on her heels and stormed out of the terminal. *I can't believe this. He is so insensitive.* She slowed her pace. She had no right to be upset. Still, last night made her feel alive and wanted. *I thought he wanted more.*

An image of Barry in front of the computer popped to mind. Did anyone want her? She took several deep breaths then stopped for a drink at a water fountain.

"Hey, Karen, wait up."

She pretended not to hear and quickened her pace. David caught up and grabbed her arm, the blonde lagging several feet away. He spoke close to Karen's ear. "I meant to tell you, but I didn't know how."

She jerked her arm out of his grip. "How about, by the way, Karen, someone else is in my life now, so all this stuff about waiting around is a bunch of...of...bull."

The woman walked up and placed her left hand on David's arm then looked at Karen with raised eyebrows. She noticed the diamond on the woman's finger. She bit down her irritation and put on her polite waitress face. The woman held herself like an inhabitant of a Park Avenue penthouse. Karen straightened her posture to mirror the other woman.

David obliged with the introductions. "Honey, this is an old friend of mine, Karen Hannigan. I ran into her in Boston. She had a layover on her way home to visit family. Karen, this is...my fiancée, Mary Tucker."

Karen stiffened her back. "Delighted, I'm sure."

Mary picked at something on the sleeve of her dress. "Yes...well, perhaps we'll run into each other while I am at home. Of course, Kansas City is such a large place. Perhaps I won't have the pleasure."

Inwardly, Karen rolled her eyes. "You are quite right. Perhaps we won't have the pleasure."

"We're bound to run into each other." David looked back and forth between them. "We both live by your folks, Karen."

"I'll look forward to it, but for now, I need to go. So nice to meet you, Mary." Karen offered David's fiancée the tips of her fingers then placed a hand on David's other arm. "By the way, I want to surprise my family. If you see them, don't tell them I'm here." She walked off to the rental car kiosk with her head held high and her face flushed.

Her heart sank. *He's engaged.* A seed of hope for something besides what waited for her with Barry had taken root after all. She would just have to do everything she could to avoid them.

She accepted the keys from the rental agent and followed his directions to her car. As she stuffed her suitcase in the trunk, her phone rang. *Barry.* She stuck the phone back in her bag and climbed into the vehicle.

Karen checked into a hotel just off of the interstate outside of Kansas City. After a hot shower, she ordered room service and selected a movie to distract her mind from the soap opera she was living. Dumping out her duffel bag she took inventory of what she needed to buy, then plopped down on the bed to look through her photo album.

She rested her hand on their wedding picture. The fitted bodice and full skirt flattered her figure, and the off-shoulder design showcased her neck. She sighed. She loved the beading on the bodice and at the time thought the designer label worth the money. She even dipped into her nest egg to make the purchase. An extravagant gown for her extravagant groom, something he fully appreciated.

When they first met, Barry had stepped in and saved her from the attentions of his boss. Then he proceeded to shower her with his own attentions. She had doubted if he was any better than his boss.

But Barry persisted. He wooed her, courted her, and won her heart within six months.

The stuff of childhood dreams.

They planned a simple outdoor wedding. Then, his boss gave them an all-expenses paid Caribbean cruise on a chartered yacht. They had a wonderful time.

She turned the page and laughed at the skewed angle of the photo. It was a picture they took of themselves. The crew turned the boat just as she clicked the shutter. She fell into Barry's arms. They were lost to the world for the rest of the day.

Through those short months of courtship and first years of marriage, she believed life could be different than what she left behind in Westfall.

At first, their lovemaking was sweet and at the same time intense. After Barry lost his job, they lost that sweetness fast. What could she have done differently? An image of Barry at the computer popped up. "It's not my fault." She slammed the album shut and started to throw it across the room. *That's what Barry would do.* She dropped it like a pan of fresh bread hot out of the oven.

A tide of emotions washed over her. *What do I do with this anger?* She didn't want to be like her dad and Barry. Megan said she needed to be angry at the addiction, but how did she do it without destroying everything in her path? Too tired to think it through, she reached for the stack of letters. Thumbing through them, she found one from her oldest brother Blake. A quick glance at his words raised her pulse.

Karen,

Stay away.

Blake.

Why did he bother writing? And why do I bother reading it? She scoffed at the thought he might change, wadded the paper, and tossed it into the trash can. "Two points." Karen laughed. "I must be crazy."

The next letter was from her older sister Joanna. She never did like Karen much as a kid.

Dear Karen,

Well, I guess you don't plan on inviting me to New York. Can't say that I blame you. If I could get away from family — I wouldn't want anyone invading my territory either.
Elinor asked me to write and catch you up on the latest. Blake was arrested — a DUI. He got his hand slapped. They need to throw him in rehab. Course they say that about me and there is no way you would catch me going there willingly — if I decide to clean up, I can do it on my own.
Mom came home finally. Not sure why — probably couldn't make it on her own. She was in St. Louis I think. I ran into Blake's wife at the store the other day — wearing dark sunglasses. Said she had a migraine. Sure. When was the last time you had a migraine and weren't lying in bed with the curtains drawn?
That's it.

Catch you later — Joanna

The letter sounded just like Joanna. Scrambled. She stood and tossed it into the can with Blake's. "Jump shot for two."

Most of the other letters contained bits and pieces of everyone's life. Like someone had orchestrated this campaign of information. She tossed another handful of letters into the trash then paused and stared at the next three. From Mom.

Her dad alluded to these letters. She paced the room, her hand trembling as she sorted them by date. Sliding her finger under the flap of the first one she pulled it out. Her eyes blurred as she read.

8

Karen set the classifieds down and took a few sips of coffee. Her mom's letter contained polite niceties. No substance. Afraid of what the other letters held and too drained to deal with it, she watched old television reruns on cable late into the night. Now she was paying for it. The quiet of the empty hotel dining room soothed her nerves.

She examined the ads and found several decent cars and a few promising apartments listed. She didn't plan to stay here forever, but an apartment would allow her to conserve money. After college, she had saved money out of every paycheck. Between her savings and investments she had enough money to start a new life. But if she spent more than absolutely necessary, she wouldn't have that nest egg for long.

She looked at her watch. *Only nine?* She wanted to sleep but her mind refused to let her. Instead, she pulled out her phone and called several hospitals until she found where her mom was a patient and verified the room number and visiting hours.

After a quick search, she found her brother's address, which she tapped into Google maps. Satisfied, she stopped by her room to grab her purse before heading out.

The smell of antiseptic filled her nostrils as she stepped off the elevator and headed down the hall to her mother's room. Before entering she stopped and leaned back against the wall, her eyes closed. *I don't want to be here.* She deliberated with herself a few moments and then hung her purse on her shoulder and turned away. When an older nurse glanced her way, she quickened her pace, looking at the floor.

"Karen? Karen Hannigan?"

She paused and looked up at the woman in front of her. "Margie?" The hair was a bit grayer, but the smile was the same. Karen smiled, leaned down and hugged her. Margie Grave's physical stature may have been short, but on the inside she stood taller than most. And Karen could still almost wrap her arms around Margie twice.

"I've been praying for you." Margie's delight at seeing Karen was evident in her smile and sparkling eyes.

Still the encourager. Karen blinked away threatening tears. *I won't break down. Not here.* "Thanks, I guess."

"I'm glad you came home. How's your mom today?"

"I couldn't bring myself to go in."

"It's hard." Margie nodded, placing a hand on Karen's arm. "She changed you know."

"No, I don't know." Karen looked away. "Sorry, Margie, I don't mean to snap. I know you mean well."

"Where are you staying?"

"Over on Ambassador Drive." She shifted her weight and glanced at the elevator.

"Nonsense. I have that apartment over my garage. Why don't you stay there?"

Karen smiled, remembering it as her own private clubhouse before Margie and her husband finished it to rent out. "That's so generous. Thank you. I'll think about it. I'm just not sure how long I'll be here."

Margie hugged her. "Well, it's yours for as long as you want."

A half an hour later Karen pulled into her youngest brother, Albert's driveway. The drive from the hospital reminded her of the opening from the old Green Acres reruns she used to watch with Barry. Trading light poles for fences, buses for horses and steel walls for the wide open spaces. It was good to see the sky again.

Albert's house stood about a quarter of a mile from the main road on a gravelled lane. Pulling close to the house, she noticed a large, well-tended garden off to the side. She climbed out of the car and took in the view around her. Not another house within a mile. She took a deep breath and relaxed. *Nice.*

She took another deep breath to muster her courage. *Someone's grilling.* She skipped the front door and walked around the side of the house where she found her brother standing next to the grill. Taller than her now, he still wore a crew cut and stood ramrod straight while he worked. If she didn't know better, she would swear he was in the military.

She smiled. Out of all her siblings, Albert was the one she looked forward to seeing.

He looked up, met her gaze and stepped back from the grill. "Karen? I can't... Where did you come from?"

"Surprise." She chuckled nervously.

"That's an understatement." He rushed across the patio and gathered her up in a bear hug. "It's good to see you. No one will believe it. Come in, meet my wife."

They stepped through the back door, and Karen followed Albert through the house. It was immaculate. Bats and baseball gloves were housed in a sports rack against the wall near the back door. Framed children's artwork lined the hallway.

The master bedroom caught her eye as they walked past. Nothing cluttered the view. Candles stood like sentinels on the dresser. The sage green walls invited her to relax. This room offered sanctuary.

The house was designed with a great room concept with a view straight from the kitchen through to the living room. She supposed that would be helpful while raising little ones. A breakfast nook nestled in one corner of the kitchen next to the windows. A stack of paper plates along with plastic silverware and cups lined the counter.

"Honey, look who showed up. It's my sister, Karen." Albert grabbed her hand as he led her into the room. "Karen, this is my better half, Haley." She stood a foot shorter than Albert with a head of hair redder than Karen's, although Haley wore hers long. Two kids came up behind her.

"I'm so glad to finally meet you." She hugged Karen. "These are our kids Charlie and Annie, they're six. Albert's talked about you so much. You know, your sisters haven't come around as much as I'd hoped when we married. I looked forward to finally having sisters since I only had brothers. I hope —"

"Mom." Charlie and Annie spoke in unison.

Haley covered her mouth. "Sorry. I do get carried away." She laughed while the kids gave Karen a quick hug and ran off.

"Come on, we'll visit while I get the rest of lunch ready." Haley linked her arm through Karen's. "Albert, you better get back out to the grill or you'll burn the meat again."

"Yes, dear." Albert winked at his sister. "I think next time you need to run the grill."

Haley's laugh reminded Karen of wind chimes. "Maybe I'll do that. I think Dad would appreciate it."

Albert kissed Haley and patted her backside, before returning to the grill. The interplay between her brother and his wife fascinated Karen. She blushed. Her parents never displayed that type of affection.

"How's mom doing?"

Haley paused. "I'm glad you made it home, there's no way to know how much longer she has." She pulled a bowl out of the fridge and set it on the counter

"Is she in hospice yet?"

Haley nodded. "And your dad hired a private nurse, too. There's someone with her all the time. We kids do our best to make sure at least one of us stops in on her every day." She handed her a bowl of coleslaw and a stack of plates. "We need to get this out before the others arrive. They'll be surprised to say the least." Haley led the way to the patio.

"I can't stay if you're having company."

"Of course, you can. It's family."

"Family? No. I'm not ready to see everyone. Especially together." Karen set the bowl and plates down on the picnic table.

"Take a deep breath. It'll be okay. Hey, Albert, come talk some sense into your sister."

Karen bolted for her car.

Albert ran up beside her. "Come on, Sis, stay. You're going to see everyone anyway. Why not get the first time out of the way?"

She shook her head. "I can't." She heard wheels crunching gravel and looked down the drive at the car rushing toward them.

Albert laid a hand on her arm. "Joanna is always early."

"Always?" Karen tossed her purse into the car.

"The family gets together every Saturday. Either here or at Dad's. His idea. Some sort of peacemaking scheme of his."

"Everyone comes?"

"If you want to receive your legacy, get a piece of the orchard or stables when I die, you'll come to lunch together once a week," Albert imitated their dad's voice, then laughed.

"Who cares about the stables and the orchard?" Karen snorted. "He's already given us a legacy I don't care for."

"Dad wants to change that."

"I'll believe it when I see it."

"The only way you'll see it is by being around him."

Karen listened to her younger brother play reconciler and wondered where his wounds were. He seemed so put together and ready with the right answers. Maybe their dad's actions didn't affect him the way they bothered everyone else in the family.

"Of course, Dad's possessions don't matter to Haley and me." Albert raised his eyebrows. "Blake on the other hand…"

"Ha. That's about the only thing that would get him to spend time with Dad."

Gravel spewed out from under the tires as Joanna came to a stop. Albert raised his chin toward their sister. "She's a good place to start."

"This is entrapment."

Albert shrugged and offered her a sheepish grin.

Karen glared at her brother and crossed her arms. "Fine."

Her older sister climbed out of the car like a cat stretching its way across the top of a couch. Her wavy blonde hair hung past her shoulders, looking more mussed than styled. But she could get away with it. Karen stifled a grin. Her sister hadn't changed. As a kid, Karen looked up to Joanna who was eleven years older. She seemed to have it all together. Lived in her own apartment, held a job, owned a car, and had friends. Karen thought her sister was cool — even though Joanna called her names, made fun of her and was downright mean at times.

Then Joanna was arrested for shoplifting. After her release, Karen visited her and found her passed out, high on drugs. Karen held no more illusions about her sister.

Joanna seemed to study Karen, then took a long drag on her cigarette, threw down the stub and ground it out with the heel of her boot. Reaching into the backseat of her car, she pulled out a couple of bags. "Here, Albert. I'm returning these to your wife."

"Joanna." Albert crossed his arms.

"What? Okay, I'm returning these to Haley."

Albert raised his eyebrows and tapped his toe. "You know what I mean."

"You can't really mean you want me to pick that up."

Albert matched her stare for stare.

"Fine. Take these to your wife." Joanna handed the bags to Albert and blew out a pent up breath while she picked up her cigarette stub and put it in the ashtray in her car. "Little brothers can be such a pain."

Albert carried the bags into the house and the two sisters waited on each other in awkward silence.

"So, you take off without a word and show back up the same way." Joanna leaned against her car with her arms folded.

"What did you expect? An I-love-you-and-I'll-miss-you note? Come on, we never got along. You never even liked me."

"That's a load of lies and you know it."

"No, it's not. And you know it."

Joanna reached into her purse and pulled out another cigarette.

Turning sideways to block the breeze, she tried lighting it, but the lighter shook in her hands and the cigarette refused to burn. She shrugged.

"You didn't answer my letters."

"I didn't open any letters from the family until two days ago."

"You kept it but didn't open it." Joanna snorted and tried to light up again. "Have you seen Dad yet?"

"No."

"He changed, or so it seems. Tried to mend bridges, too, but it hasn't worked too well." Joanna leaned against the car. "You know, I used to be jealous of you."

"Me? Why?" Karen moved over beside Joanna.

"You were his little princess. I assumed you always were. I didn't realize the truth until after you left."

"I told you, but you didn't believe me."

Joanna pushed away from the car. "Look, I'm gonna blow this joint. I don't think I want to deal with any fireworks today. They're sure to be worse than usual."

Karen moved aside while Joanna got in the car.

"Tell Dad hello. If you stay that long. Or you can hop in and we'll go get drunk and have a good cry." Joanna laughed. "Don't look so shocked, little Sis....I guess it's still a bit early in the day. Later." Joanna sped down the long gravel driveway.

Karen sighed. Joanna was elusive when they were kids. Would it be any different now? Maybe if they spent some time together. Karen smiled. But not to get drunk.

Joanna pulled out onto the street and blared her horn at a pickup pulling in the drive. Karen glanced back at the house. Albert looked nervous. She furrowed her brow. *Who's coming now?*

9

Blake stormed around the side of the house trailed by his wife, Alita, and their father.

"I thought I saw you. Why are you here?" Blake stood with his tattooed arms crossed, glaring at her.

"I'm…" She shriveled under his stare.

"Blake, so glad you could make it." Albert stepped between them. "Remember what Dad said about playing nice."

"I doubt he meant Karen." The way he spoke her name made her feel like an unwanted pet. Nothing had changed.

"I meant everyone." Her dad stepped forward. At well over six feet tall, he still carried himself like a young John Wayne.

Blake cursed, pushed past him, and stopped inches from Karen's face. "You shouldn't have come. It will only end badly." He grabbed Alita's arm and pulled her around the house. Seconds later, his truck roared to life, peppering the side of the house with gravel as he sped away.

Karen took a deep breath. Blake never liked her, but despite every taunt and threat, he had always been her brother. Today he talked to her as though she were out to get him. She clenched her teeth. *This wasn't a good idea.* She headed to her car.

"Karen, don't go." Her dad followed her. "Stay and visit. I'll leave." He stuck his cowboy hat back on and headed out of the yard.

Karen stopped and watched him walk away then went back to where Albert and Haley stood. "It doesn't mean he's changed."

"You'll see." Albert put an arm around her.

"Karen?"

She turned at the voice and saw her younger sister Elinor approaching. Although Albert was the youngest by birth, Elinor was the youngest by default. More fragile than the rest of them. Before Karen left home, she protected both of them the best she could. Once she left, Albert took over that role. Of course, she didn't think they received quite the same treatment as she did.

"Yep, it's me." Karen watched her younger sister wobble toward her in the gravel. *Heels.* Karen grinned. Elinor was the beauty of the bunch. And she still walked with the poise of a model. The tights she wore under a simple paisley tunic made her look taller than she already stood. Karen hitched her thumbs through her belt loops and waited for Elinor to make the first move.

Elinor hesitated then reached for Karen, who returned the hug then stepped back. "Love the hair cut, but what…?"

"It was too…Joanna." Her sister tucked a loose strand behind her ear.

"Ah…well, I wouldn't have thought it, but black actually looks good on you. It sets you apart. Kinda like those shoes." Karen nodded down at her sister's feet. "Prada?"

"I figure every girl deserves a vice." Elinor lifted her foot and angled it from side to side. "Like 'em?"

"As long as they're on your feet and not mine."

Elinor laughed, wrapping her arms around Karen again. "We missed you. I wish you never left."

"I had to leave."

"Sure. Listen, I'll let you guys catch up. I couldn't stay long anyway. I'm needed at the antique shop." Elinor sniffled and began backing her way out of the yard. "You're not going to skip out on us again, are you?"

"I'm not sure what I'll do." Karen didn't want to make any promises she couldn't keep.

"Okay, then. I guess I'll see you around."

Karen watched her sister retreat. "Hey. Let's do lunch sometime."

Elinor turned, her face brightened. "That would be nice. This week sometime? Get my number from Albert and call me."

"That works." If she reconnected with her siblings one at a time it wouldn't seem so overwhelming. She turned to Albert and Haley. "I suppose I should go, too."

"And leave all this food?" Haley put her arm around Karen's shoulder. The invitation of warm companionship swayed her. "I am hungry. Thanks." She piled her plate with food, then sat down at the picnic table across from Albert and watched the kids play.

A year ago she went to the doctor for birth control without telling Barry. She hadn't worried about getting pregnant before. They both wanted kids. But when she realized their relationship was a mess, she decided she would not bring a child into the same angry environment she knew as a teenager.

"Want to talk about it?"

"What?"

"You're distracted."

"Oh." Karen took a bite of cookie. "Just thinking about kids."

"You have any?"

"No." Karen looked down and touched her fingers where her wedding ring should be.

"You married?"

"Eight years." She dropped her hands into her lap and looked up into her brother's eyes as he sipped his iced tea. "We were married six months after we met. Not a very good foundation for a lifetime together, I suppose, but the first six years were good. Then he lost his job and spent more time angry than not. He reminds me of Dad. I don't get their anger." Karen glanced over at the kids tugging back and forth over a ball.

"Selfishness."

Karen nodded toward the kids. "Like a kid getting angry because he can't have what he wants?"

Albert chuckled. "Exactly. But adults throw bigger temper tantrums."

She nodded. "Barry wants a good life. But with his choices in play, it's not happening."

"So, he throws his anger at you?"

"That about sums it up." Karen gazed across the table at her brother.

"What about Dad? What were his tantrums about?"

"I don't know, Karen. I don't know," Albert shook his head.

"Barry's just like Dad when he's drunk. I walked on eggshells around him. Then a few days ago...he hit me." She grabbed a napkin and wiped her tears.

"I'm so sorry, Karen." Haley put an arm around her shoulder.

"I lost my job a couple days ago and the same day found out he was looking at porn. There was no way I wanted to hang around. Anyway, I packed up and here I am. Now, I don't know — I didn't think about being around family." She swung her legs over the bench and looked at Albert. "I need to leave. Would you go to the hospital with me to see Mom tomorrow?"

"Sure. Since tomorrow's Sunday, why don't we meet after lunch? Say about one?"

"Works for me."

Leaving Albert's, Karen drove farther out into the country rather than return to the hotel. White fences stood in sharp contrast to the green fields they surrounded. Horses grazed on the rolling hills. Her dad had always enjoyed keeping a few horses around. She remembered their after school rides together to check on the orchard. He rode alone after she turned thirteen.

She rolled the car windows down and let the summer breeze whip her hair around her face then turned the radio up loud enough for the horses on the other side of the fence to dance to. She chuckled then sobered when she turned her mind back to family.

What force brought her home of all places? All her thoughts were focused on the need to get away from Barry. Could she live through the memories? For what? Her vision blurred and she pulled off onto the shoulder.

Karen rested her head on the steering wheel and cried. *God, I don't know why you would want to hear from me, but just in case...* She slammed her palm on the dashboard. *Why am I here? I'd be better off if I disappeared to some little hide-a-hole and started over.*

A wry laugh escaped her throat at the image of some diner dump in a remote place. It sure sounded a lot easier. She escaped once before and started over. Her crying subsided as she considered the possibility again. The thought of freedom from her family and Barry tempted her, but she knew the anger and hurt would always hang over her unless she dealt with it.

Leaning her head against the headrest, she squeezed her eyes shut. She leaned over across the front seats and drew up into a ball and cried until her eyes were dry and the sadness lifted. *I'm going to make it and be better for it.*

Karen eased the car back onto the road, made a U-turn and headed back to the highway. After stopping at a department store for a swimsuit and a couple changes of clothes, she picked up supper from a local deli and headed back to the hotel.

Thankful the hotel maid forgot to empty the trash, Karen pulled out the crumpled letters she'd thrown away the night before. Her swimsuit lay forgotten on the bed and her salad sat on the desk half eaten. She thumbed through the stack. The one from Blake sat on the top. She was surprised he wrote at all.

Older by ten years, they never were close. He usually either ignored her or picked on her. By the time she turned eight, Blake had joined the Marines. For a short time after his deployment, their relationship was almost tolerable. Then her dad turned, and Blake punctuated every interaction with anger. Karen shuddered as she remembered their last encounter.

The week before she left for college, she baby-sat for Blake and Alita. Their boys, only nine and four, found a stash of porn magazines hidden in Blake's closet. She was appalled he left them so accessible, but thankful she caught the boys before they saw any of the trash.

She returned the magazines to their hiding place and confronted her brother the next day. He was working in the garage, his feet sticking out from under his pickup. She stuck her hands in her pockets and leaned back against the wall, attempting a nonchalance she did not feel. "Blake, your boys found your stash of porn."

"So? They gotta learn about it someday."

She pushed away from the wall with her foot. "Don't you care?"

Blake rolled out from underneath the car and stood up. "Look, miss goody two shoes, when you have kids, you can raise them any old way you see fit." He wiped his hands on his jeans.

"They're too young to be seeing pictures of naked women."

"It's none of your business." Blake narrowed his eyes at her.

Her dad was a tea kettle always steaming with anger, but her brother was a volcano spewing sporadic red hot embers. Her instincts shouted at her to run, but her desire to protect those boys kept her rooted to her spot. "I'm telling Alita."

"Oh, no you won't!" He stomped toward her, grabbed her by the shoulders and shook her. "This is my family. You're going to be sorry you ever brought it up." He shoved her into the wall and raised his hand, whipping it toward her.

Karen's feet refused to move as she watched Blake's hand draw closer like a slow motion film.

"Dad?" Blake's youngest son called from the doorway, a questioning look on his face.

Blake dropped his hand and turned to face his son. "I'm busy. Go see your mom."

Her nephew glanced her way, then dropped his gaze and ran from the garage. While Blake watched his son run toward the house, she slipped out the side door, ran to her car and sped home.

Nineteen years had past since that day, and she hadn't seen him once. She crumpled Blake's letter and threw it in the trash.

All hate. But it hurt to see it in writing.

Karen slipped into her swimsuit and headed to the pool. The water was too cold so she slipped into the hot tub and let her muscles relax as the bubbles swirled around her. A half an hour later she was joined by a couple in the middle of a heated argument.

She grew uncomfortable, but was enjoying the warm water, so she leaned her head back and closed her eyes, hoping they would get the hint. But the pair seemed oblivious that she was even there.

The wife railed on her husband about everything he did wrong. He offered a weak defense. Karen wanted to tell the woman to lighten up or else he wouldn't hang around long.

Memories of arguments with Barry flooded back.

Karen opened her eyes and sat up straight. The couple finally noticed her and she gave them a sheepish grin as she climbed out of the hot tub. The woman lowered her voice, turned to her husband and shook her finger in his face as Karen toweled off and stepped into the hallway.

Did I treat Barry so ugly that he didn't want to be around me? Did I drive him to his bad choices? She hurried to her room as the emotions threatened to overwhelm her.

He came home drunk at night and lost every job he found. He cheated on their marriage with…images of other women and gambled his way into a huge amount of debt. He constantly cut her down with his angry outbursts. He hit her. He destroyed their relationship without any help from her.

Didn't he?

She pushed the door to her room shut behind her and slid to the floor. Tears rolled down her cheeks as the memories flooded her mind. Yelling at Barry. Pointing her finger in his face. Turning her back on him. Refusing him her bed. Giving him the silent treatment. Demanding him to be perfect. She buried her face in her arms.

"Oh, God, what have I done?"

10

Rush hour found Barry stuck in a cab a few blocks from his destination. He checked his watch. *Time to hoof it.*

He paid his fare and joined the throng on the sidewalk and made it into view of The Plaza Hotel only a few minutes late. He wished he had told the limousine driver to pick him up on the way. It was probably already there.

Dennis told him to look for a woman in red. He paused when he saw her standing next to one of the columns in front of the hotel. He walked across the street to join her. *What a woman.* He knew what Karen would say, but appreciating beauty was a far cry from an affair.

Long legs, curly blonde hair and lips that pouted a bit. Her form-fitting dress screamed to be noticed. Any man would be a fool not to admire the scenery. Brushing aside the nagging guilt, Barry squared his shoulders and set his mind to turn on the charm.

Heather stood with her hands on her hips, foot tapping as he approached. He felt his wedding ring in his pocket. It would be hard to play the party guy if she knew he had a wife.

She crossed her arms in front of her. "I assume you're Barry Marino. You're late."

"I'm sorry, milady....Your carriage awaits." He held his breath and waited for her response. She smiled and held out her hand like a lady of the royal courts.

"Lead the way, young knight."

Barry breathed a sigh of relief and winked at her. *Guess I haven't lost all my skills.* He spotted the limo a few cars down, then bowed slightly and offered his arm to escort her through the crowd on the sidewalk. "This way, milady Heather."

Her laugh enchanted him and he relaxed a bit.

"You're from Chicago? I've always wanted to visit the Windy City. How long have you lived there?"

Her hand tensed on his arm before she spoke. "I'm fairly new to Chicago. I still feel like a tourist some days. Like when I get turned around on the bus routes."

He chuckled. *Why is she tense?* As they approached the limousine, the chauffeur opened the door and they climbed in. "Our reservations are for six. We can take a stroll through the park gardens or go on to the restaurant and wait in the bar. What do you prefer?"

"Let's wait in the bar. These heels are murder on my feet."

"I don't know why you ladies wear them, they look uncomfortable." He looked down at Heather's small feet. "But I gotta admit, they're nice window dressing, if you know what I mean."

"There's your reason."

Barry laughed. Tonight would be enjoyable.

At the restaurant they told the hostess they would be in the bar, then found a seat and ordered drinks while Heather chatted about the paintings that lined the walls. He enjoyed the melodic sound of her voice and wished he could get to know her better. He pushed aside another twinge of guilt, determined to enjoy the break from the reality of his life with Karen.

After a short wait, the hostess showed them to a table at the back of the dining room. "Will this do?"

"Very nicely, thank you." Barry held a chair out for Heather and settled himself across from her.

"Would you like to look at the wine list?" The waiter handed the list to Barry. He paused as the name of Karen's favorite jumped out at him. The one served at their wedding reception.

Regret nibbled at the corner of his mind and he glanced over the top of the menu. *I can't think about Karen right now.* He snapped the list shut and handed it to the waiter. "Bring us the best wine in the house." He smiled at Heather's raised eyebrows. "Dennis passes on his apologies. He wishes he could have made it."

"I'm sure. Not. He probably has a girl who doesn't understand the need to wine and dine a new client, so he sends you. Now I'm trying to figure out if you're married or not."

Barry knocked his water glass over, then fumbled trying to clean the mess. Her gentle laugh stopped his efforts. "It's not a big deal. Don't talk about her, though. Okay?"

"No problem." He grinned.

The waiter arrived and showed him the label before pouring a small amount into his glass. Barry checked the cork then swirled it around in the glass. One of his favorite dates with Karen was a wine and cheese tasting at a vineyard in Maine. He smiled as he recalled her delight on that trip. Everything was an adventure.

He sniffed the wine. It had a dark aroma. He tasted it and found it dry and full bodied. Dennis would approve.

Barry watched as Heather took a sip. She closed her eyes, swallowed, then let out a sigh. Her smooth skin and curve of her neck tantalized him and the deep cut of her dress teased him. The pleasure she displayed with a simple drink of wine promised more. Was she for real? *I can't let this woman get to me.* He turned his attention to the menu and ordered the house special for both of them.

"What brings you to The City?" Barry refilled her glass.

She swirled the liquid in her glass. "I tried to surprise some friends of mine from college, but I got here and found they were out of town. I suppose I should have called first." Her laugh tickled Barry's senses.

"So are you in town long? If you like, I can take you to a ball game. I think the Yankees are in town this week."

"If you suggested the Red Sox, I might take you up on it."

"A play then?" Barry cringed. *Too much.*

"I appreciate your offer, but I fly back tomorrow."

"If you're ever in town again and need someone to hang out with, just give me a call."

Heather glanced at him over the rim of her glass and smiled as she touched his shin with her foot. Barry's pulse raced. Karen hadn't flirted with him in so long he forgot how good it felt.

Heather's eyes twinkled as she reached for the bottle. Barry watched her pour another glass, but declined when she offered it to him. He met her gaze and found himself locked into place.

She told him bits and pieces about her life then reached across the table and took his hand. "Now it's your turn. Tell me about yourself."

He cleared his throat. "I've lived here for — "

"Barry?"

He yanked his hand away from Heather's and glanced up. "Megan. Robert." *Of all the luck.* He pushed his chair back from the table and stood. Ignoring Megan, he offered a hand to her husband, a man who looked like he belonged on the basketball court.

Before Barry lost his job he enjoyed hanging out with them, but now, they only reminded him of his failures. Karen pointed out Robert's good qualities on a regular basis. Barry wished she would brag on him like that. *But what have I done to deserve it?* He couldn't even do this simple favor for Dennis right.

"Barry." Robert shook his hand and looked over at Heather.

"Great restaurant, isn't it?" Barry nodded at Megan.

"I'm Heather." The woman stood and offered her hand, laying her other hand on Barry's arm. "It's so good to meet a friend of Barry's."

Megan raised an eyebrow as she shook Heather's hand. "Likewise." Megan turned her eyes on Barry. "How's your wife?"

Robert put his arm around his wife. "I think we need to go. We'll catch you later."

Barry watched them leave, then sat down. His shoulders drooped. Everyone and everything seemed bent on seeing him fail.

"You don't work for Dennis, do you?"

"How did you know?"

"Just a hunch." Heather pulled an earpiece out of her ear and laid it on the table.

Barry sat back in his chair. *A cop.* He was sure Dennis knew and intended for him to take the fall. "This was a set up?"

Heather nodded. "Tell me about your relationship with Dennis."

"Not much to tell. I used to work for him. When I found out most of his stuff was criminal, I made a few — charitable — deals in his name. He didn't like it, so he fired me. Then he made sure I couldn't find any decent work."

"You could help us put him away." Heather folded her hands under her chin.

"You want me to snitch?" He snorted. "No thanks." He stood and tossed his napkin onto the table.

"If you change your mind, let me know." She held out her card.

He ignored the offer. He didn't need another complication right now. What he needed was a stiff drink. Good thing Jack's Bar wasn't far away.

Barry weaved through the full tables at Jack's and headed straight for the bar. Megan and Robert ruined his chance to use Dennis to get his life back on track and now they would report his outing to Karen.

A hand grabbed Barry's neck and squeezed hard. "Four days."

Barry stiffened. It didn't take Anthony long. *Why did I even come here? Stupid.*

Barry nodded, downed his drink and left the bar. The lure of a bottle and the Internet called to him. With Karen gone, no one would tell him to stop. Just what he wanted.

11

Barry poured a cup of coffee, then sat down at the kitchen table. Pulling the classifieds out of the Sunday paper, he glanced through the listings as he stretched his back and neck, stiff after the last couple of nights on the couch.

The last few years no one in the real estate industry had taken a second look at him once they checked his reference. Dennis made sure every broker in New York knew about what he had done. And nobody would look at him without a reference.

The jobs he did manage to land — fast food, day labor, and the like — never lasted. He ran a hand through his hair. He needed to get a grip on his anger. It always landed him in hot water. He folded the paper and tossed it on the table. Nothing much listed today. He refused to scrub toilets.

He glanced at his cell phone and saw the voice mail icon. He cursed when he heard Megan's voice. She and Robert thought he was having an affair. He fumed and paced the floor. *Have they already told Karen?*

He dialed Karen's number and got her voice mail again. He hung up. *You're infuriating. How can we work on our problems if you won't talk to me?* "Just because they saw me with some woman, and just because I got a little mad at Karen gives them no right to doubt my faithfulness."

Doesn't it?

Barry shook the voice from his head and went to the bedroom for his wallet. He stopped in the doorway and stared at his bed. The porn magazines mocked his words. He grabbed his wallet and stormed out of the apartment.

Come to me and rest.

Where did these thoughts come from? He picked up his pace and jumped on the bus headed toward Jack's. He needed more to drink than just a beer.

Two hours and several drinks later, he paid his bill and stumbled out of the bar despite Jack's protests. He caught a bus uptown to Dennis' restaurant. The man still hadn't made up for blackballing him.

Barry looked at his watch. Hopefully he wouldn't have long to wait before he confronted his former boss. He found a place in the alley near Dennis' car to wait.

At 10 o'clock Dennis stepped out of the building. Behind him were two heavy weights. Barry ignored the paid protection and got right in Dennis' face. "What do you mean, setting me up?"

The bodybuilders reached for him, but Dennis waved them off. "This isn't a good place. Let's go back inside." Dennis took his arm and guided him inside the restaurant.

"When you first came to New York, I thought you had potential, that might be useful to my organization. But it turned out you were an albatross. So I cut you loose."

"But you didn't have to make it impossible for me to get a decent job."

"No, I didn't." Dennis smirked. "Consider it payback. And a warning."

"You said you would help me."

"Look, I needed to flesh out a snitch and distract the cops for a few days while I cleaned some stuff up." Dennis laughed. "So, I misled you about the job and paying off your debt. You should know that's how I operate. Here." Dennis stuck a wad of bills in Barry's front pocket. "For your time."

Barry glared at Dennis then pulled the money out and threw it down. "I don't want your filthy money." He exploded and dove for Dennis, but he was so drunk, he crashed into a bussing cart when Dennis stepped out of the way.

"You shouldn't have done that." Dennis motioned to his goons. "Get this trash out of here."

A hard blow to the back of Barry's head knocked him to the ground and blackness followed.

※

Barry blinked against the throbbing pain in his head. Propping himself against a wall, he took stock of his surroundings. The alleyway had enough cardboard boxes to fill a small warehouse, but Dennis and his goons were gone.

He tried to stand, but the pain in his right side sucked the air out of him and he fell back against the brick building. Dazed, he rubbed his hand across his side in an attempt to soothe the searing pain. His ribs felt broken. *I have to get out of here.*

He inched his way to the end of the alley and strained to see the street sign. The letters were blurry. Nothing looked familiar. He sat down, and with his elbows on his knees, leaned his forehead into his hands. His side ached with every breath. At least he was alive.

"Come to me and rest."

Barry looked around for a body to go with the voice but saw nothing except a church steeple across the street. The lights were on, and people were coming and going. Maybe if he could make it across the street, someone would help him.

He pushed himself to his feet, took a moment to catch his breath, and eased onto the sidewalk. He stumbled and a pair of hands reached out and lifted him up.

"Here, son, let me help you."

Barry looked into the eyes of a white-haired gentleman. He blinked and gasped for air as the man helped him to stand. The same man who helped him up when he almost got trampled on the sidewalk. Was that a week ago? "Thanks. I'm going to that church."

"That's where I'm headed. What's your name, young man?"

"Barry."

"I'm glad you found us."

"Me too."

The man's pace matched Barry's until they were across the street then the older man paused and looked around. "I need to find someone to help us. Oh, there's one of the workers. Robert, could you help me get this gentleman into the church?"

Barry shook his head as Robert Fletcher strode toward them.

"Barry? What happened to you? Let's get you inside."

He winced as Robert reached around and took the burden of weight from the older gentleman, and led him up the stairs. Barry turned to thank the man, but he was gone.

"Who was that guy?"

"Don't know, never saw him before." Robert guided him to a chair, then spent several minutes checking his injuries. "So, what happened? Was it Anthony?"

Barry jerked back. "How do you know about Anthony?"

Robert raised an eyebrow.

"Right. …Karen told Megan." He swore under his breath. "It was someone else — Dennis."

"The guy you used to work for? Some friend he turned out to be. What did you do?"

Barry shrugged his shoulders. He hated everyone knowing his business. "So, what is this place?"

"It's a rescue mission of sorts. We help people however they need it. Right now I think you need a doctor." Robert helped Barry to the car, then drove to a nearby clinic, where a nurse checked for internal injuries before wrapping his bruised ribs.

Afterwards Robert dropped Barry off at his apartment. "Call if you need anything."

"Yeah right. Like I want help from the guy who's out to ruin my marriage."

"I don't think you need any help from me on that one."

"Stay out of my business." Barry eased himself out of the car.

"I won't stop praying."

WHERE HOPE STARTS

Barry slammed the door and watched Robert drive away. "Who asked you to pray?" He stopped at his mailbox and pulled out a small package, looking at the postmark. *Who do I know in Boston?* Back in his apartment, he threw it on the kitchen table and headed to his room to change.

Stripping off his torn shirt, a wad of money fell out of the pocket. The cash Dennis offered him. *First time I've ever been paid for taking a beating.* He laid out a couple of bills for a drink the next day, then rolled up the rest and stuffed it deep into the second drawer of his dresser.

Unable to sleep because of the pain, he wandered into the kitchen and snatched a bottle of whiskey from the cupboard. He sat down at the table and reached for the mystery box to open it.

Karen's ring.

He stared at it and downed another shot of whiskey. Leaving the ring on the table, he grabbed his bottle, marched to the living room and turned on the computer.

The first site opened, his pulse quickened. Pleasure overruled all other senses, and the pain abated. Lulled into a fantasy world where women didn't expect anything and never ran away from his anger, he sat mesmerized until the first hint of sunshine poked through the curtains. He swore and shut off the machine. *Why do I do this?*

He slammed his chair back and swept the desk clear of Karen's odds and ends — the sound of shattering glass fueling his dark emotions. He tore pictures off the wall, hurling them across the room. Downstairs his neighbors pounded on their ceiling and brought him out of his stupor. He didn't want anyone to call the police.

Still feeling the effects of the whiskey, he staggered toward the bathroom to take a shower. He stopped in the bedroom doorway and stared at his favorite reading material strewn across the bed. *How could she throw it in my face like this?* He yanked one side of the bedspread up and sent the magazines flying, and then he dropped to his knees.

The sight of the rumpled bedcover brought another image to his mind — the night they spent in each other's arms a few weeks ago. He dropped his head into his hands and rocked back and forth on his heels as the tears ran down his cheeks. "Karen. Karen. I do love you. I do."

He crawled up in the bed and wrapped his arms around her pillow. The lingering scent of her perfume filled his nostrils — her whispered words hung in the air. No matter how many sites he visited or naked women he lusted after, he still longed for Karen. No fantasy could replace her softness, her laughter, her smell. "Karen, come home to me."

12

Karen pulled into a spot in the hospital parking garage and leaned her head back against the headrest. Her mind was still spinning after the scene at the hotel the night before.

Watching the couple in the hot tub argue reminded her of heated arguments with Barry. He hurt her, there was no doubt about that. But had she hurt him along the way? Didn't he carry more of the blame?

She didn't know what to think, but she couldn't dwell on it now. She had to get inside. She grabbed her purse from the passenger seat, slammed the door shut and took off for the entrance.

She was a half hour late, but Albert smiled as she emerged from the revolving doors. "I thought maybe you changed your mind."

"Great idea." She turned to leave, but Albert caught her elbow.

"Oh, no you don't, Sis. You know you need to do this."

Still drained from the night before, Karen knew there was no sense in fighting him. "Lead the way."

Albert headed toward the elevators. "Elinor called. She's looking forward to lunch."

"I'll get her number from you before I leave."

"Dad called, too. Asked how you were. I told him about our visit."

"Hmmf. Why did you bother?"

"I know it's hard for you to believe — "

"I don't want to talk about it." She hurried to catch the elevator before the doors closed. Albert apologized as they got on, but she glared at him.

"Should I just hang up on him?"

"Works for me."

"Karen."

She turned and glared at him. "What?"

"This is more than just Dad, isn't it? Did you hear from Barry?"

Karen relayed her evening in the hotel to Albert and he grinned.

"What are you so happy about? It wasn't funny."

"I think God is at work."

"If that's Him at work, I don't like it." She crossed her arms while they waited for the elevator to come to a stop.

The doors opened and they stepped off as an elderly couple got on. They were holding hands. She couldn't remember the last time she held Barry's hand in public.

Albert tugged at her arm. "Come on."

The hallway closed in on Karen and she found herself short of breath. She stopped and leaned down, hands on her knees. A pair of shoes entered her field of vision.

"Karen? You okay?"

She looked up to find her friend, Margie. She straightened, took several deep breaths and pasted on a smile. "Yeah. Thanks. Just got a little winded, I guess."

The older woman nodded and reached out to hug Karen. "When do you plan to move into the apartment?"

"I'm still thinking about it."

"Well, I've opened the place up to air out. It'll be ready for you. You need my phone number."

Karen added Margie's number to her contacts. "I'll let you know. Tell Sam hello for me."

Margie looked down at the floor. "Sam died three years ago."

"Oh." Karen nibbled on her lip. "I'm sorry."

"He lived a good life and he's with Jesus. Don't be sorry — I'll see him again."

Karen hesitated. *How can she be so confident?* "Well, I'm glad you find comfort in that."

"You haven't come back to Him yet, have you?" Margie tilted her head and looked at Karen. She squirmed under the older woman's scrutiny. Margie always read her like a book. From the day she ran to Margie and her husband for comfort and sanctuary, they formed a bond that rivaled any she hoped to have with her mother. Margie and Sam were like surrogate parents.

Margie always encouraged her to open herself back up to God. A lot like Megan. Living in Margie's apartment would put her face to face with that on a daily basis. After her father's rejection, she refused to believe God cared about her. After all, he allowed whatever took her father's love away. She shook her head. "God doesn't want me."

"Deep in your heart, you know different. Give me a call." Margie turned to Albert. "Take good care of your sister."

Albert nodded. "Yes ma'am."

Karen gave her friend one more quick hug then watched her walk away.

Albert touched her elbow. "You ready?"

"As ready I'll ever be." Karen took a deep breath and they slipped into the room.

Her mother's cheeks were sunken, bones no longer hidden by a layer of fat. Her beautiful red hair was gone. "She looks like a survivor from a POW camp."

He put his arm around Karen while the shock wore off, and then stepped back. She sat beside the woman who gave her birth and took her hand. "Mama. I'm here. I'm sorry it took so long. I know you have secrets to share. I hope I'm not too late." Karen laid her head beside her mother.

"Why are you here?" The voice bounced around the room.

Startled, Karen turned in her chair and faced Blake. "I think that's obvious."

"I told you to stay away and I meant it."

"She's my mother, too. You can't keep me away." Karen matched her brother's glare.

Blake took a step toward her, but Albert intervened.

"Look, Blake, this isn't the place to air our differences." Karen stood up. "I'll leave for now. We can talk another time."

"You can be sure of that." Blake glowered at Karen.

She picked up her purse and walked out the door. Albert followed. "What's going on between you two?"

"We didn't part on such good terms."

"You don't say." Albert matched Karen's pace.

"It's a long story." Karen pushed the elevator button.

"I have all the time in the world."

"Not today." Karen's phone interrupted them. Barry's ringtone. She let it go to voice mail again. "I need to call Elinor. Can I get her number?"

Albert crossed his arms. "You're stalling."

"You don't give up, do you?"

"Not on you. Never have." Albert gave her a crooked grin.

"Can I give you a rain check?"

"Sure. Call me." Albert hugged her and left.

Karen watched her brother walk away, then sat down in the lobby. She started shaking. Her encounter with Blake resurrected old fears. First Dad, then Blake, now Barry. She leaned back in the chair and sighed. The first two had been chosen for her, the last one only she could take credit for. She cried out to God for the love she longed for.

You are loved.

The whisper in her heart startled her. Was Albert right? Was God at work? Even after the way she treated Barry? Even after the way he treated her?

She squeezed her eyes shut. She wanted to believe the voice in her heart. She just didn't know if she could.

Taking a deep breath, Karen gathered her composure before grabbing her purse and heading out the door. She would steer clear of Blake for as long as she could.

13

Karen gave Elinor a quick call and arranged to meet her for a late lunch, then headed to the Applewood Hill Bed and Breakfast in Westfall. Her sister raved about the place. Formerly a run-down Victorian home, the owners refurbished it several years before and turned it into an upscale vacation spot and restaurant.

A real estate sign marked the turn off. Karen slowed and admired the view. White, trimmed in blue, the large house boasted a wrap-around porch complete with a front porch swing. It was an impressive sight pulling down the drive. The orchard adjacent to the Bed and Breakfast stretched out on either side. *Why are they selling the place?*

Karen tapped the steering wheel with her fingertips. It would make a great investment. *Something to think about.* Parking the car, she climbed out and looked around. Tastefully landscaped, a lot of time and attention had gone into it.

Elinor waved from the porch. Karen headed toward her. Without the whole family around, she looked forward to this time with her grown up little sister.

She gave Elinor a hug. "Did you make reservations?"

"The manager always finds me a spot."

"Someone special?"

"No."

Karen raised her eyebrows at her sister's quick answer and blushed face. "Come here often?"

"I manage an antique shop in Westfall and this is my favorite spot to eat." Elinor waved to the gentleman at the front counter.

Karen grinned. He reminded her of one of Jane Austen's characters.

"Elinor. Always a pleasure." The man's smile offered more than a simple greeting as he took her hand. "Who might this be?"

"My sister Karen. She's in town for a while because of our mother. Karen, this is James Abbott."

James turned to Karen and took her hand. "A pleasure."

His British accent reinforced her first impression. "The pleasure is mine as well."

"I wish it had been under better circumstances. Your mother came here often with Elinor. She is a kind and gracious woman."

Karen tensed. The woman who stood aloof while her dad emptied his anger on her was not a kind and gracious woman.

James tucked a couple of menus under his arm. "Now, Elinor, may I show you ladies to the dining room?"

"Yes, thank you."

James led them to a table and left with the promise of a quick appearance by their waiter. Karen turned to Elinor and chuckled. "Your Mr. Darcy is awful handsome."

"Oh, be nice. He's a real gentleman."

Karen laughed at her sister's discomfort. "Don't worry — I think it's sweet."

They ordered grilled salmon with rice pilaf and a side salad.

After the waiter left, Elinor reached for Karen's hand. "So, how are you? Why didn't you let us know you were coming?"

Karen shrugged. "Dad wrote about Mom's health and I decided to come home. Kind of short notice."

"We wrote you earlier about Mom. Didn't you get the letters?"

"Sort of." Karen rearranged the silverware on the table.

"Sort of? What does that mean?"

Karen looked up at the sharp tone in her sister's voice. "I never opened them, okay?"

"No it's not okay. How can you be so…so…so…"

"So what? You have no idea — "

The waiter appeared with their food, placed it on the table, and made a hasty retreat. Karen looked at her sister and her shoulders drooped. "I'm sorry."

"I'm sorry, too."

The silence hung between them until James approached and sat next to Elinor. "Ladies, I'm sure you have much to catch up on. May I make a suggestion? We have a beautiful gazebo next to the orchard often used for more private meals that you are welcome to use."

"I'm sorry. Have we disturbed your other patrons?" Elinor blushed.

"Not at all." James smiled and patted Elinor's arm. "I am always looking for ways to attract your attention. This is simply one of my ploys."

"James."

"It's true, you know." He stood. "Shall I have one of the waiters set the table for you in my gazebo?"

"Maybe we should leave. Karen?"

"Are you serious? I think it's a marvelous idea." She turned to James. "We would love to take you up on your offer."

"Well, I don't think we should — "

"Wonderful." James interrupted Elinor. "Come with me. I'll show you to the orchard and send the waiter back for your food." They rose from the table, and James led the way back through the foyer, down a hallway to a back door.

"How could you?" Elinor whispered.

"It looked like you needed a little help." Karen chuckled when Elinor blushed. "Come on, I don't want to tell you my story in front of all these people."

"Okay. ...For you."

"Sure. Whatever you say." Karen sauntered toward the orchard.

Karen stared out over the orchard while the waiter set up their table. The gnarled branches of the trees twisted beneath the greenery. In a few short months they would be full with fruit. A breeze lifted her hair off her shoulders and she sighed. Her life felt about as twisted as those branches. This was a peaceful place, she would have to come back.

She joined Elinor at the table after the waiter left.

"So what have you been up to since I left?"

"Not much."

"I heard you went to Europe after your senior year of high school."

"It wasn't what people built it up to be. I decided to cut the trip short." Elinor took a drink of water.

"Really?" Karen leaned forward on her elbows. Elinor was being elusive, but Karen intended to dig out some conversation.

"I mean, I liked it okay. We visited a lot of cool stuff."

"Like?"

"The Eiffel Tower, the Sistine Chapel. The usual stuff."

"Did you make any friends?"

Elinor looked around the orchard. "I traveled with a small group and everyone went their own way. I don't want to talk about it." She sloshed water out of her glass when she set it down.

"Maybe a guy is why you came back early." Karen tapped a finger against her bottom lip.

"I just didn't want to be there."

"Okay, I'll drop it. What's up with Blake?"

"He hasn't been the same since he came back from his tour overseas. He's been mad at the world ever since."

"War's an ugly place. It could affect anyone." Karen wondered what happened to her brother. She knew of several women at Megan's shelter who were there because of the changes in their husbands after serving in the military.

Elinor finished her last bite and laid down her napkin. "Enough chit chat. Tell me what's going on."

"I'll give you the condensed version."

"I don't think so." Elinor pointed to a swing next to the gazebo. "I've got as long as you need."

Karen followed her to the edge of the orchard. Nestled in among the apple trees, a white arbor framed the swing. The tiny pink roses covering the trellis reminded her of the flowers her mother used to grow.

"Do you remember the good years with Dad?"

"We had a lot of fun, didn't we?" Elinor smiled.

Karen nodded. "Do you remember when it changed?"

"Like yesterday." Elinor sat on the swing. "It happened so fast."

"Did Mom and Dad ever tell you why? I mean after I left."

"No. Don't you know?"

"Nope." Karen paced. It made her angry to think about it.

"You mean after all this time, they never told you?"

Karen stopped and faced Elinor. "Evidently Mom explained everything in one of her letters. But I can't find it. And Dad won't tell me."

"I can't believe our family. This thing has hung over us far too long. You need to get Dad to tell you what it is."

"Ha! Dad isn't going to budge. Are you sure you don't know anything? Whispers through the wall? Something?"

"Nothing. So, how long are you sticking around?"

Karen huffed. "No clue, but I can't go back to New York the way things stand with my husband, Barry."

"What's going on?"

"You name it. Drinking, gambling, porn... Last week he hit me."

"Karen, I'm so sorry."

"He hasn't always been that way." Karen sighed. "The first six years were like a fairy tale."

"What happened?"

Karen nibbled on her bottom lip. She couldn't share the blame for Barry's choices, could she? It seemed so unfair. And if she were at fault in any way for her floundering marriage, did she hold blame for the choices her dad made?

"I'm not sure."

"Can I do anything to help?"

Karen smiled at her little sister. "If you find out what the big secret is, let me know."

"You know I will."

Leaving the orchard, Karen's steps slowed. She wanted answers, but waiting for them seemed her only option. "You don't happen to have tomorrow off from the boutique, do you?"

"No. What's up?"

"I need to look for an apartment. It would be nice to have some company." Karen still wasn't ready to take Margie up on her offer.

"Try Joanna."

"Maybe."

Elinor stopped next to her car. "It was good to catch up. You should stop by my shop soon. I'll give you a good discount."

Karen laughed. "I'll try and do that. Thanks." She waved, then walked up to the porch where David stood watching her.

Her phone jingled Megan's ringtone. Karen let it go to voice mail and nodded at David. *He looks good.*

He joined her at the bottom of the stairs. "I'm sorry for not telling you about Mary."

"No concern of mine." Karen headed toward her car.

David walked beside her. "It could be."

First Boston and now here. She shook her head. All she could think about were the days she could not go back to. His nearness distracted her. She needed to leave.

"Karen?" David touched her shoulder.

"I'm sorry. What did you say?"

"Your husband is a jerk."

She stopped at her car and glared at him. "Don't talk about Barry that way."

David looked at her hand. "You took your ring off."

Karen sucked in her breath. "It had nothing to do with you."

"Are you sure?" His eyes searched her's for an answer. "You're right." He ran a hand through his hair and looked off into the distance. He leaned against the car beside her. "So, if I quit offering relationship advice, can we call a truce?"

"I'm right? That quick? I expected more."

"What can I say? How about it?"

"Sure. It would be nice to have my old friend back. Now, I better go."

"Where are you off to so fast?"

"I don't have any reason to stay." Karen shielded her eyes from the early afternoon sun.

"Why don't you join me for a horseback ride at my folks?" He flashed puppy dog eyes at her.

"Don't you have to work?"

"I have my own firm. I can leave early when I want." David laughed.

"I missed our rides." She tilted her head and bit her bottom lip. Sadness crept into David's eyes and she regretted bringing it up. "I don't think it's a good idea."

"How can I change your mind?"

Her phone rang. Megan's ringtone. She held up her finger to stop David's questioning and reached into her purse. *It must be important.* "Hey, Megan. What's up?"

"There's something you need to know."

"Go on." She shot David a look of apology.

"Robert and I tried out a new restaurant the other night. We're looking for a new favorite. We don't like the new management at the old one, you know."

Karen sighed. "Megan. Is there a point?"

"I debated telling you…" Megan paused.

"What?" Karen rolled her eyes at David.

"We saw Barry."

"And?" Her stomach churned. *How can Barry afford to eat out at a fancy restaurant?*

"He was with a woman and they looked pretty cozy. When we went over to say hello, he acted guilty."

"The jerk." She risked a glance at David. He gave her an "I told you so" look and she turned around. "Thanks. We'll talk later. I…I need to go." She put her phone in her pocket. *The audacity of the man. And I was thinking I played a part in this mess.* She thumped her car with the side of her fist.

"You okay?" David touched her shoulder.

She didn't answer for a moment. A horseback ride sounded good. She turned and faced her high school sweetheart. "I think I'll take you up on that offer."

"You remember the way?"

"Of course."

Karen followed David out of the lot and rolled down the windows to enjoy the fresh country air whipping through her hair. She never enjoyed this sense of freedom in New York. She floored the gas pedal and caught up to David as he turned into the long drive to his folks' house.

The colonial style house at the end of the quarter mile drive still gave her pause. His family had owned the land for several generations. The solidity of family it promised made her envious, but the more she hung around his family, the more she wondered if pride, not love kept the inheritance intact.

Gwen and Trent Ellis treated her with kindness, but it felt stiff and proper. They appeared the perfect family when around others, but Karen questioned what went on behind closed doors.

David was different. From the day they met, they talked with ease to each other and enjoyed one another's company. He accepted her, without reservation. She missed those times and wished she could pour her heart out to him like she used to. She shook her head. *Things are different now. He has a fiancée.*

She pulled her car to a stop next to David's and watched him get out and walk towards her. It was just the two of them alone with their memories. *Maybe this wasn't such a good idea.*

He opened her door. "Just like old times."

Not quite. She got out and followed him to the stables. "How often do you ride?"

He laughed. "More than you, I bet."

She slapped his arm playfully. "That's not fair."

He winked at her. "Did I ever play fair?" Stopping in front of a stall he clicked his tongue and a dapple gray poked it's head over the top of the half door. "Meet Line Dancer."

Karen laughed. "You didn't." She stepped forward and stroked the horse's muzzle.

"Yep. I think of you every time I take her for a ride."

"And does Mary know the story behind the name?" Karen looked around the barn.

"Now who's into someone else's business?" He turned away.

"Guilty as charged. Sorry." She held up her hands. "So which one do I get to ride?"

"I have just the one for you. Come on." He grinned and led her to the back of the barn. "Isn't she a beauty?"

Karen unlatched the stall door and reached out to the pure black mare. The horse nuzzled her fingers. "What's her name?"

"Midnight."

Karen ran her fingers through the mare's silky dark mane. "Perfect."

"She's rather spirited. Think you can handle her?"

"I'd like to try."

"Then it's settled."

They saddled up and headed out onto the five hundred acre property. Once they passed the outer pasture gate they urged the horses into a gallop. Karen thrilled at the warm breeze on her face and the refreshing country scents — so much better than the host of smells that came with city life.

David looked over his shoulder at Karen. "Race you to Round Top Meadow."

"You're on." *Just like old times.*

The pair raced back the way they came then turned west and rode toward the river. They were laughing by the time they reached their favorite spot. She couldn't remember how many times she rode here on horseback or in David's old pickup to escape the ugliness of those last few years at home.

Karen dismounted and walked to the edge of the cliff. The river below wound its way through the hills and out of sight. She closed her eyes and found herself face to face with memories of another day in this same spot. The first time David kissed her. She jumped when he stepped up behind her.

"A penny for your thoughts."

She caught her breath and turned around. His eyes told her he remembered too. His fingers traced the outline of her face and she leaned into his touch, longing for the tenderness. He leaned toward her and she closed her eyes, envisioning the kiss. Instead of David's face, she saw Barry.

She pulled back and turned away. She heard him draw in a breath. What was wrong with her? *This isn't right*. Even if Barry was with someone else, they were still... *What are we?* She clenched her fists.

She needed to sort it out. It wasn't fair to David to string him along. She took a deep breath and turned around, hoping he didn't hate her. "I'm sorry. It's not— "

"I get it. You're married and I'm engaged."

"Yeah." Karen let out a pent up breath.

"Still friends?"

"If it's possible."

"We'll make it possible."

14

Barry rubbed his eyes and moaned as he rolled onto his back. The room spun when he stood so he dropped back on the mattress, holding his head in his hands.

Everything hurts. What happened? He felt the tape around his ribs and remembered Robert helping him home. Barry cursed. *Dennis.* The urge for a drink overwhelmed him.

Come to me and rest.

He swatted at the imaginary voice. It was like an angel on his shoulder commenting about his life. He forced himself up and to the shower. Twenty minutes later he sat at the kitchen table eating pastries, drinking a cup of coffee, and staring at Karen's ring.

Where are you? He dialed her number and again it went to voice mail. He slammed the phone down and swallowed the last bite of pastry.

Megan would know where she was. He glanced at his watch — 3 o'clock. He wouldn't have to wait long before Megan got home from work. He stuck Karen's ring in her jewelry box, grabbed his keys and headed out the door.

Megan and Robert lived a few blocks north so he walked to their apartment building, then paced up and down their block as he waited. He needed a drink. *After she tells me what I want to know.*

"Barry?"

He turned and faced Megan. "I need to know where Karen is."

"If she wants you to know she'll tell you herself."

"Last time I saw her, you were with her. When I get home, there's a note. You must know something."

"Not as much as you would like."

"You're her friend." Barry clenched and unclenched his fists then stuffed them into his pockets and walked a few steps away.

Megan sat down on the steps and sighed. "She headed home. Somewhere in Missouri. That's all I know."

"Thanks." He turned to go.

"Barry?"

"Yeah?"

"I'm praying for you guys."

"Whatever."

He headed straight for the bar. He was one step closer to finding Karen, but he didn't know where to look. She never told him about her hometown, and Missouri was too big for a scavenger hunt.

Holding his sore ribs with his left arm, he hauled himself up onto a bar stool. As he settled in, he felt a hand on his shoulder. He grimaced. *Anthony.*

"Barry, have a drink on me. I like to see a man pay off his debt." Anthony motioned for Jack to serve Barry whatever he wanted, then laughed. "I got a cashier's check in the mail yesterday. Debt paid, in full."

"Who …I …?"

"You don't know? Guess it's your lucky day. I have a game running in the back room. You're more than welcome to join us."

Barry paused then shook his head. "No thanks." He had to know who he owed before he racked up a new bill. Did Karen pay it off? *I doubt it.*

Anthony chuckled and slapped Barry on the back. "If you change your mind, you know where to find me."

He watched the loan shark retreat to the back room, then downed his drink. He turned down a second round and headed out into the cool evening to catch the uptown bus.

When it neared the stop near his apartment he spotted Robert on the steps of his building. *Megan probably called him.* He considered riding the bus to the next stop then circling around to go in the back way. Robert would be none the wiser. His aching ribs convinced him otherwise.

He got off at his usual stop and waved at Robert. "Obviously you have something to say. You might as well come on up."

"You hungry? I brought some Chinese."

"Whatever."

Inside, Robert set the takeout on the table and waited.

"Want a beer?" Barry opened the refrigerator.

"Don't drink."

"Good for you. But I need more than water." Barry popped the beer top, grabbed some food and headed to the couch. "What's on your mind?"

Robert followed Barry to the living room. "You want Karen back?"

"Maybe."

"Then get help."

"I'm not an alcoholic."

"I'm talking about this stuff." Robert pointed to the magazines spread across the coffee table.

Barry grabbed them, tossing them behind a chair. "There."

"It takes more than that."

Barry sneered at Robert. "Why are you here?"

Robert stared back at him then took a deep breath. "Megan told me about your visit. Said you got a bit agitated."

"So?"

"I'm concerned about you."

"Right. If that's all you've got, there's the door."

"We are praying for you." Robert stood and headed for the door, then stopped. "God wants to help you clean up the junk in your life. You don't have to do it on your own. You just have to accept His offer."

Junk? He balled his hands into fists. "I don't need God."

"We all need God, Barry. Look, come visit my church. It's not the same one you found the other night. Here's a business card with the address on it. I've written my number down, too, in case…" Robert set the card on the coffee table and left.

He didn't need help. He just wanted his life back to normal — when no one talked about God. When he had life under control with plenty of money and fun. A great marriage. When he loved Karen and she loved him.

Why did she have to leave? Barry rubbed his chin and looked around the apartment. His eyes landed on the computer. They didn't run away from him. Not like her. He just needed to straighten out some stuff, then he and Karen could work things out. He took a deep breath, straightened his shoulders and walked over to the computer.

Come to Me and rest.

He needed to silence this voice and replace the image of his wife interrupting his thoughts day and night. He sat down and turned on the computer, drumming his fingers on his leg while he waited for the connection.

Guilt pestered him as the first image came up, but he continued clicking link after link. Picture after picture. Within minutes, numbness took over his conscious. He buried himself deeper into the fantasy world he created. By midnight his eyes were red and tiredness overwhelmed him. He shut the computer off and headed for bed.

He tossed and turned until two in the morning when he retrieved a bottle of vodka from the kitchen. On the couch he drank himself into a deep slumber.

Then the dreams came.

Karen followed him from bar to bar and card game to card game. She watched while he walked away from one job after another. Always behind him. Always silent. He tried to ignore her, but still she watched. He tried to run away and still she followed. *She knew. She knew it all.*

He woke in a sweat.

Come to Me and rest.

He covered his ears with a pillow and sobbed until he fell back into a restless asleep.

15

Karen pulled in front of Joanna's apartment building and leaned back. She enjoyed the horseback ride with David last night, but their time together left her aching for what could have been.

Lean on me, not on any man's affection or on your own understanding.

Karen gripped the steering wheel for a moment, then climbed out of the car and slammed the door. Maybe she should stay away from David, but she wanted to spend time with him.

She took a shaky breath and headed up to Joanna's apartment. Glancing around the complex she noted the manicured grounds, fresh paint and lack of junker cars up on ramps waiting for repair. *Not bad.*

When Karen reached the second floor she stopped to catch her breath, then groaned at the remaining flight of stairs.

Joanna stepped out of her apartment and locked the door just as Karen stepped onto the landing.

"You ready to get drunk?" Joanna lit up a cigarette and grinned. "Gotcha. Come on. I'm ready to see how the rich and famous live."

"I'm not rich or famous."

"Chill. It's a joke. Wanna drag?" Joanna offered her cigarette to Karen. "No? Good, I only have two more left."

Karen looked Joanna in the eyes for signs of drugs, but they were clear. She laughed at Joanna's chatter, watching her bounce down the stairs. "You sure you have time to hang out with me all day?"

"Wouldn't miss this chance to be with my little sis and see what she's made of herself... Well, maybe I would." Joanna laughed.

Karen wondered what Joanna might trade her off for. "So, where do you work?"

"I'm...uh...in between jobs right now."

"How do you pay for the apartment?"

"It's not mine. Some friends let me stay with them for a while."

"What kind of work are you looking for?" Karen cringed. She sounded like an interrogator.

"I'm taking a break — figuring out what I want to do with my life, you know?"

Karen translated that to mean Joanna was a mooch, just plain lazy or on drugs. *Some people never change.*

"Ooh...is this your car?" Joanna thumped the hood of the car.

"It's a rental. Uh...Joanna...no smoking."

"Sorry." Joanna took a few more drags before she ground her cigarette out on the pavement and climbed into the car. "So, did you have a good visit with Albert?"

"Yeah. Well, except for the Blake and Dad part. Haley's a sweetheart."

"A little too sweet if you ask me."

"Why do you say that?" Karen looked sideways at Joanna before she pulled out of the parking lot.

"She smiles all the time."

Karen laughed. "Isn't that good?"

"I think she's hiding something."

"What?" Karen stepped on the brakes a little too hard when they came to a stop sign.

"How real can a person be when they're so happy?"

"Maybe...she's hiding from her own pain?"

Joanna rolled down her window. "You sure I can't smoke?"

After a disappointing apartment search, they stopped at a local barbecue restaurant and ordered the appetizer sampler plate to share. Karen glanced across the room and let out a heavy sigh when she spotted Mary.

She picked up the dessert menu and peeked over the top. Wait a minute...that's wasn't David with her.

"What are you doing?" Joanna pulled the menu down.

"Shh. Don't let them see me."

"Who?" Joanna's voice drew several people's attention.

"Please," Karen whispered. "Be quiet and I'll tell you." She leaned forward and filled her in. "Can you see them?" Karen nodded in the direction of Mary's table.

Joanna looked at the table Karen pointed out. "Yeah. Are you sure the woman is engaged to someone else?"

"Yes. Why?"

"Come out from behind the menu and see for yourself."

Karen set it down and looked across the dining room. The man held Mary's hand as they leaned toward each other and kissed. Karen looked back at Joanna. "What do I do?"

Joanna shrugged. The waitress returned with their lemonades, set them on the table, but as she turned to go, she tripped over Joanna's purse. Her empty tray crashed to the floor and several people turned to check out the ruckus. Mary looked right at Karen, then turned back to her companion, pulling her hands away from his.

Another waitress arrived with their food at the same time Karen's phone rang. She usually liked the unique tone that set her phone apart, but she squirmed under the gaze of the patrons around her. "Hello?"

"Hey, it's me, David."

"What's up?" She turned to check on Mary, but she was gone.

"My parents asked me to invite you to dinner tonight."

"I don't know."

"Get it over with. You know they'll keep asking until you accept."

"True. I suppose tonight would be fine. What time?"

"They made reservations at the country club for seven."

"They were pretty sure of themselves, weren't they?"

"You know my folks. You remember where the club is?"

"Yeah. I'll meet you there."

Karen tossed her phone in her purse. "That'll be interesting."

"What's up?" Joanna helped herself to more buffalo wings.

"Hey. Leave some for me." Karen swatted at Joanna's hand.

"You snooze, you lose."

"Yeah, yeah." Karen filled her plate to rival Joanna. "I'm dining with the Ellis' tonight."

"Will Mary be there?"

"No clue."

"I'd love to be a fly on that wall."

"I'd rather be a fly on the wall tonight." Karen's stomach knotted up when she thought about what she just witnessed. Should she tell David? Confront Mary? She decided to leave it alone for now, but the uneasiness remained and she barely tasted her lunch.

In the car, Joanna insisted on calling friends who knew someone with a place to rent. Karen doubted any friend of Joanna's would have an apartment worth renting, but she humored her sister. When they pulled up to the apartment, she groaned. She should have recognized the address. She rolled her eyes and decided not to fight it. While Joanna waited out by the car and smoked, Karen knocked on the door.

Margie's eyes widened when she opened the door. "Karen, are you here for the apartment? Let me grab the keys."

"How much — "

"Don't even mention the word rent young lady." Margie disappeared into the kitchen and came back with the keys. "Now, there are keys to the house on here, too. I haven't changed my storage system since you left, so help yourself. Sheets, towels, food, whatever." Margie waved Karen's protest aside. "You're family. Always have been. That won't change. No matter what." Margie wiped at a tear and pulled Karen into a bear hug. "You are loved in this house, and don't forget it."

Karen relished the warmth of Margie's hug. "Thank you. But you have to let me repay you somehow."

"Seeing you around here is gift enough. I would enjoy your company in the garden, though. I need to plant some vegetables. But only as you have time. No expectations."

"It's a deal."

Karen pulled up to the valet stand to find David waiting. She would much rather park the car herself, but they required a bit of snobbery at this particular club. She handed her keys to the valet and took David's arm, then joined his parents in the bar.

"Gwen. Trent. So good to see you. Thank you for the invitation."

"We're glad you could make it."

She gave them each a polite hug and settled into the chair David pulled out for her. "Will Mary be here?"

"No. She has other plans." David declined a refill the waiter offered.

"Actually, dear…I invited her to join us. Here she is now. Mary!" Gwen waved the younger woman over to the table.

"Mother, lower your voice." David glared at his mother, before turning to Karen. "I'm sorry. I hope you won't be too uncomfortable."

Mary gushed over Karen then grabbed David's hand as they followed the hostess to their table. "Oh, honey, it's so good to see you. I had a simply awful business meeting today with that horrid Thomas. You remember him, don't you?" Mary looked over her shoulder at Karen and gave her a look that dared her to differ in the account.

She listened to Mary's chatter with David and grew uneasy about the evening ahead. She glanced behind her at Gwen and Trent and wished she hadn't come.

The hostess settled them around the table, leaving them in the care of their waiter. He handed out the menus and took their drink orders before disappearing to let them peruse the menu.

"So, Karen, how long will you be here?" Mary set down her menu.

"A while. I found an apartment today."

"Oh, Gwen, we should help her decorate. Karen, we know some of the loveliest places to find what you need."

"Well — " Karen tried to interrupt.

"What a great idea. Why didn't I think of it?" Gwen patted her future daughter-in-law's hand. "What do you think…blues?"

"No, a softer look." Mary leaned closer to David's mother.

Karen looked at the two women discussing her home like it was their own and shook her head. It looked like they would decide her apartment's fate before the evening ended. Her head pounded. She tapped David on the arm. "Order for me, please. I'm going to the ladies room."

She made her way around the table, into the hallway behind them out of sight. She could still hear their voices. Leaning against the wall, she rubbed her temples. Auras formed in her field of vision. She needed to get back to the quiet hotel to avoid being laid out with a migraine for two days. She pushed herself away from the wall. The nausea hit and she took several deep breaths. *Time to leave.*

"Stop it." David's voice rose in pitch. "She doesn't need your help. And I don't think she wants it."

"Sweetheart, she didn't say so."

Karen peeked around the wall. David's fist hit the table and his mother and fiancée both cringed. "You didn't give her a chance. I can't believe you two. Live your own lives. Quit controlling everyone else's."

"What's that supposed to mean?" Mary huffed.

David groaned and pushed away from the table as Karen rounded the corner. He glared at his mother and fiancée and sat back down.

Karen paused beside the table. "I'm sorry. I'm getting a migraine. You remember how I used to get those, David?"

"Do you need me to take you home?" He laid his napkin on the table and started to get up.

"No, I'll be fine. You all enjoy your evening." Karen started to walk away, then turned back to Gwen and Mary. "Thank you for your offer to help decorate, but I plan to ask my sisters to help me." Karen held up her hand when Mary protested. "I think their tastes are more similar to mine than yours would be."

16

Thankful the hotel dining area was empty, Karen filled her plate and sat down at a table with her back to the corner. She glanced down at the newspaper someone left behind. June third. *One week since I left Barry.* Was coming back a mistake? Last night was. She never should have trusted David's parents.

She rubbed her temples. Barry always helped her through the migraines. He used to drop whatever he was doing and rub her back. She missed his attention last night.

It's time to get this over with. She pulled one of her mother's letters out of its envelope. She held it to her nose, the faint scent of her mother's perfume still there. She laid the letter down and ate her bowl of fruit while she gathered her courage. Pushing the bowl aside and pouring a fresh cup of coffee, she focused on the words in front of her.

My dear daughter Karen,

You are so precious to me, in ways I never gave you the chance to understand. Please forgive me. I understand why you left. I ran away myself. But I think I ran more from myself and God than from your father. But God never gave up on me. I finally came home five years ago. But it's taken me till recently to make peace with God, myself and your father. Now, I hope I can help you find what you are looking for. It all starts with a story. I want to tell you face to face. Please come home and we'll talk.

Love,
Mom

Karen reached for the second letter and tore it open.

My dearest daughter,

There has been only silence from you. Are you so angry you won't even let me know you received my letters? I wait and wonder what is going through your mind. After I wrote you the first time, I waited because I wanted to give you whatever time you needed before you heard the story.
After I wrote the full account on paper for you, I waited. I thought you needed time to work through a host of emotions. But now, it is important to me I hear from you. You see, I have been diagnosed with cancer. I'm dying. I don't know how much time I have left. They've offered treatments, but realistically, they say my chances aren't very good. I can only be sure my quality of life would be nonexistent if I do what they suggest.
Whatever time I have left, I want to enjoy to the fullest. Even more than knowing whether you can forgive me or your father, I want to leave this earth knowing you are right with God.
Please, let me hear from you.

Love, Mom

P.S. Your father and I have chosen not to share the story with anyone else. We leave it for you to decide.

She stuffed the pages back in the envelope. *Where's the other letter?*
She gathered her items and headed to her car. Getting in, she rolled down the windows and called her sisters and Alita and invited them

over Friday for a movie night and sleepover.

Now she needed to buy a TV, DVD player, and plenty of junk food for Friday. Everyone could bring their own sleeping bag and pillow.

Phone calls complete, she scanned the classifieds and circled possible car ads. About halfway down the column one caught her eye. A dark green Ford Probe. *Barry would love that!* He had to sell his Probe after Dennis fired him.

This one looked like a good deal. It had low mileage and the price tag fit her budget. She dialed the number and left a message, then made two more appointments for the morning.

Her cell phone chirped.

"Hey there, good looking."

"Hey." David's voice sent a rush of pleasure through her body.

"How's my favorite girl?"

She blushed. "I thought Mary was your favorite girl."

"Not right now. She and mom were out of line last night."

Karen chuckled. "Yeah, I don't like blue. It depresses me."

"Will you let me make it up to you? I'll treat you to lunch."

"Can I take a rain check? I need to hunt for a car."

"Want some company?"

"Is that an offer?" A smile tugged at her lips.

"What better way to spend my day?"

"You sure Mary won't mind?"

"I'm not her property."

She cringed at the edge in David's voice. "Sorry." She heard him take a deep breath and let it out.

"No, I'm sorry. I shouldn't have snapped. I get so tired of Mom and Mary's plans for my life. But Mary left for Europe this morning, and she won't even know. However, I do need an excuse to get away from Mom. Do me a favor and let me tag along."

"Since you put it that way. I have two appointments over in Liberty in the next hour, but I'm still at the hotel."

"Funny. So am I."

Karen looked around and finally spotted David's car in a side lot.

"Have you been watching me this whole time?"

"Actually, I just got here. Where are you?"

"Turn to your right, the red Sable on the front row."

"I see you now. Nice view."

Karen blushed again as she watched David climb out of his car and walk toward her. He wore dark blue jeans and a forest green button-down shirt that complemented his hazel eyes and blond hair. The sleeves were rolled up, the tail untucked. He looked good.

She remembered how her heart flipped every time she saw him after that kiss under the stars when she was fifteen. Karen tucked her phone back into her purse and took a few shaky breaths while David climbed in beside her. *Maybe spending the afternoon together wasn't such a good idea.*

"Where to, gorgeous?"

"You behave or I'll drop you off at your mom's." She grinned.

"You wouldn't."

"Probably not." She pushed her doubts aside and smiled at David. She started the car but paused before she backed out. She turned in her seat and squinted across the parking lot.

"What is it?"

"I thought I saw Blake."

She shrugged and continued onto the highway. She turned the radio to a classical station. "If you're so tired of being treated like property, why Mary?"

David straightened up and looked out his window. "It's expected."

"Marriage in general or to her?"

"Both." He turned back to her and placed his arm on the back of the seat. He touched her hair. "The only reason I can think of to go against what is expected of me is — "

She glanced his direction and the desire in his eyes caught her breath. "Don't say it. Please don't."

"As you wish." David turned the radio to an oldies station.

Boy, he is making this hard. Sitting next to David stirred a desire for their old relationship. If only she had read his letter all those years ago.

You never would have loved Barry.
She squeezed the steering wheel. Why did God have to remind her? *I don't like Barry.* And David was eager to pick up the slack.
Do not lean on your own understanding or any man's affections.
Karen blinked back the tears that threatened to betray her emotions. She didn't want to listen to God. It wasn't fair.

By early afternoon, they had looked at five cars, all duds. They stopped for a drink and to regroup. As they ordered their slushies, she got a call back about the Probe. It was part of an estate sale and the executor seemed anxious to sell.

The moment she saw the car, she knew she had to buy it. They had a mechanic look at it and a few hours later she owned a new car.

Karen swung the car into the parking garage and picked out a spot. She got out and admired her new ride. If Barry ever saw it, he would think she bought it with him in mind. She recoiled at the thought. *I didn't buy it for him.* She grabbed her purse out of the passenger seat, locked the door and headed for the hospital entrance.

Why did he have to get so angry? *If only... No.* It would never happen. Megan believed God still did miracles, but Karen didn't buy it. Not in her marriage. Divorce felt like the only answer. Then she could think about taking David up on his silent offer. She shut out the voice that reminded her to keep David at arm's length. Even Megan said she would be justified if she left Barry.

She stopped outside her mother's room and took a deep breath before pushing the door open.

A beeping monitor greeted her as she stepped in the chilly room. The smell of disinfectant mixed with the fragrance of flowers beside her mother's bed turned her stomach. She nodded at the nurse closing the curtains. The florescent light above the bed flickered, sending shadows across her mother's pale face. She looked worse. Karen bit her lip. Emotions she thought long gone stirred inside her. Despite the rejection and the hurts, she missed her mother. *I should have come home sooner.*

Setting her purse in a chair, Karen stood next to the bed and stroked her mom's face. "Please, wake up, I need to know why…to understand why you and…"

She turned at the sound of footsteps and tensed. "Dad."

He pulled off his cowboy hat. "Karen." He walked into the room. "I'm glad you're here. Maybe we can visit while we sit with your mother."

She reached for her purse. For years she wanted to just sit and talk with her dad. To have him love her. But now, the thought of staying in this room with him made her sick. "I need to go."

"Please. We haven't talked since you've been back."

"We have nothing to say. Unless you plan to tell me what she can't."

Her dad walked over and laid his hat at the foot of the bed. "Didn't you get your mother's letters?"

"I have three letters from her. But they don't tell me anything new. It's time you told me yourself. I deserve to know why you rejected me. What did I do wrong?" Karen clutched her purse tightly. How could he leave her in the dark?

"You're right. You deserve to know. But I promised to let her tell the story. I intend to keep my promise." Her father took her mother's hand in his. "She deserves that after all the other promises I broke." Tears trickled down his face.

Why is he crying? I'm the one who was hurt. "What about the promises you made to me that you broke?" She turned to go.

"Please forgive me, Karen."

She rushed out of the room and down the hall before stopping to lean against the wall. She bent over, supporting herself with her hands on her knees. Deep breathing brought her some release from the pressure of an oncoming migraine. She heard her father's approaching footsteps and cringed.

"Karen…come by the house. I'll tell you what I can."

Karen looked up. "Just like that. You'll tell me what I want to know?"

He ran a hand through his hair. "I can't tell you everything."

"No, of course not." She shook her head.

"It's for your mother to tell."

"I can't believe how stubborn you are. Mom isn't going to wake up and I need answers." Karen walked toward the elevator.

"The offer stands if you change your mind." He called after her.

She ignored his pleas and got on the elevator. It deposited her into the underground garage and she hurried to her car where she slid into the seat and locked the doors. Only then did she let her emotions go.

Karen wrapped her arms around her waist and leaned her head into the steering wheel as sobs wracked her body. How could he ask her to forgive him? Memories of the day her life changed came unbidden into her mind like it was yesterday.

It was Valentine's Day, the year she turned 13. Her mom wasn't in the kitchen when she came downstairs, so she walked down the hall and peeked into her parents' room. Her mom lay on her bed. Karen tiptoed into the room and sat on the edge of the mattress.

"Mom? Are you sick?"

"Karen? Oh, sweetie." Her mother turned over to face her and reached up to cup her cheek in her hand.

Karen sucked in her breath at the look of sadness on her mother's face. "What's wrong?"

"I'm so sorry." Her mom turned back toward the wall.

Karen patted her mom's arm then left to find her dad. He would know what to do.

She heard Elinor and Albert scramble down the stairs and start to argue when they discovered there was no breakfast yet. She ignored their questions and made a beeline for the back door. Her gaze fell to the garbage can where she saw the card she made for her dad. Bewildered, she pulled out the card and walked across the yard to the barn.

"Dad?" Silence greeted her. Finally she found him in the tack room. "Dad, what's wrong with Mom?" He continued his work in silence. She thought she heard him cry and inched closer to touch his arm. "Dad?"

When he turned, his body shook and tears streamed down his face. He shrugged her hand off of his arm. "I can't stand to look at you, much less have you touch me."

"What did I do?"

Her dad turned away, and his voice rose in anger. "Get out of here. And don't bother me at work ever again."

Karen couldn't believe her ears. She dropped the card on the floor as the tears pooled in her eyes. She turned and ran from the barn, almost colliding with Blake. He laughed.

She ran crying into the woods behind their house. She skipped school and around noon made her way to Margie and Sam Grave's house. They fed her lunch and allowed her to stay the rest of the day after they listened to her story.

Sam gave her a ride back home where her dad waited on the front porch. "The school called." He opened the door and she followed him inside. He took off his belt. "Bend over."

"Mom?" Karen's mom sat in the rocker next to the fireplace. She turned her head away.

Her dad had spanked her only once before and he cried as he punished her. But that Valentine's Day everything changed. She felt his anger every time the belt contacted her body. Even through her jeans. When her father stormed out of the room, she crumpled to the floor, choking back her tears. "What did I do?"

Her mother rose from the chair and followed her dad out of the room, silent tears streaming down her face. Karen hobbled upstairs past Elinor and Albert, and crept into bed where she cried herself to sleep.

It was the first and last time he touched her in anger. After that, all it took was a look or a barrage of hateful words spat at her for the rejection to embed itself deep into her heart.

A knocking sound brought her back to the present. *How long have I been like this?* She looked up. Karen's father stood with Margie next to the car. *What do they want?* She rolled down the window.

"Are you okay, sweetie?" Margie leaned toward Karen.

"Yeah, why?" She looked from one to the other.

Margie looked over at Charles then back at Karen." Your dad saw you in your car. He was worried and waved me down."

"Um, I have a headache and decided to rest a few minutes before I drove back to the hotel."

"Call if you need me. I know you're hurt." Margie put her hand on the door. "Your dad wants to make it right. Your mom and I talked a lot before she went into the coma, and I think if she were awake right now, she would tell you how much God loves you and that He has good plans for you."

Karen laid her hands in her lap and snorted. "I need to go, Margie." She started the motor.

"I'll be praying for you." Margie stepped aside and Karen pulled out of the garage.

A glance in the rearview mirror showed her dad standing next to Margie. His face filled with concern. Karen had no desire to forgive him. She couldn't trust him. Running away sounded like a good idea. She took a deep breath. *I need to get my mind off things.* Maybe David would go to the movies with her.

She ignored the growing knot in her gut. "I don't care if I'm playing with fire."

17

Karen tossed and turned, her dreams invaded by scenes from last night's movie.

She was a spy running from the enemy and no matter how fast she ran, he remained one step behind her. She darted into an alley, he followed her. She sprinted through a building — still he was on her heels. Fear stole her breath. *Who is chasing me?*

A dead end. She turned and faced her predator. Shadows hid his face; she shuddered as he reached for her. *Someone save me!*

Another figure stood in the shadows. She reached out to him, gasping for breath. "David, help me."

She fell at the man's feet. Light from the street lamp blinded her. She threw her hand up to block out the light, hoping to get a better look at his face. Instead, her arm hit something solid, launching it across the alley.

The crash woke her.

Karen looked at the clock. Five in the morning. There was no point in trying to go back to sleep. She had a lot to do and her mind was already racing with the details. Today, she was moving into the apartment.

She rolled out of bed, threw on her shorts, and headed down to the hotel gym, thankful to find it empty. Her frustration fueled her workout. Would David really walk away from Mary and his family's expectations?

Do I want him to?

He was the hero in her dreams, offering tenderness and rescue, did she expect him to fill that role in real life? Was it fair to ask it of him? She could almost hear Megan ask if it was right. Karen turned the speed up on the treadmill and sprinted until she gasped for air. After a minute of punishment, she slowed to a walk and drained her water bottle.

David was trying to rekindle their love, but every time she got close to him she thought of Barry. She shut off the machine then grabbed a towel and wiped the sweat off of her neck. *What am I supposed to do?* David was her first love. But Barry's love was more. More intense. More romantic. More real.

Those pictures, though, made her skin crawl. *If I were enough…* She wiped her tears on her shirt. Did she really want to go through all the work of forgiving Barry and trying to be happy again? Or should she just grab David's offer and run?

I know the plans I have for you.

Karen dropped her head in her hands. First she was to blame, then she was supposed to forgive everyone. Now God had plans for her life? Megan claimed He worked miracles. Karen didn't trust His intentions. Or David's or Barry's. The only plans she could trust were her own. She wiped her eyes and took a settling breath. *I have options.* Like the Bed and Breakfast.

Relief flooded her and a quiet smile stole over her face. She could buy and run that place without help from anyone. Tossing her water bottle in the trash, she headed to her room to pack. Excitement nudged the confusion out of her mind as she thought of the bed and breakfast.

A new beginning. No matter who she ended up with.

Karen stood in the driveway between the main house and the apartment and admired her new home. The front door at the top of the stairs was now painted yellow and trimmed in white, instead of sea foam green. "Much better."

She bent down to smell the potted Gardenias sitting on either side of the door. She used to help Margie plant some every year. Stepping inside, she paused when sunshine hit her face. The bay window to her right in the living room let in more light than she ever had in her apartment in New York. Karen smiled.

The kitchen sat to the left of the front room. A vase of fresh flowers stood on an old worn mahogany table which occupied a cozy breakfast nook. Karen ran her hand across the top. It looked like her grandparent's. She clapped her hands. "I love it."

Through an open door behind the kitchen she spotted a four poster bed filling the room. She gasped at the elegance of her new bedroom. On the far wall, she discovered French doors that led to a deck overlooking the property. To her left, she could see Margie work in her garden and to the right an open field and woods reminded her of childhood explorations. *I wish Sam were still here.* She sighed. Two chairs and a small table took up the far side of the deck. Flowers hung from the overhang.

She hugged herself and breathed in the country air. *I'm home.*

She headed over to thank Margie for her welcome and caught up with her in the tool shed. She laid down her hand tools as Karen approached. "You're already here?"

"I woke up early and wanted to be in my new home."

"Good. It gets quiet around here without Sam. I haven't rented that place since he died. Can you join me for lunch?"

"I'm sorry. I need to pick up a few things before I get moved in. By the way, I love the furniture."

"I'm so glad. It's been in my friend's attic for years and she wanted it to have a good home. Do you need anything else?"

"I think I'm good. If it changes, I'll let you know." She had already imposed, she was going to buy the rest of the furniture herself.

"If you're sure. When you have time for a visit let me know."

"I will. I better go." Karen hugged her older friend and waved goodbye. She needed to ask Margie about the past. She and Sam picked up the slack where her family left off and while they never gossiped, they seemed to know everyone's business. They hung out with her parents before she came along. *What happened with that?*

Karen stopped at a local thrift store and bought a few towels, dishes, and a set of sheets, before heading to an electronics store for a TV and DVD player. She would buy groceries after visiting her mom.

She arrived at the hospital and found Albert already in their mom's room. He gave her a hug. "How's the new place?"

"Wonderful. You'll have to come see it."

"Yeah, but I hear no men are allowed tonight."

Karen laughed. "I'll have you and your family over next week."

"I'll look forward to it." Albert motioned to the only chair in the room. "I'll sit on the window ledge."

"Thanks. How is she?"

"The same. The doctors don't know how long she has. Most people have about a month when they get to this stage."

"Oh." Her shoulders slumped. "I want her to wake up."

"The doctors say it's unlikely."

She sat down in a nearby chair. Stopping by every day might be a waste of time. "Did I tell you she wrote a letter explaining everything that happened? But I can't find it and Dad won't tell me himself." She nibbled her bottom lip. "Are you sure you don't know what happened to turn Dad against me?"

"I'm sure." Albert knelt beside her chair. "Look, even if you don't find the answers you're looking for, God can help you move past this. Besides, Dad will tell you if Mom isn't able to."

She shrugged. "Maybe, but I don't know if I can trust him. In the letters I do have, Mom spoke about forgiveness."

"It's the only way to find any peace."

"Whose peace? Dad's?"

"No, yours. Forgiveness isn't about the perpetrator of the pain. It's about the person they hurt."

"Yeah, right. I forgive him, and then he gets away with it. I'm still left with what happened."

"When you forgive him, you let go of the right to exact justice yourself. You trust God with his consequences and you're no longer tormented by the fact you can't punish him. It becomes God's job and you're free to let God heal the pain in your heart."

"Then I'm supposed to act like nothing happened?" Karen crossed her arms.

"Of course something happened. But--"

She snorted. "Of course there's a but. But there is no way I can go back to any kind of real relationship with him."

"Maybe not. But you make room for it."

Karen huffed. "I don't want to make room for it. Besides, I don't like the idea that if God forgives him, he gets off easy."

"That's God's decision. Jesus already took our punishment when He died on the cross. Besides, only God knows what Dad has already been through because of his choices. How much he has suffered."

"Suffered? Dad's the one who made me suffer when he betrayed me."

"Okay, so Dad betrayed you when he turned his back on you. But didn't you do the same to God?"

Karen drew in her breath and stared at her brother. "No."

"When was the last time you talked to God?"

Karen hung her head. "Until recently, it was the day Dad rejected me." She stood up and turned to go, then stepped back.

Her father stood inside the doorway, tears streaming down his face. "I am so sorry, Karen, for everything. It torments me. I know I can't change how I treated you. Please, give me another chance."

She shook her head. "I have to go." She moved past him and noticed Blake standing in the doorway. He laughed. She glared at him, then headed down the hall toward the elevator.

She stepped onto the elevator and leaned against the wall as it descended, her arms wrapped around her waist. She longed for someone to hold her close and keep the ugliness at bay. She thought of Barry, then remembered his betrayal. *And Dad's.* Betrayal on both sides.

Albert, her mother, and Megan all urged her to let it go. "I can't." But she hated how her gut twisted every time she thought about it. Did forgiveness really set people free? She shook her head. Barry and her dad didn't hurt over this. Not the way she did.

Her dad claimed to be tormented by his choices. Barry didn't appear to be bothered by his. She didn't want to spend her days focused on revenge — she just wanted them to feel the same pain. If only she could trust God to take care of it.

I know the plans I have for you.

"The only plans…" She stopped talking to herself when someone else got on the elevator. The only plans she cared to think about were her own. But she was starting to rethink the bed and breakfast. She needed something farther away. Starting over where she knew no one sounded better than being so close to her dad.

She sighed. The thought of relocating made her tired. Why did she have to be the one to go somewhere? It wasn't fair. Tears moistened the corners of her eyes and a knot formed in her throat.

When the elevator reached the parking garage, she rushed to her car and locked the doors. The emotions of the day flooded her. She banged her fist on the steering wheel. Her family was messed up. She was messed up and stuck in their mess, too. She didn't want forgiveness to be the answer.

Sobs threatened to pour out of her. She bit her lip. *I'm tired of this. I will not break down again.* She longed to go straight to her new apartment and hide from the world, but she had a girl's night to prepare for. She took a deep breath and shoved all her scrambled thoughts to the back of her mind for another day, like she had done for years.

On her way home, she stopped at the store. Darting through the aisles, she tossed her items into the cart and hurried to the checkout. The lines were three carts deep. Her watch read a little after four. Her sisters were arriving at six.

As she pulled into her driveway, she called David. She needed help installing her new television. She gave him quick directions to her place then headed inside.

Thankful for the convenience of a dishwasher, she loaded up her thrift store dishes. She tossed towels and sheets into the washer and stacked paper plates and napkins on the kitchen counter. David arrived as she filled the fridge with groceries.

"Nice place."

"Thanks. You're the first to see it, other than Joanna. She helped me find it."

David walked through the rooms and nodded his approval. "Where does the television go?"

"Over here." Karen walked to the corner opposite the couch. "But I don't have a console yet. We'll have to put it on the floor." She led David out to her car. "Can you get it? Or do I need to call Albert?"

"I got it. Why don't you grab the DVD player and hold the door."

David finished just as the first car pulled in the drive. She looked out the window, then darted out of the apartment and down the stairs. "I'm so glad you made it." She gave Haley a hug.

"I wouldn't have missed it." She waved toward David's car. "Who beat me here?"

"David Ellis stopped by to help me take the TV upstairs and hook it up." She turned to watch David come down the stairs. Haley sighed. David joined them under the shade of the pin oak.

"I better go before the whole gaggle of ladies gets here."

Karen laughed. "David, this is Haley, Albert's wife. Haley, David."

Haley nodded. "I better get my stuff in." She pulled out her sleeping bag and headed up the stairs.

"Thanks for your help." Karen walked David to his car.

"No problem." David looked towards Haley. "What's up?"

Karen watched her sister-in-law walk away. "Nothing."

He looked over his shoulder at Haley, then back at Karen and shrugged. "Whatever you say. Do you want to hang out tomorrow afternoon?"

Karen hesitated. "Sure. I'll call you when we're done." She waved and watched him drive away.

Haley walked up beside her. "Be careful."

"What do you mean?"

"You know."

"I need a friend." Karen shifted her feet and looked away.

"You're married, Karen. Be careful." Haley started to walk away then turned back. "You know, God has plans for you."

Karen's head jerked up, her brow wrinkled.

"He does, Karen."

"If God cared about me, why didn't He take care of my future a long time ago?"

Haley took Karen's hands in hers. "Who do you think has watched out for you all these years?"

"I took care of myself."

"I hope someday you'll see how God watched out for you. He loves you." She gave Karen a quick hug and returned to her car to get her other things.

Karen watched and fought to keep away the tears. She balled her fists and dug her fingernails into her palms. She jumped when a pillow hit her in the face.

Haley smiled. "Come on, help me get unloaded. Joanna's here and I think she brought Elinor."

18

Karen led Haley and Elinor inside. "Joanna, you coming?"

Joanna held up her pack of cigarettes. "Need one more before I call it a night."

Karen rolled her eyes. "Could you call Alita while you're out here and make sure she remembered?"

"Sure." Joanna lit her cigarette.

Haley and Elinor explored Karen's place until Joanna finished her smoke and joined them.

"Did you get hold of Alita?" Elinor plopped down on the couch and smoothed the pillow she pulled into her lap.

"No answer. I hope Blake isn't up to his same old tricks."

"When I talked to her this morning she planned to be here. So unless Blake gets in one of his moods, she should be here." Haley joined Elinor on the couch.

Karen looked around at the somber faces of her sisters and sister-in-law. "It's that bad?"

"You'd know if you had stuck around." Joanne stuck her cigarettes into her purse and made herself at home on the floor. "Hey, I hear a car."

"It's Alita," Elinor looked out the window. "She's with somebody."

"Let's help her unload." Joanna got up.

"She's not getting out," Haley got up from the couch. "I'll go see if she's alright. You guys get the pizza in the oven and pick out a movie."

A few minutes later, Haley and Alita walked into the apartment.

Karen was taken aback. She hadn't gotten a good look at her sister-in-law that day at Albert's, but now she could see the changes. Alita no longer looked like the cheerleader who married her brother. Her shoulders stooped, she looked like a wilted flower. What had Blake done to crush her spirit?

The evening passed in a blur of pizza, ice cream, movies and giggles. One by one, they drifted off to sleep on top of their sleeping bags spread out in front of the television screen. Karen turned off the light shortly after the last movie ended around midnight and settled herself on the floor with the others.

What a great night. She relished the idea of her sisters for friends. At seventeen she never dreamed it would be possible. *If I had stuck around...* she stopped herself. *Dad. He always gets in the way.* If she stayed and bought the bed and breakfast, she would probably run into him on a regular basis. Would it be worth it to have a relationship with her sisters? Mulling over the possibilities, she fell asleep within a few minutes.

Several hours later Karen sat up straight from a deep sleep. What woke her? Footsteps. She looked around and noticed Alita's spot was empty. The numbers on the clock glowed four o'clock as Karen tiptoed across the floor toward her bedroom. "Alita?"

The door to the balcony stood open. She heard sniffling and approached with enough noise not to scare her sister-in-law. "Can I come out?"

"I'm sorry. I didn't mean to wake anyone."

"Don't worry about it." Karen sat in a patio chair. "Is it Blake?"

Alita nodded.

"Want to talk about it?"

"No."

"Because he's my brother?"

"No, it's just hard." Alita got up and walked to the railing.

Karen waited.

"Blake refused to marry me when he joined the marines. Said I should forget about him. After he deployed, I found out I was pregnant, so I wrote and told him I planned to wait for him despite what he thought I should do.

"When he returned, he had changed. He carried a heavy sadness. But he wanted to get married. The first year we got along pretty good." Alita huffed. "I thought I could make him happy."

She sat back down and faced Karen. "When your dad turned on you, any steps he and Blake had made to mend their relationship stopped. Blake went from sad to unreasonable."

"I had no idea."

"I think the anger simmered in him until the night you discovered his stash." Alita nodded. "I already knew. Soon after, the abuse started. He blamed you, so I blamed you, too. But a few days after he hit me the first time I noticed a bottle of prescription pills in the trash. I asked him about them, but his answer was vague. Something about Marine Corps doctors, and he didn't need them anymore."

"But he did?"

Alita shrugged. "The nightmares started after he threw them away. And every time he had one, he became violent. Still works that way. If I stay away from him for a while, sometimes it passes. Now I know it's PTSD."

"Have you talked to him about getting help?"

"Once." Alita scoffed. "I learned my lesson."

"Why do you stay?"

"I tried leaving once. Loaded up the kids and headed for who knows where. We made it a week before he found us." She shook her head, then began to chew her fingernails. "I didn't go out in public for two weeks after that. Took that long for the bruises to fade." She looked Karen in the eyes. "You tell me. Would you be eager to leave again after that?"

"It would be hard." Karen looked down at her hands.

"Besides, how would I have provided for the boys? I don't have any special skills. Maybe now that the boys are grown I could support myself, but I don't know how to walk away. I think about leaving, but I can't think straight when I get around Blake. I'm rational when I'm with you or Haley. But the minute Blake walks into the room, I let him walk all over me. Besides, he needs me." Alita hugged her knees to herself.

The two sat in an uncomfortable silence for a few minutes. Karen unsure of what to say.

"What about you?" Alita finally asked. "Elinor told me you were married, but I don't see a ring."

Karen bit her lip. "We had six great years, but now…he drinks. He's into pornography. Magazines. Websites. I feel dirty and unwanted. He's angry all the time…and he hit me. Once. I left before he did it again. Last weekend my best friend saw him at a restaurant with another woman. I'm gone two days and he's out on the town with another woman."

"Do you think you'll give him another chance?" Alita drew in a shaky breath.

Karen walked to the edge of the balcony and looked out into the moonlit night towards Margie's garden. Every time she repeated her reasons to someone, she felt the pain dig deeper. Maybe she should put an ad in the paper and get it out for all the world to see and quit talking about it. She sighed. Pain didn't obey any laid out plan.

"I don't know. Sometimes when I consider divorce I feel relief and sometimes I hurt. But I don't trust him and for now I need some time away. I haven't been through what you have, though."

"Your bruises are as real as mine." Alita joined Karen at the railing. "Whether they're one or a hundred. And the bruises on the inside from the anger…just 'cause we can't see them, doesn't mean they're not there. Your dad left lots of those on Blake and you."

Karen put her arm around Alita and drew her into a hug.

Alita rested her head on Karen's shoulder for a moment then pulled away. "Have you walked through Haley's garden yet?"

"No. I noticed someone did a lot of work though."

"She built a pond surrounded by reeds and at one end she placed a bench with a plaque next to it. It says God doesn't break a bruised reed or snuff out a smoldering wick, that He'll make sure justice happens. It's my favorite spot when I feel broken."

Karen walked to the opposite side of the deck. She turned back to face Alita. "Don't you think walking away and drawing a line in the sand might be a part of that justice?"

"Maybe. But for me, getting out is kinda like trying to get out of quicksand."

"So how do you survive?"

Alita looked up at the stars. "You know I used to go to church all the time before I married Blake. But it was just religion. Over the years, it's become my lifeline. If I don't hope in God, what would I have? Even though I don't make it to church much since Blake watches me like a hawk, I'm on my knees an awful lot."

"After everything you've been through, you still hope God will come through for you?"

"God comes through for me every day."

Karen crossed her arms. "Maybe God wants you to come through for yourself."

"Maybe someday I'll be able to leave. But I can't do it without God."

Karen met her sister-in-law's gaze. She couldn't decide if she despised Alita's faith or was jealous of it. For a moment she remembered the peace that accompanied such faith. A shudder went through her and she dismissed the thought. "You think He'll stop coming through for you if you stand up for yourself?"

Alita opened her mouth then closed it. Tears ran down her face. "I don't know how to stand up for myself."

"If you need someone to stand beside you, I'll be there." Karen put an arm around Alita.

"Thanks."

They fell into a tired silence then jumped when the patio door opened. Haley joined them and stifled a yawn. "You're up early."

Karen laughed. "What time is it?"

"Around 5:30 I think."

"Guess we'll need a lot of coffee this morning," Alita stretched her arms over her head and yawned.

"I'll be right down." Karen grabbed her purse. She looked forward to finding some unique furniture at garage sales. She heard a car door slam and looked out the window. Blake stood next to his truck. She hurried outside and joined her sisters at the bottom of the stairs.

"What do you think you're doing?" Blake stalked over to Alita.

"I told you where I would be."

"And I told you to stay home." Blake grabbed her arm and pulled her toward his truck.

Karen took a step toward them, but Joanna caught her arm. "It would be better if you didn't interfere."

Karen looked at her sister. "Someone needs to stand up to Blake."

"But not now, and not you." Joanna tossed her cigarette, pulled out her phone and dialed 911.

"I don't get you." Karen hurried to help Alita.

"Karen, don't. You'll just make it worse. I'll go with him, it'll be okay." Alita winced.

"You should listen to her." Blake pulled his wife toward the truck.

Karen hesitated, then stepped in front of Alita and Blake. "I won't move."

"Then I'll have to finish what I started nineteen years ago." Blake released his grip on Alita and towered over Karen. "You need to learn to stay out of other people's business." He took her by the shoulders, threw her to the ground, then stood glaring down at her, his fists clenched.

"Don't." Alita grabbed his arm.

He turned to his wife, his chest heaving with each breath. She released his arm and backed away.

"Don't ever tell me what to do." His slap came quick and knocked Alita against the truck. Glaring at the other women, he grabbed Alita's arm and opened the passenger door.

"No, I'm not going." Alita grabbed at the door frame.

"No?"

"No, I won't get in."

"You'll do what I say." He slapped her again and her lip started to bleed. "You want me to break your arm, too?"

"You've broken the last bone of mine you'll ever touch. I have witnesses now." Alita straightened and matched his stare.

"It doesn't matter. They won't report it. They never do." He grabbed her by the shoulders, and threw her to the ground. He pulled his leg back and aimed his foot at his wife.

Karen grabbed a two-by-four from next to the garage, then ran behind Blake and swung it at his legs. They buckled and he fell to his knees. He got up, turned to grab Karen, but came face to face with four women holding two-by-fours. Joanna stepped forward. "Don't think about it, Blake."

He dropped his arms and stared at Joanna. "You? I thought we had a pact."

"We do." Joanna dropped her piece of wood and walked up to Blake. "But it doesn't include hurting Alita. I should have stepped in a long time ago."

He dropped to his knees. Joanna paused, then kneeled beside him. She wrapped her arms around her big burly brother as he held onto her and wept. "It hurts, sissy. I can't make it stop."

"Shh. It'll be okay." She cradled his head against her shoulder.

The others watched the scene before them as though in a dream.

"You better go, now." Joanna held Blake away from her and angled her head towards the road where the sound of sirens could be heard. She leaned over and whispered in his ear.

He nodded, wiped his eyes, and got up. He turned to Alita. "I'm sorry." He climbed into his truck and sped out of the driveway.

Joanna helped Alita off the ground. "I'm so sorry. I should have stood up for you before now."

"But you did today. And he said he was sorry. He's never done that before."

Karen, Elinor and Haley gathered around Alita and Joanna. Alita's hands shook. She brushed away her tears then touched Karen's face. "Thank you."

Karen hugged her. "You need to file charges and get a restraining order. Change the locks. And get some ice on your face."

"I think the police want to talk to us first."

Alita, Haley and Elinor walked toward the officers getting out of their car.

Karen turned to Joanna who had already lit up a cigarette and held her back until the others were out of hearing. "What was that little scene with Blake about? I've never seen him like that."

Joanna stared at her, then tossed the half-smoked cigarette to the ground. "There's a lot you've never seen." She turned and joined the others.

How could I be so blind? Karen was so focused on her own hurts, she hadn't seen how her dad's actions had affected everyone else. *Another reason not to forgive him.*

Karen's phone chirped. Grateful for a distraction, she answered.

"Hey, want to go line dancing with me?"

Her heart raced at the sound of David's voice. She touched her arm where Blake had grabbed her and shuddered. An evening of dancing would get her mind off of him and the rest of her family. "Sure."

"You remember how?"

"How does a person forget?"

"By living in New York City?"

She glanced over at her sisters to make sure they were out of earshot. "Be nice or I won't go."

"Okay. See you tonight? About six?"

"I'll be ready with my boots on."

19

Barry stared at the online job listings. His visit with Anthony last night left him confused. *Who paid off my debt?* With his luck, it was probably some sort of mistake and once Anthony figured it out, his life would be over.

In the meantime, he needed to find a job. In the last few days he filled out more applications than in the past year — from a job fair, signs in windows, and the classifieds.

All week he stayed away from the bar. He was so busy he had no time for his favorite Internet sites. He ran a hand through his hair, then got up and refilled his coffee mug. He was no closer to Karen's return. And she wouldn't pick up the phone so they could talk about it. What else could he do?

He slammed his coffee mug on the counter. Barry swore under his breath as he grabbed a napkin and wiped up the spill. He couldn't make Karen any happier than he had made his parents.

"No. I won't think about what I did to my parents. I can't undo it and besides, they'll never forgive me." He paced through the apartment, attempting to shove his emotions deep down inside himself. *I haven't thought of Chad in years. Why now?*

He stared at the computer. He needed to continue his job search. What else could he do?

Come to me and rest.

"Where's the rest in this?" He sat back down at the desk. "Great, now

I'm talking to the voice." He scrolled through the classifieds. Sales were out once they checked his references and called Dennis. A waiter? He didn't have the patience for all the cranky customers. And again, there was the trouble with Dennis' reference. Janitorial work? Not very glamorous, but he needed an income, and they may not check his references as closely. No jobs in the janitorial section.

The jobs that required no specific skills wouldn't even pay enough to cover the rent and utilities every month; he'd need two jobs. No way he was going to work that hard.

He tried leaving Dennis off the reference list on a few applications, but then they wondered about the big gap in work history. He had searched hard all week. *And what do I have to show for it?*

A couple of articles caught his attention, then an ad popped up promising escape. Frustrations boiled inside him. Even when he tried to do the right thing he couldn't. His hand rolled the mouse to hover over the button. He almost felt Karen breath down his neck as if watching his every move. He pulled his hand back. He hadn't looked all week. He got up and put his mug in the sink.

He was ten the first time some older kids pulled him aside and showed him the pinups in their locker. He quickly discovered the high that came with fantasy and it became his easy fix for the pain in his life.

He swallowed. Could he ever overcome it? Karen deserved better, but he was tired of trying and seeing no results. He sat back down in front of the computer.

Come to me and rest.

He shook his head, clicked the button and allowed himself to be seduced away from his thoughts of being the man Karen wanted. He clicked link after link to escape her and the voice. She kept watch over his shoulder and the voice whispered in his ear.

Come to me and rest.

Barry threw the mouse across the room and pulled the plug out of the wall. He grabbed his keys, but paused when he saw the business card Robert left behind the night before. He stuck it in his pocket, then walked out the door and headed toward Central Park.

Come to me and rest.

He picked up his pace, ignoring the ache from his bruised ribs. When he reached Central Park West he was panting. He leaned over with his hands on his knees to catch his breath. *This is stupid. I don't even know where I'm headed.* People stared and gave him a wide berth.

He stood up and looked around in time to see an older gentleman with white hair walk south. *Is that the same man who helped me?* Barry tried to follow, but soon lost sight of the man. He stopped after a few blocks and rested against the fence bordering the park.

He didn't visit the west side very often. He looked at the street sign to get his bearings. "No way." He pulled out the card Robert had given him and looked at the address. He stood a block from Robert's church. "How...?"

Come to me and rest.

Barry paced in front of the park entrance and argued with the voice in his head. He never had much use for his parents' God and he wasn't about to start now. He could handle life on his own.

"I don't need you."

20

*K*aren followed David as he guided her across the large deck overlooking the river. Stomping boots echoed out into the night air. Shadows danced across the wooden planks in the bar's leftover light. A short flight of stairs led to a dock below.

"Having fun?" He leaned back against the railing.

"Can't remember the last time I had so much fun. Thank you." Karen stood next to her former beau and watched a barge move downriver.

"I never stopped loving you." He turned her face toward him.

"David…"

"Shh." He touched her lips with his thumb.

Karen stood mesmerized as David leaned closer. Her pulse raced. She closed her eyes and sighed. As David's lips grazed hers, shockwaves pulsed through her body. She pulled away and ran down the stairs into the darkness.

David slumped into a chair, holding his head in his hands. She kept an eye on him as she tramped back and forth across the dock. Her thoughts jumbled together. Why didn't he leave their relationship at friendship until she decided about Barry? *I only have myself to blame. I know it leads to this every time.*

Her phone rang. She reached for it, but her pocket was empty. Looking up, she saw David reach down and pick it up off the ground. She strained to hear what he said, but couldn't. By the time she reached the stairs, he had ended the call and stood smiling down at her.

"Who was it?" She made her way up the steps.

"Some guy." David shrugged and handed her the phone. "He asked if this was your phone. I said yes, then he wanted to know my name, but he wouldn't tell me his. He hung up."

Karen scrolled to her call log. "Oh no. That was Barry!"

"Why do you care? The man's a jerk." David huffed.

She glared at him, then tried to dial Barry, but got his voice mail. He probably assumed the worse. *Which is close to the truth.*

"Why do you keep pressing things? I told you to back off the romance." Karen scowled at him.

David matched her stare then held up his hands in surrender. "Fine, I'll back off."

"Take me home." She turned and marched to the car.

※

Barry found a bench inside the park and sat down to call Karen. After three rings a man's voice sounded on the other end. He held the phone away and verified the number he dialed. Maybe she lost her phone. "Is this Karen Marino's phone?"

"Yeah. Is this her husband?" the voice said.

"Where's Karen?" *Why does this guy have her phone?* His face got hot, and he bolted from the bench ready to fight as though the man stood in front of him.

"If you ever loved her, let her go. I'm better for her than you ever were. You don't deserve her."

"I want to talk to my wife." Silence. He clenched his fist for a moment, breathed out a string of cuss words, then stuffed the phone in his pocket. How long has this been going on? His phone rang, but he didn't even look at the caller ID. *How can she point the finger at me?*

He caught a bus to SoHo, entered the first bar he found and ordered a beer. Scanning the crowd, his eyes were drawn to a boisterous group of women sitting at a table toward the back of the bar.

He caught the gaze of one woman, held up his glass and nodded.

She smiled, then leaned over and whispered to a friend who looked his way. She smiled and whispered something back. The first woman shook her head and covered her face. She was pretty in an uncommon way. Not the delicate perfection of a model, but she had poise.

When she laughed she leaned her head back and he could see the whiteness of her throat framed by her shoulder length black hair. He imagined what it would feel like to run his hand through it. She turned her attention back to her companions. He toyed with his wedding ring as he stood watching her. *Is Karen having an affair?* He banged the bar with his fist. Two could play this game. He took off his ring and tucked it into his pocket.

He ordered two drinks and headed to the woman's table. When he paused next to them, they looked up expectantly. He focused on the woman with black hair. "Can I buy you a drink?" He held up the extra glass he carried.

She flashed him a Mona Lisa smile and looked at her friends, then shrugged. "Sure." She joined Barry and they found a spot at the bar. As the crowd grew so did the noise, and Barry and the woman struggled to hear each other. Finally they gave up on chit chat and moved to the dance floor.

A few hours and several drinks later Barry staggered out of the bar with her. He couldn't even remember her name. Just as well. They flirted their way to her apartment building and she invited him upstairs. Too drunk to care, he followed her up.

Karen deserved it.

The morning sun hit Barry full in the face. He blinked and sat straight up in bed. This wasn't his room. What have I done?

The events of the night before blurred together. He recalled drinking and dancing with a woman. He'd been mad at Karen, but it wasn't supposed to go this far — almost naked in a strange woman's bed. The pictures were one thing, but this? His skin crawled. How could he face

Karen? He threw the pillow across the room then found his clothes and got dressed.

He found a note on the kitchen table.

I ran down to the corner store. Be right back.

Christy

He shuddered at the thought of how he spent the night. Even if Karen looked past his other shortcomings this would probably end their marriage if she ever found out. If it wasn't finished already. He felt the sting of tears against his eyes and sat down. Dread filled him at the thought of losing Karen. He had to find some way to fix this. She never needed to know. Unless, of course, Christy had some disease she passed on to him. He groaned. *I've messed up again.*

Come to me and rest.

"I already told you I don't need you." Barry laughed when he realized he had accepted that God talked to him. His parents would be elated. "I can fix this on my own. Really."

He found a basket with mail in it and pulled out the top envelope. Christy Malhoney. He jotted down her name and address on a scrap of paper, then grabbed his keys from the bedroom and left by way of the back stairway. He emerged from the building, shaded his eyes against the sunlight and groaned when his head started pounding. He passed several bars with a closed sign on them before he caught a bus back to his apartment.

He stopped at the grocer for beer, then settled on his apartment steps and drank several cans before numbness silenced the guilt riling his gut. He decided to walk to Megan's place. No matter what she claimed, she must know about the guy with Karen's phone and where exactly in Missouri she was.

When he arrived, he waited at the bottom of the stairs until he saw an elderly woman coming out. Dashing up the steps, he held the door as the woman exited, then slipped inside. He found Megan's mailbox.

Apartment 2D. Perfect. He passed up the elevator and took the stairs two at a time. At his knock, she called for him to enter. *That was easy.* Now she wouldn't be able to get rid of him.

Barry let himself in and examined the Fletcher's uptown apartment. They had a nice size kitchen and a dining room. Along the hallway, three doors stood slightly ajar. Cheery and spacious, the kind of place he had wanted to provide for Karen. No wonder she preferred Megan's place.

Barry sat on the edge of the couch, grabbed a pillow and punched it. Megan probably convinced Karen to leave. He threw the pillow across the room and knocked over a lamp.

"Robert?" Megan came out from one of the rooms. "What — Barry? How did you get in here?"

He stood and faced her. He had forgotten about Robert. Barry hoped he wasn't there. "Where is Karen?"

"You need to leave."

"I'm not leaving until you tell me Karen's address."

"I told you what I know. She's in Missouri. Now, please leave." Megan tried to edge around him toward the door, but Barry blocked her path.

"I don't believe you." He stepped toward Megan until he stood inches from her face.

"You're drunk, Barry. Sit down and we'll talk."

"Yeah, let's talk about Karen's boyfriend."

"What?"

"Don't act dumb. I called her last night and some guy answered her phone. Told me he was better for her than I was. I'm sure you know all about it. How long has she been involved with him?"

"Karen doesn't have a boyfriend." Megan moved backwards, tripped over some books and fell. Barry moved closer and kicked the books out of the way. She covered her rounded stomach and cowered in the corner. "Please, don't hurt my baby."

He hesitated. He just wanted information. Maybe if he calmed down he could reason with her. He took a long slow breath.

His knee buckled when someone stomped on his calf. An arm reached around his throat, pulling him back. He struggled, but darkness crept into the edge of his vision. He stopped resisting and the arm around his throat relaxed its squeeze though still holding him secure. His vision returned to normal.

"Are you okay, Megan?" Robert asked.

"Yeah."

"Are you done?" Robert spoke in Barry's ear.

"Let me go." Barry jerked his elbow behind him and caught Robert in the ribs.

"I asked if you're done." Robert tightened his hold around Barry's neck. He twisted away. The two men glared at each other, Robert blocking his path to the door.

"You gonna call the cops?" Barry glanced at Megan.

"I should."

"He's just upset about Karen." Megan struggled to her feet.

"That's no excuse to come at you the way he did. Maybe some time in jail will cool his heels."

Barry wasn't about to spend time in jail. He rushed Robert, shoving him onto the couch as he past, and bolted out of the building and to the bus stop. He boarded the first bus to arrive and made his way to an empty seat in the back. How did he get so out of control? *I just want to get it right for a change.*

Come to me and rest.

"I'm not..." Barry caught the looks of a couple of passengers and closed his mouth. *I'm not ready to try it your way.* Besides what did God mean by rest?

Barry transferred twice before he circled back and disembarked a few blocks away from his apartment. He stopped at the liquor store for some beer and several bottles of liquor, then at a newsstand for his favorite magazines that promised an interesting evening. He intended to rest. His way.

He dropped off his purchases at the apartment and walked to the corner grocer to pick up some TV dinners and cereal. When he returned, Robert waited in front of his apartment building. Barry tried to ignore him and walk past, but Robert followed him up to his apartment.

WHERE HOPE STARTS

"What do you want?" Barry unlocked the door and went inside.

"Look, you're lucky I got back to our apartment when I did or I would have had to call the police."

"Don't expect me to thank you." Barry set his groceries on the counter. "I can handle life without your help."

"I'm not so sure after the way you intimidated my wife."

"I wouldn't hurt Megan."

"You could have fooled us. Maybe after you sober up you'll realize what a lie you're feeding yourself. I just hope it doesn't take you hurting someone to get it through your thick skull that you need help." Robert pointed to the liquor on the table. "And that is inviting trouble."

"I don't need a nanny."

"You need God." Robert stared Barry down.

"Look, I have stuff to do." He put his hand on Robert's shoulder and nudged him toward the door.

"Megan and I are praying for a miracle, and I believe God will come through. But if you ever pull a stunt like you did today, I will call the police. No matter what my wife says in your defense."

"Whatever. And I don't need God."

Barry slammed the door behind Robert and locked it. "I need to rest." He pulled out a bottle of Jack Daniels and raised it to the unseen angel on his shoulder. "My way."

21

A fresh morning breeze stirred the curtains at the window and cardinals called to each other in the yard. The sun dappled the floor around Karen and she tapped her feet to the country music playing in her head.

Last night's line dancing had been fun until David kissed her, then Barry called and everything fell apart.

Karen groaned. *Why does it bother me so much?* Did she hope for reconciliation? Thinking about the work involved made her tired. She sighed.

I know the plans I have for you.

She shook her head. *I want simple and Barry is not simple.* She touched her lips and remembered David's kiss. "I won't feel guilty."

A glance at the clock told her church started in an hour. She didn't care to go this morning, but what else was there to do? She might as well get ready and see if she changed her mind.

Karen pulled up to the church building and found a spot to park at the side. She stared at the building, then put her car in reverse to pull out. A knock on the window stopped her.

Albert's kids waited with big smiles on their faces. She smiled. She couldn't say no to them. Resigning herself to an hour of religion, she followed the kids into the sanctuary. They scooted into a pew next to their grandpa, but she kept walking and sat by herself.

Filled with bitterness, she didn't listen to the sermon. During worship she stared at the words displayed on the wall, but never opened her mouth. After church, she rushed out, refusing to give anyone a chance to corner her.

She found a spot under a shade tree to wait for Albert and his family. She pulled out her phone and dialed Megan.

"Karen? I thought you fell off the face of the planet."

"I'm sorry I haven't called. How are you?"

"I had an ultrasound last week."

"And…"

"It's a boy."

"Congratulations."

"Thanks. Now tell me what's up with you. How's your mom?"

"There haven't been any changes since I arrived. And they really don't know how much longer she has."

"I'm sorry."

Karen huffed. "Yeah well, that's the way it is."

"Karen!"

"Megan, my mom gave up on me. There's nothing to mourn."

"I hope that changes."

"I'm not holding my breath." She didn't understand Megan's capacity to hope. There was nothing there with her mom. Just like she felt about her marriage. "Uh…have you seen Barry?"

"He's stopped by a couple of times to find out where you are."

"I guess it's good I didn't tell you."

"He's…" Megan cleared her throat. "Never mind."

"Go ahead. I know you're dying to say whatever is on your mind." Karen closed her eyes.

"Barry is acting out of his own wounds. That's where this stuff gets its hook into him."

Karen held the phone away from her ear and stared at it. How could Megan even go there? "What about me and my pain?"

"Understanding how this addiction works will help you get through your pain and make forgiveness and reconciliation possible." Megan's gentle voice were a contrast to the words she spoke.

"I don't know if I want to understand or forgive, much less save my marriage. Even if he wanted to change, how can I trust him after all this?"

"It takes time. Look, I didn't mean to sound like I was defending him. I just want you to heal."

Karen choked back a cry. "Right now, I just want him to feel as much pain as I do."

"I understand. I was there once myself, remember? But trust God. He'll get you through it."

"Look, I need to go. I'm supposed to have lunch at my brother's." Karen rubbed her temples. Trusting God wasn't in her vocabulary.

"Karen? Uh..."

"Yeah?"

"When Barry stopped by this morning — "

"He came by this morning?"

"Before church. He's pretty angry. He asked me what I knew about your boyfriend. Said he called and some guy picked up your phone. You aren't seeing anyone are you?"

"He must be talking about David, a friend from my high school days. We went line dancing. That's all. Barry called and David picked up. Barry must have jumped to the wrong conclusion."

"Did he?"

"What are you accusing me of?"

"Playing with fire. You're still married, and hanging out with other men doesn't give God much of a chance."

"Didn't you hear anything I just said? I don't care about my marriage right now. Besides, David and I are just friends." Karen grimaced. Were they?

"Can you honestly tell me you don't have any feelings for this guy?"

Heat flooded her face. Megan was right. David was a big part of her confusion. She squeezed her eyes shut. "I'm not ready to let go of what might be with David until I know what will happen with Barry."

"You're leaving your options open?"

"Sounds kind of cold when you put it that way."

"Trust God. He has good plans for you and Barry. Wait on Him and give Him time."

"I don't know if I can." Karen leaned against a tree. Maybe she needed to file for divorce and move on. Check into a loan to buy that bed and breakfast. And take David up on his unspoken offer. Those were plans she could count on. "I have to go. Albert and his family are headed to their car."

"Don't do anything rash. I'll pray for you."

"Bye. Call you later."

Karen stuck her phone in her purse. A visit with one of Albert's congregation might have been preferable to her talk with Megan. Karen pushed away from the tree. Despite Megan's words, she doubted God wanted any part of her.

How did she trust a God like that?

22

"Be quiet." Barry banged on the wall and pulled the pillow around his ears.

The knocking continued, then he heard a key in the lock. He pulled himself out of bed and the room spun. Steadying himself, he grabbed an empty liquor bottle from the floor and stumbled to the bedroom door. "Who is it? And what do you want?"

"It's your landlord."

Barry came into the living room. "What do you mean barging into my apartment?"

"Had some complaints." The man kicked some beer cans out of his way. "What happened here?"

"None of your business. What day is it?"

"Thursday."

"The date." Barry rubbed the back of his neck.

"The 25th, bozo." The man stood with hands on his hips.

"The 25th? How in the world…?"

The landlord looked around the apartment at all the empty liquor bottles and beer cans. "Drink makes the time fly. But it don't pay the rent. Where's your wife?"

"That's none of your business either."

"It is if you can't pay your rent. You gonna have it next week?"

"Yeah."

"If you don't, I'll change the locks and call the police." He turned to go.

"Wait." Barry returned to his bedroom and dug around in his drawer for the wad of money from Dennis. "Here, if you're so concerned, I'll pay you now." He threw the money at his landlord.

The man counted the bills. "That'll do. Stop by the office later, I'll have a receipt for you."

Barry locked the door behind the landlord, then turned and kicked cans out of his way. Two weeks wasted. At least the rent was paid. *No thanks to Karen. She's too busy with her boyfriend.* He swung a fist at the wall and left a gaping hole. Swearing, he headed to the shower. *I'm always messing up.*

After his shower, he gathered up his dirty clothes and threw them into the laundry basket. Grabbing a trash bag from under the kitchen sink, he stuffed it with beer cans, liquor bottles, and magazines then took it out to the dumpster.

Satisfied with the cleanup, he stopped by the fridge for something to eat. It was empty and his big wad of cash just walked out the door. He needed some money. A game at Anthony's? That was a stupid idea. Maybe Karen stashed some money somewhere. She always hid her fun money from him — like she didn't trust him.

Barry looked through her dresser and dug through her pockets, finally finding a few bills forgotten in one of her coat pockets. *Twenty-three bucks* — just enough for supper and a drink or two. He slammed the closet door shut.

He knew their joint account had a couple hundred dollars in it earmarked for automatic bill pay. If he got to the bank first, he could withdraw it. Who cared if the utilities didn't get paid? At this rate, he would be on the street soon anyway.

Come to me and rest.

"You don't give up, do you?" He put his shoes on, grabbed his cell phone and hurried out of the apartment. He opted for the stairs, his head throbbing with every step. He stepped out of the stairwell and spotted Robert at the elevator. Barry ducked his head and hurried to the front door, out the door and down the sidewalk.

"Barry, wait up."

Barry cursed. Not fast enough. He stopped at a crosswalk. "What do you want?"

"I've been trying to get hold of you the last couple of weeks, but you never returned my calls."

"Been busy."

"Well –"

"If you want to talk you'll have to keep up." Barry crossed the street at a near jog.

"Karen called Megan." Robert strode next to him. "Said you didn't pick up her calls, so she asked me to stop by."

"You know, Karen left me with no warning, no money, and no hint where she is and now she acts all concerned? Tell her to come back and check on me herself." He continued to the bus stop.

"So, are you alright?" Robert followed Barry onto the bus.

"Didn't you hear anything I just said?"

Robert rode in silence to Barry's stop, then followed him off the bus. "I can ask around at my church and see if anyone knows about any jobs available."

"Knock yourself out." Barry's phone vibrated and he pulled it out from his pocket. He pressed his lips together when he saw Karen's name on the caller ID. He turned his back on Robert and answered the phone. "What?"

"You sound mad."

"What did you expect?"

"Right. Well, I'm staying here for a while."

"And where is here?"

Karen hesitated. "You don't need to know for now."

Barry swore. "You afraid I'll come and ruin your party?"

"What are you talking about?"

"Your boyfriend."

"There is nothing going on."

"Not according to him."

"Who are you to point fingers?"

Barry cursed under his breath and ran a hand through his hair. She always turned the tables on him. "Are you going to send money for the bills?"

"Get a job."

"I've tried."

"Right."

She always thought the worst of him. *Of course, what have I done to prove otherwise?* "What about your precious stuff? We lose the apartment, we lose that."

"I don't care what happens to it."

He narrowed his eyes. "What about us?"

"I'm not sure. But right now, I don't want to see you."

"Well, I don't want to see you either. Why did you even bother calling?" Barry heard her gasp as he hung up. He jammed the phone into his pocket and started walking.

Robert caught up with Barry. "Where you headed?"

"To find a drink and who knows what else." Barry called over his shoulder. "Maybe I'll get into a poker game." He stepped around some workmen coming out of an apartment building.

"You've had enough to drink." Robert grabbed Barry's shoulder.

He turned and brushed off Robert's hand. "Back off."

Barry continued his trek. Hearing footsteps behind him, he spun around and came face to face with Robert. "I don't need a nursemaid." Barry shoved Robert back a few steps, knocking him into a construction worker.

"Hey, watch it!" The man cursed and shoved Robert back.

The crowd parted around the two men. Robert got in Barry's face. "You need help."

"Not yours." Barry threw a punch, hitting Robert in the jaw with a right hook.

Robert stumbled back. He caught his balance and rubbed his jaw. "You should take up boxing."

"Maybe I will." Barry held his fists in front of his face and moved around Robert looking for an opening.

Robert took a defensive stance.

Barry threw a left towards Robert's head. He blocked it and came back with an uppercut, sending Barry stumbling into the crowd. Hands pushed him back into the fight.

"Not bad yourself. But not good enough." Barry rammed his head into Robert's midsection, knocking them both to the ground. Robert rolled out from under Barry, jumped up and backed away. A voice in the crowd warned them to stop, saying the police were on the way. Robert held up his hands in surrender.

"Dumb move." Barry kicked Robert in the side, dropping him to the ground. "Come on, finish this."

"Barry, this is stupid." Robert rested on a knee, looking up at him.

Barry bounced from one foot to the other, like a prize boxer ready for a take down. He motioned for Robert to get back in the fight, daring him to continue. Robert's gaze locked on something behind him. Suddenly, Robert lunged, slamming him to the ground, then rolled to the side.

Barry lay stunned, looking around. The crowd began to disperse. Robert lay on the ground. Blood covered his head. Barry tore off the bottom edge of his shirt then crawled over to him, and held it to his head to stop the bleeding. "Someone call an ambulance."

"They're on the way. The police too."

"What have I done?" Barry stayed by Robert's side and waited for the ambulance. He was angry, but he didn't mean to hurt Robert. He hadn't planned to hurt his brother, either, but Chad was gone and now Robert lay on the street with a bloody head.

What happened? He remembered Robert rushing him and knocking him to the ground, but how did he end up with a bloody head? Had he been so out of control? Did he black out and forget part of the fight like he forgot the last two weeks?

He glanced around at the shrinking crowd and saw people looking his way, pointing and whispering. A two-by-four lay on the ground nearby with blood on it. *Where did that come from?*

The sound of a siren broke through the fog in his mind. He struggled against the hands that pulled him away until he saw the paramedics. A few minutes later they loaded Robert into the ambulance and took off.

"You almost killed a man." A police officer cuffed Barry and read him his Miranda rights.

"We're friends. We had a disagreement."

The police officer looked him over as he put him in the squad car.

"Right."

I messed up — again.

Come to me and rest.

Really, God? Barry looked upward, then leaned his head against the squad car window, squeezing his eyes shut against the tears.

He needed a drink.

23

Karen stuck the phone in her pocket. Her lawyer had the divorce papers ready to sign. Was she ready to say goodbye to Barry? *I can't wait around forever.*

That's why she was checking into buying the B&B. She had an appointment later with the owners, then tomorrow with the banker. She would make her own way, even if Barry wasn't a part of it.

She grabbed the flowers from the counter and headed to Margie's for breakfast.

Knocking gently on the back door, Karen walked into the kitchen. Square in shape, the walls were lined with cupboards and a massive island took up the center of the room. The kitchen was big enough to feed a house full of kids, though Margie and Sam never had any. An eating nook jutted out of the north wall.

"Hi, Margie."

She glanced over her shoulder from the sink. "Be right with you."

Karen took a deep breath. She had often retreated here after an episode with her dad, and she and Margie would bake cookies or cakes or just sit and talk. She still felt invited to make herself comfortable and stay awhile.

She glanced around at the improvements that had been made over the years. The linoleum floors had been replaced with wood and the appliances updated, but the curtains looked like the same ones that hung over the windows the last time she was here. She walked over and fingered the fading fabric of yellow dotted with blue flowers . "Are these the same curtains?"

Margie laughed. "I couldn't make myself part with those. Too many memories, we spent so much time laboring over them."

Karen shook her head. "And I still didn't learn how to sew worth anything."

"But worth every minute. Besides, I love the colors."

"I brought you some flowers. I think they match."

A big grin lit up Margie's face. "They're beautiful. Why don't you grab a vase from the pantry while I finish scrambling these eggs?

Karen arranged the flowers and set them on the island. "Margie, can I ask you a question?"

"Sure, what's on your mind?"

"Why did you and my parents stop doing stuff together? You were friends, weren't you?"

"We're still friends." Margie sighed as she slid the eggs back into the refrigerator.

"But after Dad turned on me, you guys didn't talk much. Was it because I hung out at your place all the time?"

Margie turned and looked out the window.

"Margie?" Karen couldn't imagine what caused the rift.

"There's a time for everything. Now, it's time to eat. Set those beautiful flowers by the picture window and come to the table." Margie set down two plates full of bacon, eggs and fruit.

From the little Karen heard about their relationship, she knew Sam and Margie played a large role in her parents becoming Christians. What was Margie not saying?

"Sorry. I'm not very hungry." Karen pushed her plate away.

"You need to eat." Margie pushed the plate back toward Karen and felt her forehead. "You aren't sick, are you?"

"I don't think so. I feel fine."

"It's probably all the stress. You'll feel better after you eat something."

"I hope so." Karen sipped on her tea and nibbled on sliced peaches.

"Any news about your mom?"

"No. I visit her every couple of days, though."

"You really need to talk to your dad."

"Why? So he can reject me again?"

Margie's soft hand covered her own. "He's changed."

Karen pulled her hand away. "It doesn't let him off the hook."

"Seems like you have a lot of hooks you're hanging onto lately."

Karen looked down at her uneaten food.

"Have you heard from that husband of yours?" Margie poured a cup of coffee.

Karen grimaced. "Yeah, and when I told him I wasn't coming home, the conversation went from bad to worse. He thinks I should send money for rent and food. But I don't know."

Margie reached across the table and patted Karen's hand. "Barry is a grown man and needs to take responsibility for his choices. Don't rescue him. Let God work on him, then you'll have a second chance at your marriage."

Karen squirmed in her chair. Margie never left God out of her conversation. "I'm not sure I want a second chance. I had a lawyer draw up divorce papers."

"Sweetie, don't do anything rash."

Karen sat up straight. "I'm not going to wait around here like a bag of discarded clothes for the thrift store."

"I'm not saying that. But you can trust your heavenly Father. Just wait and see."

"I'm looking at buying the Applewood Hill Bed and Breakfast." Karen nibbled the inside of her cheek.

"Oh, Karen. We would love to have you back home. I just wish you would wait on the divorce."

"I have to move on." She stood up and grabbed the edge of the table.

"Are you okay?" Margie moved to her side.

"I think so. Just a bit light-headed."

"Oh." Margie grinned.

"What?" Karen sat back down.

"Little appetite. Light-headed. Tell me, have you been extremely emotional lately?"

"With all the junk going on in my life? Sure."

"Tired?"

"Yes." Karen tilted her head.

"Felt like throwing up?"

"Yes. What are you…wait." Karen met Margie's gaze as she thought through the last few weeks. "You think — I might be pregnant." She gasped. Her cycle was always irregular. She hadn't thought anything of being late. She calculated the weeks…then placed a hand over her stomach. "I suppose it's possible. I need to pick up a pregnancy test."

Margie laughed and gave her a hug. "Let me know what you find out."

※

Karen pulled up to Applewood Hill and parked. Taking the pregnancy test out of the bag, she read the instructions. It was simple. Two blue lines meant yes, one blue line meant no.

What wasn't so simple, was being a single parent. And if Barry was not a part of her future, that's what she would be.

She nibbled on her lower lip. Regardless, she would love this child. And provide for him…or her. Karen smiled and looked out at the bed and breakfast. The pregnancy test would have to wait. Getting out of the car, she headed up to the entrance where James waited for her.

"The Walkers will be ready shortly. You can wait in the guest library." James led the way across the foyer to a set of French doors. He pushed them open and moved aside. "Would you like some tea while you wait?"

"No thank you. I'm fine." She stepped into the room and was immediately struck by the huge collection of books. The shelves seemed to hold every genre imaginable. The dark moss green walls and cherry trim framed the room while overstuffed chairs waited for visitors to curl up with a good read. A grand piano sat in one corner banked on either side by windows. Guests could truly relax in this space. She wondered if the furnishings would stay. She walked the perimeter of the room, her hand trailing the spines of the volumes displayed.

"Karen Marino?"

Karen turned as a white-haired man about the same height as Barry arrived with a woman, also white-haired and small in stature, close behind. They made a striking couple.

"I'm Ben Walker and this is my wife, Sheryl. Are you ready for the fifty-cent tour?"

Karen laughed. She liked them already. "Lead the way."

"We hate to part with this place. We bought it ten years ago and had so much fun renovating it." Sheryl looped her hand through Karen's arm and led her out of the library. "But our kids live on the east coast, and we aren't getting any younger. It's time we moved to be near them."

"We haven't told the kids yet, but we're not going to sit around — knitting and playing golf all day." She giggled, then glanced over her shoulder and winked at her husband. "We plan to find another B and B to run out there." Sheryl led the way up the stairs to look at the bedrooms.

Trailing her free hand on the curved mahogany banister, Karen listened with one ear as the Walkers told one story after another about the bed and breakfast, their kids, and early days of their marriage. Her heart wandered to her own memories and dreams of growing old with the love of her life. *That used to be Barry.* She turned her head to hide her tears.

"Sweetie, what is wrong? Did I say something to upset you?"

"Don't mind me." Karen shook her head. "I'll be fine."

"Well, if you're sure." Sheryl patted her hand. "If you don't want the orchard we can sell that separately from the bed and breakfast, but they do so well together. Right now we just use the fruit in the kitchen and sell it at the roadside stand, but you could do more with it."

Karen laughed at the constant stream of information. "I like the idea of keeping them together, but it will all depend on what the bank says."

Sheryl nodded and the couple led Karen down a back staircase and through a short hallway. They stopped outside a door. "Here it is." Sheryl threw open the door. "What do you think?"

Karen looked around the well-equipped kitchen. They could serve some major crowds. "It's bigger than I expected."

"This was phase two of our plan." Ben smiled.

"Phase one, of course, being the rooms and front part of the house that you have already seen," Sheryl chimed in. "And you get to take over phase three. At least we hope you will."

"And what is phase three?" Karen lifted her eyebrows in question.

"Our plans included adding on a conference center with a dining hall that would seat up to two-hundred, as well as additional bathrooms and storage. We have the zoning permits and contractors lined up. All they need is the go ahead."

"Wow." Karen ran the revenue numbers in her head. The restaurant already had a faithful clientele. Her dream of running her own place was within reach. "If I get the approval, that's exactly what I'll do."

"Wonderful," Sheryl exclaimed, clapping her hands. "Also, did you realize there is a separate house in back? You'll have your own place. And James has an attached apartment."

"We're hoping you'll keep him on," Ben said.

"I see no reason why not." She smiled at the couple. "I guess I better talk to the bank." She shook their hands and headed home. Exhausted from her morning, she looked forward to a nap.

Back in the apartment, Karen kicked off her shoes and poured a glass of water. Staring out the window she thought about the last few weeks. Her last conversation with Barry made all of her uncertainties clear. David was willing to take up where they left off so many years ago and every time she thought about Barry's anger, her heart turned to David. *But what if Barry changed?* A shiver ran through her. Could he ever be the man she married or would she always have to fear his anger and betrayal?

She enjoyed her outings with David — he was so calm and even-tempered —but when she spent time with him, she fought guilt. Why couldn't she just enjoy being with him?

She grabbed her purse and pulled out the pregnancy test. A child would change everything. She might consider taking Barry back on her own, but she would not put a baby at risk.

She put her hand on her stomach. Time to find out if her suspicions were correct.

24

Tears filled Karen's eyes. Two blue lines.

I am going to be a mommy.

A sigh shuddered through her. She held her belly. She and Barry dreamed of having a family. What would he say if he knew?

"I can't tell your daddy yet, little one. I need to figure a few things out first." But it wouldn't hurt to wait a bit on those divorce papers.

She drew the curtains to darken the room, then changed and climbed into bed, her body relaxing into the softness of the mattress. Just as she drifted off, her phone rang. She grabbed it and looked at the caller ID.

"Hey, Megan, what's up?"

"Uh…Barry's in jail."

"What? I just talked to him this morning. What did he do?"

"He beat up Robert. Put him in the hospital."

"Oh no. Will he be okay?"

"He has some brain swelling, but it's receding. It's pray and wait now."

"I'm so sorry, Megan." Karen took a deep breath. "I shouldn't have been so hard on Barry when I called. I probably made him mad."

"It's not your fault. Barry has to take responsibility for his choices. Past and present. Losing his temper is a choice. You need to let him face up to that."

"Someone else told me that this morning. It's hard to do."

"I know. I need to get back to Robert. I'll let you go."

Karen hesitated. Should she tell Megan about the baby? Probably better to wait until Robert was out of the woods. "Keep me updated."

She hung up the phone. *What is going on with him?* Her eyelids began to droop. She turned off the ringer on her phone, eased back onto the pillow and fell into an uneasy sleep.

She dreamed of running into Barry at the bed and breakfast. She and David were picking apples in the orchard when Barry started following them. David became angry when he saw her husband. She was worried too, until he caught up to her and she saw his expression. He reached out to touch her face with a gentle caress. She reached for him, but he slipped away in the manner of dreams. David held on to her, refusing to let her go after her husband.

She woke in a sweat, the covers twisted, half on the floor. She laid her arm across her face and cried. *God, if you are really out there, I do need your help.*

Trust me. I have good plans for you.

"I'll try."

Wiping the tears from her face, she sat up and looked at her alarm clock. *Lunchtime.* She yanked a tissue from its box and blew her nose. She hated crying. Of course, being pregnant didn't help. *A baby.* She smiled. No matter what happened between her and Barry, she was thankful for the child she carried.

She stood up to head to the kitchen, but dizziness forced her to sit back down. She took a deep breath and made a mental note to call the doctor for a prenatal checkup, then headed to the bathroom and splashed water on her face. A knock sounded at her front door.

Karen opened the door and motioned her sister inside. "Joanna."

"Been trying to reach you all morning." Her sister tossed her purse on the couch.

"I laid down for a nap so I turned the ringer off."

"I just came from seeing mom and thought you might like to grab some lunch."

"Can we eat here?" The thought of getting dressed tired her out.

"But I want to take you out. I won last night at the casino."

"You shouldn't waste your money like that." It was a wonder her sister had a roof over her head and food to eat. Of course, she was a consummate mooch.

"What are you talking about? I won."

"Whatever. But I don't feel like going out for lunch."

"Fine. But you could have eaten anywhere you wanted."

"A rain check?"

Joanna shrugged and followed Karen into the kitchen. "What can I do to help?"

Karen pulled out cold cuts and veggies from the fridge and put her sister to work slicing bread for sandwiches. After filling their plates, they took their food onto the balcony.

Karen nibbled on her sandwich. Whether she felt like it or not, she needed to eat for the baby. She pushed her plate to the side and waited for Joanna to finish.

She noticed the circles under her sister's eyes and wondered if she was using again. Maybe she would consider rehab. Joanna finished her lunch then leaned back in her chair, let out a sigh and pulled a pack of cigarettes out of her pocket.

Unbelievable. "Please, Joanna."

"We're outside."

"On my patio." *And I'm pregnant.*

"Whatever." Joanna laid the pack down and looked around. "It's peaceful here. Not like where I live."

"Why don't you move?"

"Leaving isn't always the answer. Even if it is, it's not so easy for some of us." Joanna walked over to the railing. "You ran away after college and stuck your head in the sand. But the rest of us — we stayed put and handled things in our own way. Dysfunctional as it was."

Karen blinked. Joanna had no idea what she went through. "Is that what this lunch is about? Putting me in my place?"

"I hadn't planned it, but while I'm at it, I'll say it like it is. You ran away from your husband, just like you did Dad. It's easier to try and find someone better than to work on what's wrong."

Karen glared at her. How could Joanna judge something she knew nothing about? She threw up her hands. "You're one to talk, when do you plan to work on your problems?"

"At least I know what my problem is. Look, I'm not saying you should be a punching bag or let someone step all over you. But maybe it's time to stick around so you can work stuff out."

"I came back."

"You came here to leave there. To find resolution for yourself. Not to make peace with Dad or to make your marriage work. What about Barry?"

"What about me? He hit me, cheated on me and constantly berated me with his anger."

Joanna looked away, then began pacing the patio.

"I don't like what Barry and I have become, but I'm not going to stick around and wait for it to get worse. I just want to be happy." Karen swiped at her tears.

"With David?" Joanna stopped and crossed her arms. "You're married."

Karen stood, nose to nose with Joanna. "Where do you get off judging me? You don't stick with one guy long enough for the family to meet him. I gave Barry eight years of my life. He's the one who threw it away." Karen stepped back, taking a long slow breath. "David loves me; Barry hits me. Tell me which one you'd choose."

Joanna held her sister's stare then looked away. "There's no quick fix. Believe me, I keep trying to find it. I'm always going where the invitation is better. It rarely works." Joanna picked up her cigarettes. "Either you let me smoke or I gotta leave."

"Fine, go ahead."

The conversation was going nowhere. Karen closed her eyes and took a deep breath. "What happened the other day — with Blake? You said I didn't see what's been going on. What did you mean?"

Joanna put out her cigarette in a potted plant. "You know those last four years you were at home?"

Karen nodded.

"Blake's first ten years were worse."

"He always talked like he was the poster child for child abuse. I thought he was exaggerating." Karen looked down.

"He didn't carry black and blue marks or end up in the hospital, but his punishments were harsh and driven by anger," Joanna shook her head and resumed her pacing. "I know kids whose parents spanked them and they turned out better than any of us. You know what made the difference?"

"Anger. The lack of acceptance and love."

"That's all he knew. Then you came along." Joanna sat back down. "You have no idea what it's like to be beaten down all your life, then have some snot nose kid come along and be treated like a princess. Blake hated you. Sure, Dad stopped treating him like the whipping boy, but he still couldn't do enough to please him. He ignored Blake most of the time."

Karen slumped in her chair, struggling to hold back the tears.

"I tried to protect him and we made a pact. Kind of like the three musketeers. One for all and all for one." Joanna smiled. "We promised to always stand up for each other. And we did…until that day at your apartment." Joanna lit another cigarette, her hands trembling.

"I…I didn't know." Karen bit her lip.

"How could you? Look, it is what it is. Maybe now Blake will get the help he needs and Alita will be safe."

Karen waited until Joanna put out her cigarette. "So, do you ever think about rehab?"

"Nice change in subject." Joanna laughed. "I think about it sometimes. But don't push it. If it happens, it will be in my own time."

Karen held up her hands and smiled. "Can't blame a sister for trying."

25

Six days in jail and a forced dry out was not Barry's idea of a good time.

He sat alone in a corner of the dining hall at the county jail, grateful the other detainees ignored him. He hoped Robert would be well enough to tell his version of events before Barry's next court appearance. His lawyer said witnesses were pointing the finger at him for Robert's injuries. Unless things changed, Barry faced jail time.

He still didn't know what happened, but if he was guilty, he deserved whatever they threw at him. He wanted Robert to recover regardless. *He tried to be a friend me.* Barry shook his head. *I don't get it.*

He never understood that sort of kindness. When his parents became Christians, they tried to be nice. His brother certainly was. He shifted in his chair. His brother hadn't deserved what happened.

Come to me and rest.

This God of his parents and brother and Robert got on his nerves. He didn't need God's help.

What you've been doing is working so well, isn't it?

Barry sat up straight. Maybe he did need to try a different approach. But God? Barry remembered his brother lying in the coffin and his parents' grief that drove him away. He pushed his tray away and slammed his fist on the table.

Someone bumped Barry's table knocking over his water glass. He jumped up and blocked the man's path. The man tossed his tray down and shoved Barry in the chest. Barry shoved back.

An arm shot out between them. "Stop it."

"Stay out of it." Barry pushed the arm away without looking up.

A hand clamped down on his shoulder. His opponent backed away. Barry turned and looked up into the face of a ponytail wearing, tattoting detainee who looked like he could bench five-hundred. He took a deep breath, nodded at the man and sat down. The anger stirring in his gut fizzled, leaving him worn out.

He had been blaming everyone and everything for his angry outbursts, but he knew the truth. He was to blame. He allowed himself to get angry, and then didn't know how to stop it, so he did the only thing he could think of — he drank. But it always made things worse.

He had hurt his parents, his brother, and Karen with his anger. And now Robert. Barry sighed and headed back to his cell. It was best if he stayed away from everyone else to avoid any more trouble.

He heard footsteps behind him and glanced back. The tattooed prisoner followed him up the stairs. He ducked into his cell and willed the man to pass by, but the man stopped in the doorway. "Listen, gettin' mad is only gonna get ya in trouble. I oughta know. It's what landed me in here."

"And you're preaching at me?"

"Nah, I ain't no saint, but...well, here." The man held out a small, black book.

"A Bible?"

"It's not the whole Bible, just the New Testament. The preacher man that comes to visit, gave it to me. A lot of stuff in there makes sense. It's helped me some. I thought I'd pass it on. Maybe it's not too late for you." The big man left Barry staring at the tiny book in his hands.

After breakfast the next morning, Barry returned to his cell and pulled the Bible out from under his mattress. He skipped past the chapters with the long names. The Christmas story he knew about, so he flipped over a couple of pages to Jesus teaching on a hillside. Barry chuckled. I'd like to go to that church. He propped himself up against the wall and began reading.

"You're blessed when you're at the end of your rope. With less of you there is more of God."

He sat up. The rope felt tight around his neck, and that was supposed to be a good thing? Where were the thous and thees?

He looked at the front of the Bible. *The Message. Hmm. Well, it's easier to read than any version my parents pushed at me.* Maybe he could understand this one.

"You're blessed when you feel you've lost what is most dear to you." His eyes teared up and he glanced around to make sure no one else was watching. *How can that be a blessing?*

"Only then can you be embraced by the One most dear to you."

He laid the Bible down and leaned his head against his knees. These things Jesus taught were topsy-turvy to what he believed. Yet they cut through the thick layers he wrapped around himself to keep from hurting. He took a deep breath.

Come to me and rest.

Barry paused. Nothing else seemed to work. He picked up where he left off. More blessings and upside down thinking. *I'll never get all this.*

"Your heart can be corrupted by lust even quicker than your body. Those leering looks you think nobody notices — they also corrupt."

"I'm doomed." Barry swallowed.

Each verse showed him more that needed changing. A heavy weight settled on his chest, but he continued reading.

"I'll show you how to take a real rest."

"I really did hear from you." He started laughing. Ready to embrace rest, Barry pressed on. "Jesus fed five thousand with only five loaves of bread and two fishes?"

"Man. What are you mumbling about over there?"

Barry looked up at a couple of tattoo covered detainees. "Just something I'm reading."

"Keep it to yourself."

Barry nodded. He looked at the next story and sat up straight. "He walked on water?"

"We told you, keep it down." One of the men towered over him.

"I'll work on it." He held up his hand.

The man glared at him and returned to the other side of the cell.

Barry continued to read, amazed at the miracles Jesus did. He healed the sick, the cripples, and the blind. He even raised people from the dead. The Easter story seemed fresh, uncluttered by bunnies and eggs. He was beginning to appreciate his parents' enthusiasm.

Jesus did a lot for the fishermen who followed Him. Simon Peter's changes impressed him. He went from a loud mouth, rough-around-the-edges traitor to the guy preaching the day so many people became Christians. *If Jesus has all that power, maybe he can help me. What do I do now?*

Keep going.

"More?"

"How many times do we have to tell you to shut up?"

"You could go somewhere else." Barry chided.

The man narrowed his eyes at him, got up and motioned for the other guy to follow him.

Barry watched them leave, then turned his attention back to the Bible. Acts told stories about the disciples after Jesus returned to heaven. When he finished that book, it was time for lunch. He put the Bible under his mattress and went to the dining room.

He found a spot away from the others. In Acts, everyone who decided to be Jesus' disciples turned their back on the way they lived before.

Was it possible to turn away from his anger? To close his eyes to the fantasies? To stay away from the alcohol? *I've done so much wrong. Would God forgive me?* He hurt so many people. Could he change? Was he ready to change?

Come to me and rest.

He grinned and drank his coffee. God's rest sounded nice.

"Can I join you?" The preacher man sat down across from him. "I'm Steve."

"Barry." He shook the man's hand.

"You have a chance to read any of the Good Book, yet?"

"Pretty interesting stuff."

"How much you get read?"

"Through Acts."

Steve let out a whistle. "You mean business."

"Nothing better to keep me busy in here." Barry smiled. The weight off his shoulders was amazing. Was it just from reading the Bible and beginning to understand who Jesus was?

"When's your court date?" Steve asked.

"Tomorrow. You?"

"Not sure. They gotta send me back out to the Midwest first. Won't be a trial though. I'm guilty."

"What did you do?"

"I killed a man with my bare hands. Been running from it for some time, the law finally caught up with me." Steve looked down at his hands. "I wish someone had given me a Bible before it went too far."

Barry nodded. God was giving him a gift. "I got in a fight with a friend. At least he tried to be. Kept telling me how much I needed God. I pushed him away one too many times and he ended up in the hospital."

"You know, I used to consider myself a pretty good man. I don't smoke or drink too much and I don't cheat on my wife. I had a job. We weren't rich, but we got by. I thought everyone got mad. But when I stood in front of the judge with the blood of an innocent man on my hands, I understood how bad I am. I just wasn't good enough. Not for this life or the next. But Jesus, he makes me good enough for the next, no matter what I done."

Barry thought about that. Could Jesus make him good enough? Barry's name sounded over the intercom, and he rose to leave. "Hey man, thanks for the Bible."

"Pay attention to it." Steve reached out and shook Barry's hand. "If Jesus can help me, He can help you."

Barry followed the guard to the visitor's room, expecting to see his lawyer. His eyes widened when he saw Megan at one of the tables. Her smile surprised him. "How's Robert?"

"Better. The swelling is down and he woke up a couple of days ago. Your lawyer is talking to him now, then he'll be over. Robert asked me to come and tell you myself." She clasped her hands on the table in front of her.

"Tell me what?" Barry tilted his head.

"Some guy from the crowd picked up a two-by-four from a nearby construction site and aimed it at your back, but Robert knocked you out of the way and got hit instead. Someone caught it on their phone and actually posted it online. The prosecutor is dropping the charges. You'll be out of here soon."

Barry breathed a sigh of relief. "I'm sorry I started that fight. I was stupid. Robert could have died. Even if I didn't hold the two-by-four, it's my fault. He didn't deserve the way I treated him."

"Robert said to tell you he forgives you."

"Why would he? I don't deserve it."

"God forgave him. He couldn't do any less." Megan reached out and touched his arm. "Once you're out of here, we'd love for you to come to church with us."

"I want to."

"Really?"

Barry nodded. "Someone in here gave me a Bible and…well, I've been reading it. A lot of it makes sense, but I need to check it out more."

Megan clapped her hands. "Robert will be glad to hear that."

"Don't tell Karen though. Not about the church or Jesus part. She wasn't big on God herself, and I'm not sure where this is headed. I want to tell her myself."

"I've prayed about this for so long."

"So I've been told."

Megan laughed. "I better get back to the hospital. Robert is coming home tonight."

"Before you go, I have a question for you. Do you ever hear…God… talking to you?"

"God's been chasing you."

"You could say that," Barry said as he ran a hand through his hair.

"Kind of like a quiet voice inside your heart?"

"Exactly. I never believed God cared about me so much."

"Did you read about the shepherd that goes after the lost sheep?"

"I was the lost sheep? And He wanted me?" Barry's eyes lit up. Megan nodded. "He never gives up."

"I'm starting to get that. Thanks."

"Sure. I better scoot now. We'll be in touch." Megan headed toward the door.

"Megan?"

She turned. "Yes?"

"Uh…I need to ask you to forgive me, too. For the way I came after you in your apartment. I'm sorry. I promise I'll never do that again."

"I forgive you."

Her smile encouraged him. "Do you think Karen can forgive me, too?"

"With God, yes."

"I hope you're right." Barry watched her leave. He knew he deserved punishment but God offered forgiveness. Just maybe he could make some changes with God's help. And find that rest He talked about.

26

June was ending on an upbeat note. Only a week ago she found out she was pregnant and toured Applewood Hill. Since then, she had applied for a loan and bought a baby name book. Karen rubbed her belly. And she told her lawyer to wait on the divorce papers. For a while.

Now she was helping Alita find a dog. Hopefully for protection. No one had seen or heard from Blake since the scene in front of her apartment. But he was bound to show up.

"How about this one?" Karen pointed to a hairless Chihuahua.

"It looks like a giant rat." Alita walked to the next kennel. "Here's one. If Blake comes around, he can pick on someone his own size."

"He would just lick Blake to death." Karen laughed at the massive St. Bernard. "I think you need a Rottweiler. They're protective of their family."

Alita paused beside the next cage. "Here's a German shepherd. The sign says a family surrendered him because of an international move. He's trained and housebroken."

"That's more like it."

At the front desk they arranged for Alita to visit with the German Shepherd and then waited in the get-acquainted room.

"Has Blake been around?"

Alita shook her head. "He showed up once after I changed the locks. I told him about the restraining order and haven't seen him since."

"How are you doing?"

Alita laughed and twisted her wedding ring on her finger. "I actually miss him. The house echoes with only me in it. Don't worry, I won't take him back. He'll have to prove he's different for me to consider it."

"Joanna said they made some sort of pact when they were kids."

"She has a way with him. It's almost like…" Alita shrugged, "like he'd prefer to spend time with her than me."

Karen sat in silence, watching Alita chew her thumb nail, unsure of how to respond. She knew the pain of a fist went deeper than the external wounds.

She looked up as a kennel volunteer led the dog into the room. The German Shepherd sniffed around a bit, then headed straight for Alita, putting a paw on her knee. When she leaned over to pet him, he licked her face.

"He's perfect." Alita laughed and wrapped her arms around his neck. "I'll take him."

Karen looked in the rearview mirror and did a double take. Was that Blake? Why would he follow her? She looked again, but the truck was gone. She must have imagined it.

She stopped off at the store for a few groceries. Maybe David could join her for dinner and a movie at the apartment. He had backed off the romance and they spent several evenings together the last couple of weeks, just enjoying each other's company.

She parked in the drive, then grabbing the bag of groceries with one hand and keys in the other, she climbed the stairs to her door. Struggling to hold her bag of groceries she dropped her keys as she stepped inside. A movement caught the corner of her eye as she reached down to retrieve them.

"It's about time you got home."

Karen dropped her bag in surprise. "Blake." She backed into the living room. Where was his truck? "You need to leave."

"Maybe I don't want to."

"What do you want?" Karen stood with the couch between them.

"About the other day…"

"Yes?"

"You don't know how it's done around here."

"Oh, I think I do."

"If you did, you would know a man needs to control his home. You butted in. If you had kept your nose out of it, I'd be in my own home right now. With my wife."

"You can't hurt people just to get your way."

"You don't have any idea what hurt is." He pressed the palms of his hands to his temples. "No one does. You just need to leave me alone. Stay out of my business."

"I can't if you're hurting people."

"Then I have to finish what I started years ago." Blake slapped the edge of a nearby table.

Karen jumped. Scanning the room, she looked for a way to escape, but Blake stood between her and the door. He slammed it shut and walked toward her.

"I don't want to hurt you." He held one hand against his head and closed his eyes. Then he tapped his head with the heel of his hand. "I just want it to stop."

"You're not making sense."

He paused at the sound of sirens. "Just leave us alone, or I'll have to finish this later." He jerked the door open and rushed down the stairs.

Karen watched from the window as he sped off in his truck. Moments later a police car pulled in the drive. She took several deep breaths and headed out to meet them.

Margie joined her and the policemen on the front lawn. "I saw the same truck the other night when the police were here," Margie said. "I knew it couldn't be good. So I called. He just left in an awful hurry."

The police officers took their statements and told them to call if there was anymore trouble.

Margie pulled Karen into a hug. "Why don't you stay over at the house for a while? At least until they find your brother."

"I'll think about it." Karen headed back up to the apartment as an old beat up truck pulled in the drive. Squinting against the sun, she smiled. *David.* He stepped out of his truck.

"What happened? I just passed the police."

Karen filled him in, playing down her fears. She patted the hood of his truck. "I can't believe you still have it."

"It's actually just a look alike. Want to take it for a spin?" David teased. "I have it on good authority some fields need some tearing up."

""Sounds just my speed. Let me lock up first."

Karen slammed on the brakes, bringing David's old truck to a stop. She laughed as she put it in park and climbed out. They clambered up on the hood and leaned against the windshield. "I haven't had that much fun since the first time you let me take the wheel and spin donuts."

"My dad got plenty mad when he discovered us sneaking off in the truck." David chuckled. "Hey look, a shooting star." They rested in the quiet and watched the stars.

Karen glanced at David. What would it be like if they got back together? Would he be a good father? "David?"

"Hmm?" He glanced at her.

"Back in the day, we never talked about kids. Do you want any?"

"You offering?" David winked at her.

"David!" She blushed and slapped his arm.

"Just teasing."

"So?"

"Why do you ask?"

"Barry and I always planned on having several."

"That turned out." David snorted, then turned toward her. "Is it important to you? I could probably be persuaded by the right woman."

Karen struggled to find the right words. Would he welcome another man's child in his home? She might not want to know the answer. "It's nothing. Just wondering."

David didn't respond and after a few minutes he hopped down. She leaned around the corner of the windshield and watched him walk toward the back of truck. "Where are you going?"

"Be right back."

A few seconds later, the night air filled with the sounds of Lionel Ritchie. "Would you like to dance?" He offered his hand.

Karen looked down into the eyes of the man she once loved. Forgetting her determination to keep her distance, she took his hand and let him help her down. He wrapped his arms around her, holding her tight as they danced through the grass.

She sucked in her breath as he cupped her face in one hand and used the other to pull her close. He slowly moved closer, his eyes searching her face before his lips claimed hers. She closed her eyes and allowed her feelings free reign, wrapping her arms around his neck and pressing into him, deepening the kiss.

A ringtone brought them back to reality.

She slowly pulled away, steading herself against the truck. *What am I doing?* She walked over to the stereo and turned off the music as he answered his phone.

"Hey. Good. And you?" He looked at the ground.

Karen turned her back, pretending not to listen.

"Not much. Just hanging out…no one. Are you enjoying your trip? …yeah, I miss you too… okay, call soon. Love you, too."

Karen felt hands on her shoulders. "So…where were we?" David turned her around and tried to draw her into his arms.

She stepped back. "I think you were about to take me home."

"But, I thought…"

"I'm sorry. I lost my head for the moment."

"You need to lose it more often." He put a hand at her waist and pulled her towards him, then kissed her lightly on one cheek, then the other before moving to her lips.

She sighed.

Trust me.

But I need this, her body screamed.
Trust me NOW.
Karen pulled back and wiped her tears. "Please take me back."
"Are you sure?" David searched her face.
"Yes." She turned to get back into the truck. She needed to get away from David before she betrayed herself. What if Blake was waiting for her? *I can't risk my baby getting hurt. I'll just have to stay with Margie, just for tonight.*

27

Karen walked to the stables where her sisters waited.

Last night's dance under the stars was a mistake. *I'm stupid for letting my guard down.* She blushed to think of what might have happened if Mary's call hadn't interrupted them.

Karen climbed up to the top of the corral and sat next to Elinor. "You sure Dad won't be here?"

"You can't stay away because of him." Joanna joined her sisters.

"She's right." Elinor hopped down and put a halter on one of the horses, then handed the lead rope to Karen.

"I just don't want to run into him today and have to act like nothing happened." Tying her horse to a post, Karen grabbed a saddle and bridle from the tack room.

"Deal with it." Joanna hopped down from the railing and pulled herself up onto a black mare. She lifted her hands above her head. "Look, no hands." Squeezing her legs against the horse's sides, she guided her mount around the corral.

"Show off." Elinor tied her horse next to Karen's and whispered. "Being around Dad gets easier."

Jerking the cinch tight, Karen watched Elinor head to the tack room. *I don't see how.*

"Dad told me I could live here if I helped out with the horses and orchard." Joanna slid to the ground and checked her horse's hoofs.

"Why don't you?" Karen adjusted the stirrups on her saddle.

"You aren't the only one who likes to keep away from Dad." Joanna grabbed her tack and saddled the mare.

Looping the reigns over her horse's neck, Elinor laughed. "Besides, can you really see the two of them getting along to run this place?"

Joanna led her horse through the gate. "Last one to the creek is a rotten egg." She jumped on her horse and headed into the woods.

Elinor and Karen mounted and raced after Joanna. They were all laughing by the time they pulled to a stop at the creek's edge.

"We didn't have this much fun when we were little." Karen dismounted and pulled her boots off before stepping into the creek.

Joanna joined her. "That's because you were a pain."

Karen splashed water on Joanna, starting a water war. Soon they were soaked. Elinor watched from the bank. "Such children."

Joanna and Karen looked at each other and then sloshed Elinor.

"Stop it. I didn't want to get wet. Who knows what is in that water?"

"Spoilsport." Joanna stepped out of the creek.

"Nah. She probably has plans at the Bed and Breakfast." Karen said. "Look at her blush."

"Stop it." Elinor said, crossing her arms.

"Does Elinor have a beau?" Joanna teased.

"Please."

"Come on, Elinor. James is sweet on you. You need to marry him and have a dozen kids," Karen enjoyed the bantering. It made her feel closer to her sisters.

"I doubt he wants to marry me."

"You don't see the way he looks at you." Karen winked at Joanna.

She pretended to swoon. "James and Elinor sitting in a tree…K…I…S—"

Elinor climbed on her horse. "I'm leaving"

"Please don't leave. We'll be nice." Karen pleaded.

"Do you promise?"

"Sure." Joanna pulled out a cigarette and lit up. Taking a long draw, she sat down on the bank and waited for Elinor to join them. "So, do you think the kids or the married part bothered her more?"

"Shh. Here she comes. Behave." Karen sat next to her.

"So, Karen, about Dad?" Elinor sat down between the two of them.

"I wouldn't go there, Elinor." Joanna blew out a puff of smoke.

Elinor squinted at Joanna then turned back to Karen. "He changed you know."

"Maybe." Karen kicked the water with her toes.

"He cried when you left for college. He didn't know I saw him. Then he boxed up your stuff and put it in the attic."

"Even the snow globes?"

"Yeah. I missed you and wanted to have one in my room. But Dad wouldn't let me. So, I snuck up into the attic and found one. I kept it hidden and only played it when he left the house. I'll give it back."

Karen leaned over and gave her sister a hug. "You keep it."

"Thanks."

"Enough mushy stuff." Joanna took a last puff of her cigarette, then mashed it out in the dirt. "I'm ready to go back." She stood and pulled on her boots.

Karen took a deep breath. When was she going to tell them? "I have something to tell you guys first."

"You've decided to go back to New York?" Joanna stood with her hands on her hips.

"Trying to get rid of me?"

"Ignore her." Elinor leaned into Karen. "Tell us."

She took a deep breath. "I'm pregnant."

Elinor and Joanna looked at each other, then at Karen. Silence surrounded them as they stood, speechless.

"Well?" Karen wrinkled her brow.

"I guess that's what you call a pregnant pause." Joanna laughed, bent over and slapped her knees. Elinor hesitated then joined in.

"Come on, seriously." Karen rolled her eyes.

"What are you gonna do?" Joanna sat back down next to Karen. "You're not thinking about keeping it, are you?"

"It?" Elinor raised her voice. "This is a baby we're talking about."

"It. Her. Him. All the same till it comes out. I just didn't think you would want a baby with Barry after the way you've talked about him."

"Get real, Joanna. No matter who the father is, this child is a part of Karen. What were you suggesting anyway?"

"Stop it." Karen looked from one sister to the other. What had gotten into Elinor? She had never seen her so upset. And Joanna? Surely she wasn't suggesting abortion. Karen shook her head. "No matter what Barry's done, I did love him. And I love this child. I'll start over and provide for us both. I just want you guys to be happy for me."

"I am." Elinor looked at Joanna.

"Me too." Joanna nodded. "So do you know if it's a boy or girl yet?"

"It's too early for that. I haven't even been to the doctor yet."

"Shows you what I know. Can we go back now?" Joanna stood up and Elinor followed suit.

"I suppose." Karen stood up from the bank.

"You wanna race me back?" Joanna ran for her horse.

"No fair." Karen scrambled for her boots as her two sisters jumped on their horses and raced back.

She jumped on her horse and caught up. She could imagine Barry sitting tall on a horse. He would love it. She swiped tears with the back of her hand and passed her sisters on the trail. "You snooze, you lose," she hollered as she galloped ahead.

After her sisters left, Karen went to the house and climbed the stairs to the attic.

Her dad had chosen a new globe for her birthday present every year. Thirteen in all. She looked all over the attic but they were nowhere to be found. Disappointed, she went downstairs. She would have to ask Elinor about it again. When she reached the main floor, she heard music chiming from one of the bedrooms and followed the sound down the hall.

She opened the door and there stood her father with his back to her, next to a shelf containing her snow globes. Her favorite tune, *Listen to the Mockingbird,* played in the background.

"I brought them in here after I came back to God." Her dad turned to face her. "I listened to the music while I prayed for you, pleading with God to bring you home. Now you're here. Can you forgive me?"

Karen looked at her dad and tried to find it in herself to forgive him. Bile rose in her throat. He had hurt her and refused to help her understand. If she ever forgave him, it wouldn't be today.

She stiffened her back, turned and left the room, her father's weeping echoing in the hallway.

28

Barry stared out at the faces waiting for him to speak. He wanted to remember this day. June 29. Eight days since his fist fight with Robert.

"My name is Barry Marino, and I am an alcoholic. I've been sober for eight days." The room exploded with applause. He took a deep breath and continued with his story. Relief swept through him as he finished and sat down.

After the meeting, he smiled as he walked out into the sunlight. He was free from so much more than a jail cell. On his last night in custody he decided to follow Jesus. God forgave him, but there were people he hurt and he needed to ask their forgiveness, too.

Karen topped the list. Tears stung the back of his eyelids. *How can I ever make things up to her?*

It would take a lot of work to overcome his vices and restore his marriage. He needed to understand why he defaulted to addictions, what drove his need for all those things. It would take counseling. But more than anything, he needed God. He took a deep breath. *I can do this.*

Grateful for a small loan from Robert and Megan, Barry picked up a few things from the grocer on his way home. Stale air greeted him when he opened the door. His gaze paused on the computer. Good thing he had cancelled his Internet service.

He grabbed a trash bag and reached for a magazine to throw away. His eyes rested on the cover and he felt the familiar buzz. He glanced back at his computer and thought about his neighbor's unsecured wireless router.

"No. God help me. No more." He grabbed the magazines, stuffing them into the bag as fast as he could, then ran to the dumpster out back of the building. They needed to be gone before he spent any time in the apartment.

He headed back inside to finish cleaning. As he worked on straightening up the desk, he came across Christy's address. *The woman from the bar.* He slammed his fist down on the desk. "Stupid, stupid. Karen will never forgive me for this."

Come to me and rest.

Barry closed his eyes and took a slow breath, then dropped to his knees on the carpet. He held his head in his hands and sobbed. "Jesus, forgive me. I've sinned against You. Against Karen. Against Christy. Help me to be the kind of man Karen will be able to forgive."

A peace washed over him. He was forgiven and whatever happened, God stood with him. Before the night ended, he intended to ask Christy to forgive him. And find out if he needed to be tested for STD's.

When he faced Karen, he would face her with the full truth. That meant he needed to tell her about Chad, too. All of it. Fresh shame filled his heart and again he bent in repentance before God. He had caused his family so much grief.

Fear gnawed at him when he thought of facing his parents. He needed their forgiveness, too. "Lord, help me." Sobs wracked Barry's body. For the first time in his life, he allowed the ache full access to his heart. He longed to be loved. It's all he ever wanted from his parents.

Could the friends and family he pushed aside with his anger and bitterness forgive him? Could they ever have a relationship? He stayed on his knees until his emotions calmed, then rose, determined to change.

After a quick sandwich, he slipped Christy's address into his pocket and headed out to catch a bus. He paused outside her building. *Maybe I should have brought someone with me. Or better yet, why didn't I just call? Because this needs to be done in person.* But maybe this wasn't the right time. He turned to leave and nearly ran into a young woman.

"Uh, Christy?" He backed up.

"Yeah?" The woman sidestepped him then appeared to recognize him. "I need to talk to you."

"Better come inside," she said.

"No."

"If you want to talk, come up, my ice cream will melt if we stand here." Christy shifted her bag of groceries from one hip to the other.

Barry looked around uneasily before following her to her apartment. He waited at the door while she put away her bag of groceries. After several minutes of silence, she stopped and faced him.

"What do you want?"

"I'm here to apologize."

"Apologize?" Christy crossed her arms, her brow furrowed.

"Yeah, I got mad at my wife — and I ended up here. It was wrong. I need to ask your forgiveness."

"You don't need to apologize."

"Yes, I do."

"Why?"

Barry took a breath and plunged forward with his story. "I found God. Or more correctly, He found me."

Christy turned back to her groceries.

"I've never been with anyone but my wife. You don't need to worry about any STDs on my part... Do I need to be checked?"

Christy sat down. "No, you don't need any tests run."

"Will you forgive me?"

"Nothing happened." Christy whispered.

"What?" Barry took a step closer. Maybe he heard her wrong.

"We didn't do anything," she said looking up at Barry. "I went out with some friends to have a good time after my boyfriend broke up with me. Funny...he broke up with me because I wanted to wait." Christy laughed. "I brought you here because you didn't look like you would make it home. We danced for a while and then you passed out on my bed. I slept on the couch. When I got back from the store, you were gone. I didn't know how to contact you to tell you what happened.

I'm glad you came back and that you know."

Barry let out a heavy sigh. "Me too. Thank you." He turned to go.

"Did God really make that big a difference?"

Barry turned back around. "All the difference in the world."

"Do you think…" Christy dropped her gaze. "Do you think God is interested in someone like me?"

Barry grinned. "He's interested in everyone." He gave her the address of Robert and Megan's church and their names and number in case she had any questions.

As he strode to the bus stop, he looked heavenward. *Thank you for protecting me against my own stupidity.*

He got off the bus in front of the Metropolitan Museum of Art and walked through Central Park toward the Great Lawn. People rushed past him to whatever entertainment they had planned for a Friday night, couples strolling hand in hand toward Shakespeare in the Park.

He chuckled as he remembered the night he took Karen to *The Taming of the Shrew*. When she realized it was about a powerful husband teaching his shrewish wife her place, she leaned over and threatened to throw all of his belongings out onto the street if he didn't get up and leave with her. He dutifully followed despite the snickers of those around them. He enjoyed himself immensely making it up to her.

He watched couples out on the lawn laughing together, eyes for no one else. An elderly couple sat on a bench, holding hands while they talked. Would he and Karen have a chance to grow old together?

He used to plan dates just to make her happy. When did he stop trying to please her? He became so selfish he resorted to hitting Karen to avoid admitting guilt in their marital problems.

Barry closed his eyes and wondered what Karen was doing tonight. He sat down on a bench to call her. It wasn't the time to tell her all the details of his mess ups, but he wanted to apologize and ask her to give them another chance. He let the phone ring until it went to her voice mail then hung up. He couldn't apologize to a recording.

Fear invaded his mind. Was she with that guy? He clinched his fist. His breathing quickened. He wanted to smash whoever it was. *Oh,*

God, will I ever stop being so angry so quickly?
Come to me and rest.
Barry bowed his head and confessed his anger, pouring out his anxieties before God. He cried out to Jesus for strength and self-control. His breathing slowly returned to normal and his body relaxed as the anger dissipated. Only sadness over what he may have lost remained. "Jesus, forgive me for hurting Karen."

Memories surfaced of times he hurt his wife emotionally, mentally and physically. He got up from the bench and walked into the wooded area surrounding the Great Lawn. People were less likely to notice him as he lost the battle to hide his tears. He sat down next to a tree and leaned back. As each memory surfaced, he wept afresh and asked God to forgive him. He prayed Karen would forgive him, too.

He remembered his fantasies and shuddered. All those pictures of naked women on the Internet and in the magazines. Shame overwhelmed him. Resting his head on top of his knees, he wrapped his arms around his legs and rocked. He felt dirty. *Will I ever feel clean again? How can I face Karen?* "Oh, God help me."

Come to Me and rest.

Tears spent, Barry regained his composure, dusted off the back of his jeans, and headed out of the park. Returning to his apartment wasn't an option right now. It held too many shameful memories....and his computer. Instead he roamed around the block eventually stopping at a grocery store for a soda. Then he called Robert.

He picked up on the fourth ring. "Hello."

"Hey, this is Barry. Am I calling too late?"

"Not at all, what's up?"

"I...uh...you guys doing anything?" Barry figured it would sound crazy if he said he was afraid to go back to his apartment. But Robert was the only true friend he had.

"We're about to watch a movie. Want to join us?"

"I don't want to barge in." Barry took a deep breath, relieved he didn't have to explain.

"Hey, I'm lucky to have a wife who caters to my every whim while

I'm in my invalid state, but—"

In the background he heard Megan's mocking reply. "I didn't say you're an invalid."

Barry smiled at their banter and hoped Karen and he could be that way again.

"No, you just treat me like one." Robert laughed. "Hey quit that. Barry, please come over. Maybe then she'll be nice to me."

"Can I bring some food?"

"Maybe some chocolate mint ice cream and we'll use it for a peace offering to Megan. Be nice to me, Megan, or I'll tell the doctor."

Barry chuckled.

When he arrived at their apartment with the promised peace offering, a pillow in the face greeted him. He shrugged and set the ice cream down on the table. A good pillow fight always relieved the tension. The only thing missing was Karen.

29

Why did I let my sisters talk me into this? Last week, she walked out of her dad's house, refusing to forgive him, hating to be around him. Yet here she was, coming to another of his family picnics, and tomorrow she planned to join the family for the Kansas City baseball team's July Fourth game and fireworks. *I must be crazy.*

She leaned back in the seat and watched David maneuver his Mustang through the winding back roads to her parent's home. She had put off filing for divorce, why wasn't she putting David off? She remembered their dance beneath a canopy of stars and sighed.

If she had stayed all those years ago, they would have married. Kindness would be the norm. And whether from his own hard work or from family, money wouldn't be an issue.

She caught her breath. But then she wouldn't have the baby. She placed a hand over her stomach. Barry provided all of those things in their early years, but other than the baby, all she had to show for it was memories. She didn't know what would happen with her and Barry, but she wasn't ready to give up on a future with David.

I know the plans I have for you.

"But I don't know those plans." Karen muttered into the wind.

"What?" David reached over and took her hand.

She jerked her hand back. *I need to make up my mind.* "Just talking to myself." She turned toward him so he could hear. "You're sure about going with me? I don't know what kind of reception you'll get."

"I can handle myself. Let's sneak off to the orchard for another dance."

Karen blushed. She spent the last week avoiding him. They still hadn't talked about what happened.

They arrived early and found her dad at the grill. He looked up and paused. "David. Haven't seen you in a while."

"Charles. Good to see you." He glanced at Karen and then back at her dad. "I'll let you two catch up."

Her father nodded and watched David walk toward the stables, then turned to Karen. "I thought I told you family only."

"We've known David forever. He's almost like family."

"But he's not."

Karen locked eyes with her dad. Who was he to tell her who she could hang out with? "We're going for a ride while we wait on the others." She stomped off to the barn. *I can't believe the audacity of that man. Why does he even care?* She kicked a bucket out of her way and opened the tack room door.

David came up behind her. "What's up?"

Karen whirled around. "I don't want to talk about it. You helping, or what?" She blew her wayward bangs out of her eyes.

"Yes, ma'am." He held up his hands and ducked when she threw a sharp look his way. "Hey, I'm not the enemy."

"Here, smarty pants." She handed him a saddle and bridle then led the way to their mounts.

When they left the stables they saw more family arriving. They headed to the trail head and ignored Joanna and Elinor calling out for them to wait up. Karen urged her horse into a run and David stayed close behind. "Where you off to in such a hurry?"

"Anywhere but here." She pulled farther ahead of him and ducked under a low branch. She glanced back and snickered when it almost nailed David. "Sure you can keep up?"

"The challenge is on." He pulled his horse neck to neck with Karen's.

They rode the trail for a few minutes each attempting to pass the other until the trail opened up next to the creek. They reined to a stop,

Karen slightly in the lead. David grinned. "You better let me win on the way back or else."

"Or else what?" Karen taunted.

David turned his horse until he faced her then sidestepped his mount until their stirrups touched. He reached over and touched her cheek. "This feels like a good or else," he whispered, his lips brushing hers.

She sucked in a breath, forgetting about her earlier caution, and gave herself to David's control like a butterfly trapped in a spider's web. Powerless to break the bond. He looked into her eyes before he leaned toward her again. She returned his kiss.

The sound of horses running through the trees broke through to her, and she pulled away from David as Elinor and Joanna rode into the clearing.

"How come you didn't wait up?" Joanna locked eyes with her.

Karen narrowed her eyes. *It was just a kiss.*

And it was just dinner with another woman.

Karen gasped. She pulled at the reins and urged her mount deeper into the woods. Tears rolled down her face. David filled an ache in her that Barry stopped satisfying when he turned to gambling, drinking and other women.

She pushed to a gallop and dodged the branches that blocked her path. She ran her horse to the end of the trail. *God, if you care, show me what to do next.*

She slowed her horse to a trot. She couldn't just chase after what she wanted anymore. She had her child's future to consider. But what did that look like? She wiped tears on her sleeve and headed back down the trail. A few minutes later she found the others following her at a more leisurely pace.

She straightened in the saddle and pasted on a smile. "You guys are slow pokes. Race you back." She took off before they could question her.

By the time they rubbed the horses down and returned them to the corral, the food was ready. The family gathered next to the food table and formed a circle. Her dad grabbed the hands of the grandkids. The others joined hands and waited for to her to complete the circle.

Really? She grabbed David's hand on one side and Joanna's on the other. This whole togetherness thing drove her crazy. Didn't her dad understand some things just could not be fixed?

At the amen, she dropped hands and glanced around the family circle. Albert and Haley whispered and looked in Karen's direction. She looked at David. He noticed, too. She rolled her eyes and grabbed a plate from the food table.

David and Karen filled their plates then found a spot at one of the picnic tables. Haley and Albert sat across from them. When David left to retrieve some soda, Haley leaned forward and caught Karen's attention. "I need to talk to you."

"Yeah?" Karen took a bite of steak. She had to hand it to her dad. He knew how to cook a steak.

"Maybe after we eat."

"Sure, whatever." They probably wanted to talk to her about David. Seemed everyone had an opinion.

I do, too.

She shook her head. *I'll take care of it in my own time.*

30

Tomorrow was the Fourth of July. A fitting day for his baptism, a symbol of his freedom. Juggling his armload of food, he stepped into line and waited his turn. He stared at the magazine rack in front of the register.

Look away.

Barry closed his eyes. It was everywhere. *How can I do this?* He moved to the counter and paid for his groceries. Last night he watched an entire television ad for a lingerie show, fighting his desires the whole time. He was weak. Tomorrow he planned to be baptized but he felt unworthy to receive the grace that God offered him.

That's what grace is.

God, I want to give you my best. Not a second rate effort to obey.

Barry stepped off the bus and greeted Megan with a hug and Robert with a handshake. Barry smiled. *It feels good to not push people away.* Anger kept a man tired.

"Come on, church is about to start." Megan put her hand through his arm. I'm so happy you're getting baptized today."

"Me too." He followed them to a seat near the middle of the sanctuary, where several people came over to welcome him before the service. Their kindness surprised him. During worship he watched the lyrics displayed on the wall and sang when he grew comfortable with the tune. The words poured over him and he found a connection with God he didn't understand.

Why did I go so long refusing to acknowledge you, God?

Barry slid to his knees under the weight of his guilt and bowed his head in repentance. Robert's hand on his shoulder reassured him. He remembered the words of God he read the previous day. He received full forgiveness for his past sins. Though grief for his actions would follow him for a long time, he did not need to carry the guilt.

Hope filled him and he raised his face toward heaven and allowed the joy of God to overcome the guilt and shame. The heaviness left and he rose to his feet. He joined in the chorus of a song and lifted his hands, reaching for God like a child might reach for his father.

Before the last song, he and Robert left the sanctuary and went behind the stage. Barry changed and then climbed the stairs to the water tank where Robert waited. He grinned and motioned for Barry to join him in the water. Robert then faced the audience and placed one hand on Barry's back. "Do you believe in Jesus Christ the son of God and confess Him as Lord of your life?"

"You bet I do." Barry grinned.

"I baptize you in the name of the Father and the Son and the Holy Ghost." Robert immersed Barry in the water and brought him back up.

He imagined Jesus bursting out from his grave of three days. Barry let out a whoop of excitement and shook the water off of his face. The congregation clapped and he joined them in their song of worship as he stepped out of the tank.

During lunch with Robert and Megan, Barry pulled out his notebook and peppered Robert with questions.

"Slow down; we won't be able to get to these all in one day." Robert chuckled.

"Sorry. Guess I got carried away."

"I wish more people got carried away. Let's move over to the couch."

Megan brought them coffee, then cleared the table while they talked. Barry sat on the edge of his seat. "How do I keep away from the pornography when it's everywhere?"

Robert sighed. "The best way to beat this is to keep close to Jesus and let someone ask you the tough questions. Have you kept your eyes away from that junk? Are you reading your Bible, praying, and treating your wife right? If you stay isolated, it's too easy to fall back into."

"It seems impossible. My body responds so quickly. It's almost like I don't even have time to make a choice."

Robert nodded. "The visual part of sex is huge, and that's great in the marriage. But the world turns it into something God never intended. And it's everywhere. A man has to choose to dwell only on his wife."

"I want to." Barry set his coffee mug down.

"It takes retraining your brain. After you've been steeped in the world's perversion of sex, it takes about ninety days away from the stuff for your brain to detox and reset its chemical balance. After that, you'll enjoy Karen like you never have since this stuff became a part of your life."

"That would be my whole marriage." Barry shook his head. Even though he had avoided STDs by not sleeping around, he still brought a disease into their marriage bed. He leaned forward and propped his arms on his legs. "The first time you called this an addiction I didn't get it, but now it makes sense."

"How many days have you been away from it?"

Barry hung his head. "Not even a whole day. There was an ad on TV last night, and..."

Robert placed a hand on Barry's shoulder. "Don't bury yourself in regret. You can get through this." Robert put down his coffee mug. "In addition to someone holding you accountable, you need counseling to get to the root problem. Restoration is possible. But it will take hard work and time. It takes longer than a ninety-day detox for your brain to completely rewire, so new habits replace the old."

"You've already been holding me accountable, do you mind keeping it up?"

"I'll be tough on you."

"Good. I'm serious about getting this out of my life."

"I'll call you every day and ask if you're keeping on the straight and narrow, but we can also get together for prayer and Bible study, if you're interested."

"I'd like that, but it may have to wait a while." He ran a hand through his hair.

"Oh, yeah?" Robert sat on the edge of the couch.

"There are some people I need to see first."

"Karen?"

Barry shook his head. "I don't even know where she is. And she won't pick up my calls."

"Then…?"

Barry pressed his lips together.

"Want to talk about it?"

"I need to ask my parents' forgiveness for some stuff I did a long time ago."

"Where do they live?"

"Maine." Barry hadn't seen them since he left for New York City, so he did a white page search to make sure they still lived in the same place.

"Hmm. You flying?"

Barry shook his head. "No money for that. Thought I'd take a bus. A couple days of day labor should pay for that."

"Barry…the doctors told me to take some time off from work — let my head heal a bit more before I return to the stress of the firm. Are you interested in some company? My car is available, but we'd have to go this week."

Barry leaned back and stared at Robert. "You would do that?"

"Sure. Besides, I can't just sit for another week. I'll go stir crazy."

No one ever offered him anything without strings attached. "I can't pay you for gas. Not up front anyway."

"Consider it an investment in your future. I'll even cover a hotel stay if needed."

"You're sure? What about the baby?"

"I'm sure. We're still in the second trimester so Megan should be fine. I'll check with her though."

"What will be fine?" Megan gathered the empty coffee mugs and listened to their travel plans. "I'll pack you some sandwiches and snacks."

"You don't have to." Barry faced Megan.

"When my wife sets her mind to a project, she doesn't take no for an answer. Do you, Megan?"

"Nope." Megan laughed. "So when do I need to have it ready?"

Barry shrugged his shoulders and looked at Robert.

"How about in the next hour or so?"

Barry sat back in surprise. By this time tomorrow he would be face to face with his parents. "Sure, but I hate to impose."

"I'm like my wife." Robert put his arm around Megan." I won't take no for an answer."

Barry slapped his knees. "Well then, okay."

"Megan, we'll leave the food to you. I'll go throw a change or two of clothes into a bag." Robert turned to Barry. "Then we can stop by your place and pick up what you need."

Robert kissed his wife and then went to pack.

Barry pitched in and helped Megan.

"So you still can't reach Karen?" Megan pointed out the cooler on the top shelf for Barry to pull down.

"If you hear from her, try to find out where she is. Or at least convince her to pick up when I call. If she won't talk to me, what can I do but wait?"

Thirty minutes later, Robert stuffed his bag into the trunk of his sports car and Barry put the food within reach in the back seat.

"Nice ride." Barry stood back to admire the red convertible.

"Yeah, picked it up from this guy I designed a house for. He moved up to a newer model. It's fun to drive." Robert tossed the keys to Barry. "The doctor said I can't drive for at least a week. You do have a license, don't you?"

"Yeah, but it's been a while."

"It's like riding a bike. At least it's a Sunday and the traffic won't be too bad." Robert got in and waited for Barry.

Maybe he should have taken the bus. *Naw.* He grinned, climbed behind the wheel and buckled his seat belt. Turning the key, he let the engine purr for a moment, then put it in gear and eased out into traffic.

Barry stopped briefly at his apartment for some clothes, then headed toward FDR Drive, relieved to be on the way. They should arrive in Maine between ten and eleven that night, then tomorrow continue to his parents' house outside of Portland.

On the outskirts of Boston, they lost reception to the Yankees' game. Robert searched for another station then turned it off after several minutes of static and talk shows. "How long since you've been home?"

"Twenty years."

Robert whistled. "Why so long?"

"Didn't think they wanted to see me." Barry gripped the steering wheel so tight his knuckles turned white. He couldn't blame his parents. Not really. He had been selfish and it had cost them what they loved most.

"That's a hard one. What happened?"

I could really use a drink right now. When would the desire for the stuff go away? Barry swore then grimaced and looked at Robert. "Sorry. Still working on that."

Robert waved a hand. "You should have seen me when I turned my life around. Robert laughed. "You'll get there."

Barry chuckled. "It's hard to imagine you any different."

"That's a story for another day. Tell me about what happened with your folks."

"I'm responsible for my brother's death." Silence filled the car.

"Tell me about it."

Barry glanced at Robert and saw no judgment, no censor. He focused back on the road. "My brother, Chad, was the good son. I was the other one. After my parents and he became Christians, it only got worse.

I hated their religion, their Bible and their God and wanted to ruin it for all of them. Barry wiped his eyes with the back of his sleeve, then slammed on the brakes and swerved when the car in front of them stopped. All he could see was a long line of vehicles ahead. "Probably an accident. Want to wait it out or take the back roads?"

Robert glanced at the fuel gage. "We need gas anyway. Let's fill up, then find a place to eat."

After gassing up, they stopped at a local bar and grill. Inside, the waitress greeted them with crossed arms. "You want a seat?"

Barry raised an eyebrow. "That would be nice."

She nodded over her shoulder. "Take your pick. Menu is on the table. Specials are on the board. I'll be over to take your order in a few minutes."

Barry looked around. A jukebox occupied one end of the dining room and a wooden floor in the middle hinted at late night dances away from prying eyes. "Hope the food is better than the atmosphere."

Robert laughed. "I agree."

After ordering the special, Robert handed the waitress their menus then faced Barry. "So, you were telling me about your family."

Barry rolled his eyes. "I was hoping you might forget."

"I want to hear."

Barry nodded. The thought of facing his parents tomorrow twisted his gut. Maybe talking about what happened would help.

Come to me and rest.

At a time like this, rest seemed so far away, but God had already given him rest through so many things. He could trust Him with this. Barry propped his elbows on the table. "My plan included ruining Chad's reputation. I should have left him alone."

"What happened?"

"I took him to a lot of parties and he never once compromised his convictions. Made me sick. But at the last one a couple of college guys crashed the party. Of course, we looked up to them like they were gods. They spiked Chad's soda, and we all thought it funny when he lost his inhibitions. He laughed at all the dirty jokes and when the guys brought out the magazines, he gawked along with the rest of us. They even planned on a girl in the mix.

He passed out from the drugs and I went on with the party. I planned to embarrass him with all the pictures I took. My own high school graduation present to myself. But he never woke up."

"I'm sorry."

"Yeah, me too."

The waitress brought their food to the table. "Anything else?"

Barry shook his head. "Just the ticket, thanks."

She laid the ticket on the table and left.

Robert chuckled. "Guess she needs a day off."

Barry agreed. "Let's leave her a good tip, that'll make her day."

Digging into their food, they turned their attention to a baseball game being broadcast over the speakers. Barry was glad to leave the subject of his family for another time.

31

Karen pulled up a handful of weeds from Margie's garden. Pausing, she wiped sweat off her forehead, thankful the humidity from the fourth hadn't followed them through the week. She stood up and admired her progress. Flowers hidden earlier by a curtain of weeds now dominated the area. She grinned. This part of her life was rewarding and satisfying. Unlike her relationship status.

She squatted and yanked on more weeds. They came up and she lost her balance, falling backward into the dirt. *Drat!* Tears trickled down her cheeks. *Why did you become such a jerk, Barry?*

Their marriage sparked for a while. Even more than she and David ever had. She blushed. She never should have let him kiss her last week. But she had been so mad at her dad telling her what to do, she hadn't wanted to stop. She closed her eyes and Barry's face filled her mind. An ache overwhelmed her heart. *I miss what we used to be.*

She retreated to a nearby bench and took off her gloves. *Do I still love him?* She didn't want to love an angry man. *This isn't fair God.*

"Karen? What are the tears for?" Margie joined her on the bench.

"I guess its' pregnancy hormones," Karen buried her head in her hands and cried harder.

The older woman put her arm around Karen's shoulder.

Karen leaned against Margie until the tears subsided. "Thank you. I'm sorry I didn't get much done."

"Pshaw. None of that. Now tell me what's really wrong."

"Just the same old stuff. I'm so tired of my erratic emotions."

"I'm worried about you. Why don't you go clean up and visit one of your sisters or hide away with a good book?"

"But I haven't finished. And then I was going to visit Mom."

"You've been here all morning, not to mention all week. Besides, haven't you figured out the work is simply an excuse to have you around?" Margie gave Karen a squeeze. "I'm going by to see your mom later today. I'll let you know how she is. Now you go on and have a fun afternoon."

Karen smiled and returned the hug. "Thanks."

Weary, she longed for a soak in the shower and a nice long nap, but the phone was ringing when she entered her apartment. She caught her breath when she heard David's voice, and her face flushed when she remembered the way she returned his kiss.

"Hey, good looking. Want to hang out a while?"

Moisture gathered in her eyes. How did her feelings turn on her so fast? She wanted to go with him. She stomped her foot and let out a pent up breath. "We need to cool things."

"Didn't realize they were hot. Not that I haven't tried."

"That's my point. I'm still married, and we can't be pretending I'm not." She kicked off her shoes and plopped down on the couch.

"I promise to be on my best behavior. You need to have some fun."

"I'm just tired, and I probably won't be good company." Maybe this excuse would get David to stop his pleading.

"Nonsense. I enjoy your company no matter what. Wear jeans and tennis shoes."

"David, didn't you hear anything? I'm not coming." She wanted to scream at him.

He chuckled. "I'll be by in an hour. Might want a jacket, too."

Karen hung up the phone. *I'm asking for trouble.* She clenched her fists and screamed inside her head. Why didn't I say no?

David lowered the top on his Mustang and after a few miles, he reached for Karen's hand. Her skin tingled and she gently pulled away. He was already breaking his promise of good behavior. She had a feeling it wasn't going to stop. "Where are you taking me?"

"It's a surprise."

She crossed her arms. "Fine. I bet I figure it out." A few minutes later, they passed the sign for Smithville Lake. Karen clapped her hands. "Your family still has their boat?"

"So much for a surprise." David shook his head. "Do you still enjoy sailing?"

"I haven't been in a while." The last time she went out on the water she and Barry were honeymooning on a yacht. Karen watched the other boats out on the lake. "I forgot how beautiful it is out here. Thank you, David." She relaxed into the warmth of the seat.

The boat was prepared to set sail when they arrived at the marina and they soon left land behind them. Karen sat in the bow, the wind blowing her hair. It was a perfect day to be sailing, the water sparkling with the reflection of the sun. Maybe this was a good idea after all.

When they reached the middle of the lake, David called out to Karen. "I've got snacks if you're hungry."

She stood up and turned to join him, then grabbed her stomach and hurried to the side. Holding her head out over the water, she lost her breakfast.

The waves rocked them back and forth. Her grip on the rail tightened. Her stomach lurched, and threatened to send her leaning out over the water again. She needed off the boat. Yesterday.

"You sea sick?" Concern etched David's face.

"Guess I lost my sea legs. I don't know if I can do this."

"We can go back."

"I'm sorry, David, but could we?"

"Sure." David turned the boat back to land.

Karen stayed close to the side of the boat until they docked and David helped her off. Back on solid ground, they found a bench and Karen sat down.

David disappeared into the clubhouse and returned with a couple of cans of cold club soda. He waited while Karen drank some. "Do you feel any better?"

"A bit. I'm so sorry I ruined our outing. You went to such trouble to make it a special day."

"Let's do something else."

She really wanted to go home and rest, but didn't feel like fighting for it. "If it's on dry land." She offered him a tired smile.

"What about horseback riding or a movie?"

"Why don't we go to the zoo?"

"The zoo? I haven't been since I was a kid. Maybe a museum?"

Karen's posture slumped. Although she and Barry enjoyed museums, the zoo was more fun, and Barry catered to her whims. Once he took her on a promotional midnight tour of the Bronx Zoo. She loved it. "A museum is fine."

David took her to the Nelson-Atkin's Museum of Art in Kansas City, where they spent a couple of hours roaming the rooms. While he pointed out the value of each piece, she imagined Barry entertaining her with stories of the artists or a game of museum eye spy. *Why do I keep thinking about him?*

After the museum David suggested a picnic. Not caring where he took her, she watched the buildings zoom by as they left the city and headed north. *What do the days ahead hold for me?*

Her emotional outbursts in the garden indicated she still cared for Barry. But even if she loved him, she didn't know if she could stay married to him, especially if he didn't change his abusive behavior. But with their baby on the way, should she give Barry a chance?

Driving through a small town along the river, she admired the old houses lining the streets. If the loan came through, she had no doubts about running the bed and breakfast. She looked forward to owning her own future, but at the moment, the thought of doing it on her own overwhelmed her. *If only he would change.* She sighed.

Trust me. I have good plans for you.

Karen shook her head at God's gentle reminder.

"A penny for your thoughts."

"I'm sorry." Karen looked over at David. "I haven't been much company today."

"I still enjoyed the time with you. What's got you so serious?"

Karen hesitated. "Stuff. I'm not sure what I need to do."

"Barry?"

"Partly. I've applied for a loan to buy the Applewood Hill Bed and Breakfast."

"Does that mean you're staying?" David parked the car near the riverside park and turned to look at her. "I like the idea of you staying."

"If the loan comes through. If not, I don't know what I'll do."

David came around and opened her car door. "We'll have to walk a bit." He retrieved the basket and led the way to a spot where they could see the wide Missouri stretch in both directions.

"It's beautiful," she said.

"One of my favorite places." He spread a blanket on the grass.

Karen pulled crackers, cheese, some grapes and a bottle of wine out of the basket. She frowned.

"I'm sorry. Do you not drink wine?" David put down the cork screw.

"No alcohol – period." She shuddered. Knowing the effect it had on Barry was enough to keep her away. And now she had the baby to think about, too.

"Then we'll drink water." David put the wine back and pulled out two bottles of water. Karen nibbled on her food while David plowed in and went back for seconds. "I guess it's more of a snack than a meal."

"It's fine with me."

After they ate, David stuffed their plates into the trash and sat next to her with his arms wrapped around his knees. Sitting in silence, they watched the sun set. Karen shivered from the breeze coming off the water. David put his arm around her and she leaned into the warmth of his body.

David nuzzled the top of her head, then he reached down and turned her face up to his. A warning bell went off in her head, but she ignored it. As his arms tightened around her, she closed her eyes. The intensity of his touch grew and she put her hand up to his chest and pushed away.

David looked into her eyes and tried to pull her back into his arms. "I love you Karen. Marry me."

"What?" She scooted away from him on the blanket. "Where did that come from?"

"Dancing under the stars the other night made me realize how much we belong together. We have ever since we were kids. Didn't you feel it?"

Karen tried to clear her mind, but his presence muddled her thoughts. She shouldn't have kissed him. But she didn't have it in her to speak reason at the moment. "It's not so simple."

"Divorce Barry. He's no good for you. You told me how he was."

"But…"

"I'll call it off with Mary."

"David. This is all too fast." Karen tried to slow her breathing.

"Fast? I've waited nineteen years."

"I can't give you an answer. God hasn't — "

"God? I thought you didn't want any part of God."

How did she explain the voice in her heart? "I don't know. He just keeps coming up."

"If that can change, then how you feel about us can change."

Karen looked away from the hope in David's eyes. What would he say if he knew about the baby?

Tell him.

She rubbed her hands up and down her arms. *I don't know if I can.*

"Karen, look at me." David turned her face toward him with a finger under her chin.

"I'm pregnant." She looked down and placed a hand on her stomach. "With Barry's baby."

David dropped his hand and stared at her, then got up and paced for a bit before kneeling in front of her. "We can work around that."

"What do you mean?" Karen's gut tightened. "Can you love another man's child as your own?" She thought she knew the answer. Did he?

He shrugged. "I can only try. But there are other ways."

She wrinkled her eyebrows together. What was he saying?

"Forget I said that." He ran a hand through his hair. "I can love your child. It won't matter who the father is."

Karen didn't think he believed himself. "When I know what I'm going to do, I'll let you know. But if you love me like you say you do, you won't pressure me." And if he was saying what she thought he was saying, he could never be the man for her. She would protect her child no matter what it cost her.

"You drive me crazy, Karen." David's shoulders slumped.

"I've enjoyed the day, but I'm tired. Please take me home now."

32

Karen drummed her fingers on the steering wheel. For the most part, she had enjoyed yesterday with David, but how could he ask her to marry him? And when she told him about the baby –did he really imply what she thought he did? She shivered. She wished he would just be her friend.

She glanced at her watch. She already missed Albert's sermon this morning, she better not be late for lunch. At least it was just his family. Huge drops of rain splashed against the windshield. Speeding up, she made it to their house and inside before the sky turned loose its downpour.

Taking off her shoes, she joined Haley in the kitchen and set the table. "Hope it eases up before I have to drive to Westfall. I don't like driving in the rain."

Haley peeled the last potato and tossed it in the pot then leaned against the counter and watched Karen. "We went dancing at The Old Corral a few weeks ago. We thought we saw you there."

Here it comes. "So?"

"You were there with David."

"Do you have a problem with me having a bit of fun?" Karen placed the napkins on the table.

Haley hesitated and wiped her hands on the towel. "You're married."

"To a jerk." Karen bit her lip. She already decided to back off from David. Why get so agitated?

Haley took a deep breath. "I know you've been through a lot and it's tough to wait on the best when you have something good at hand. But God has better things in store for you."

Karen squeezed her eyes shut and rubbed her temples. Haley was clueless. "I wouldn't call the last couple of years best."

"We can't always understand when we're going through something. But he will be there. He loves you."

Tears blurred Karen's vision. No one ever loved her the way she longed to be loved. She thought Barry did, but then he went and….she pulled in a shuddering breath. "I don't trust God."

Lightening lit up the sky.

Haley stepped closer to Karen. "He promises to walk through our storms with us."

"I've walked through each one of my storms alone."

You didn't invite me in.

Thunder rattled the cupboards and Karen jumped. She shook her head. "I can't." She pushed past her brother in the doorway. "I won't be staying for lunch."

"Stay until the rain stops." Albert said, following her to the door.

"I'm used to storms." Slipping on her shoes, she grabbed her purse and rushed out the door. By the time she reached her car she couldn't tell the difference between the tears and the rain on her face. She had second thoughts about driving in this downpour, but she didn't want to be with anyone right now.

Everyone insisted God had big plans for her and He loved her. If He loved her so much why didn't He show her? She hit the steering wheel with the palm of her hand. "I can't do this on my own anymore."

She looked upwards. *Show me you care.* She sped up when the rain relented enough for her to see farther down the road. She turned the wheel into a curve and the car spun out of control. Fear grabbed at her as she worked to regain control of the car. With a deep ditch on one side and a rock wall on the other this wasn't going to turn out well.

"God, help me!"

Peace enveloped her. The car spun in slow motion, as if unseen hands took control. She lifted her hands from the wheel and leaned back in her seat. The car turned to the side of the road with a rock wall. *I'm going to crash.* She closed her eyes and waited. The car stopped with a soft thud.

She opened her eyes and glanced out the front window. Her car rested at the only break in the wall on either side of her. She looked out the back window in time to see a van come around the curve. A couple of seconds longer coming to a stop...her body shuddered.

She climbed out of the car expecting to see a dent or two in the front fender. She did a walk around inspection, but there were no marks whatsoever. She sank down to the wet ground and bent over, holding her face in her hands, tears mingling with rain. God heard her cry and answered. "Why do you care for me?"

You are a bruised reed blowing in the wind and I will not let you break. I love you and I have plans for you. Trust Me.

Karen heard a car pull to the side of the road behind her.

"Karen?" Albert approached slowly.

She looked up at him and the tears came harder. "He does love me."

He knelt down beside her and wrapped her in his arms while she turned loose of all of her anger and hurt. When her crying subsided, Albert helped her up, then took the keys, and pulled her car onto the shoulder.

"What were you doing out here?"

Albert's eyes twinkled and he nodded toward heaven.

"God?" Karen tilted her head.

"I think you've got the idea." He pulled his sister into a hug.

33

Barry yawned. He and Robert pulled into Portland after midnight the night before and he hadn't slept at all. Thinking about seeing his parents kept his mind racing about what kind of reception he would get.

His hand shook as he drank his coffee. He chuckled and sat the mug down. "I guess I'm a bit nervous."

"It'll be fine." Robert added creamer to his coffee.

"I hope. You know, I've always believed my parents blamed me for Chad's death. They were so sad, they wouldn't even look at me. I thought if I left and made something of myself, maybe then they would forgive me." Barry scoffed. "I fooled myself into believing success could make up for what I did."

"We all fool ourselves sometimes."

"I did big time. After I lost my job, I felt like there was a big sign on me that said failure. I hated myself and that spilled over in anger against Karen. I didn't know how to stop it."

"There's more to your story than failure."

Barry smiled, remembering God's forgiveness, and began to hope his parents' and Karen would forgive him, too. He scooted his coffee mug out of the way when the waitress brought their food. The men ate in silence for a few minutes then Barry set his fork down. "I don't think I can finish this. I'll eat after I've seen my folks."

"Well, I'm eating now." Robert forked another bite of pancakes.

"These are good." Fifteen minutes later, he tossed his napkin down and grabbed the check. "Now I'm ready."

Barry drove to his parents' home then circled the block before stopping a few houses down and staring at the house where he spent the first eighteen years of his life. *What does it hold for me now?*

"Let's pray before you go in." Robert's voice filled the car as he led them in prayer.

When he finished, Barry offered a smile of gratitude then pulled into the driveway. He hesitated, fighting back the tears. "I don't know if I can do this."

"Take it one step at a time."

Barry nodded and got out of the car. He slammed the door shut and walked to the end of the sidewalk leading to the porch. His feet seemed glued to the cement.

Robert got out of the car and joined him.

Barry stared at the house, still unable to move any closer to the door. "How can I face them?"

Before Robert could answer, the front door opened, and a woman stepped out onto the porch. A long denim dress accented her trim figure, and a headband held back dark, shoulder-length hair. She stared at them for a second then with a sharp intake of breath placed a hand over her mouth. Without taking her eyes off Barry, she stepped back and called through the screen door. "George, come out here."

Barry trembled and tears ran down his face. The woman on the porch came down the steps and a man came to the door, then stepped outside, his shoulders stooped.

"Barry?" His mother walked toward him.

He hurried to his mother and wrapped her in his arms. "I'm so sorry. Can you forgive me?"

"We forgave you a long time ago, son." His dad joined them, tears running down his cheeks.

The three stood in an embrace and cried, then slowly moved toward the house. Barry turned toward Robert and motioned for him to follow. "Mom, Dad, this is Robert. He's a good friend of mine. A big part of the reason I'm here. Robert, my parents, Belinda and George Marino."

As they stepped inside, Barry looked around in surprise. Signs decorated the living room welcoming Barry home. "What's this?"

"We want you back."

"But how…?"

"It's a long story."

"Well, I have time."

His parents smiled and gave each other a hug. His dad motioned for them to have a seat. "First, tell us how you are."

Barry sat on the love seat with his mom next to him. His dad sat in a rocker across from them and Robert took the easy chair.

"Well… I guess I'll start with the most recent news. I'm a Christian now." Barry gave his mother's hand a squeeze. His parents forgave him and welcomed him with waiting arms. He offered a silent prayer of thanks to God.

"Oh Barry." His mother's hands flew to her face and her eyes teared up. "We've prayed you would come to know Jesus." She reached over and hugged her son.

"That's the best news of all." His dad nodded and smiled.

"But my life is pretty messed up. Karen, my wife, left me. I don't know if she'll come back." Barry hung his head.

"It's possible. After all, God is on your side," his dad said.

Barry nodded. "Yeah. Look at us…here, together. I never thought it possible." He looked his mom and dad in the eye. "Thank you."

His dad reached for his wife's hand. "It took us about two years to climb out of our grief over Chad's death. We didn't realized until then how much his death affected you. We were new Christians and messed up a lot, but God showed us our own part in all of it. At that point, we were determined to find you so we hired a private investigator. He caught up with you in New York."

"Why didn't you contact me?"

"What would you have done?"

"Tell you to leave me alone." Barry hung his head.

"You weren't ready. So we prayed and watched out for you the best we knew how." His mother placed her hand on his knee. "Those years were the hardest for us. We waited and hoped."

"You watched out for me? How?"

"We asked some friends in New York to check up on you from time to time. About six months ago, they ate at the restaurant your wife managed. You showed up drunk and made a scene."

"I'm sorry you had to hear about that."

"You're forgiven, Barry." His mother's smile reassured him. "At that point we hired another private investigator. He found out about your debt and explained that the man you owed money to would likely have you killed or at least badly injured. Then he might have gone after your wife. We refused to stand by and let that happen."

Barry was stunned. "You did that for me?"

"Yes, son, we paid off your debt." His father stood up and walked over to the picture window overlooking the front lawn. Barry cried and his mother put her arms around him.

"It was the only way we could help you," she said.

His father returned to his chair and sat down, leaning forward. "Our investigator also told us about your friend Robert here. He was an answer to prayer."

"You knew about Robert?"

"Not a lot. We knew he loved the Lord and he dogged your steps." Barry's dad smiled at Robert. "Like an angel sent to watch out for you."

"That's Robert." Barry grinned and looked around the living room at the signs that proclaimed his welcome and their love for him. *An angel?* "Did your investigator look a bit like you, Dad? Older with white hair?"

"No, he was a young man, in his twenties I think. Why?"

Barry shook his head. "Just curious. So did your investigator tell you when I would get home?"

"No. After Robert entered the picture and your debt was cleared we didn't see the need for an investigator. But your mother and I both became convinced you would be home soon. We just didn't know when."

Barry's mother put a hand on his knee. "Yesterday morning when I woke up, I had this crazy idea to decorate the place for your homecoming. Your dad agreed. So last night after church, we invited a few friends over who have prayed with us for your return, and they helped us decorate."

"I'm blown away. I was baptized yesterday and started the trip home in the afternoon." Barry leaned back on the couch. He wiped at his tears and took the tissue his mother offered.

The doorbell interrupted their conversation.

Belinda looked at George. "I forgot we invited some friends for lunch. A young couple we mentor. We can rearrange if you'd rather, but I do think it's good timing. You should meet them while you're here." His mother stood to answer the door.

"Fine with me." Barry wondered about the looks exchanged between his parents. She answered the door and chatted with the couple before they came into the living room. Barry thought the man looked familiar, but couldn't place him.

"Barry, do you remember Todd Johnson?"

Barry stared at the man. Then it hit him and his muscles tensed. His parents befriended one of the boys who spiked his brother's drinks? Anger stirred inside him. His heart rate picked up. He moved to the edge of his seat ready to get up. This man was responsible for his brother's death. He clenched his jaw and balled his fists. An urge overcame him to hurt this man who stood next to his mother.

Forgive.

Barry turned his face and took a deep breath.

You have been forgiven much. Forgive.

He slumped back in his seat and buried his face in his hands.

"We've forgiven him. It's an important part of healing and finding peace." His mother put her hand on his shoulder. "He's a Christian now, too. Your new brother in Christ."

Barry leaned forward and sobbed. He covered his head with his arms. Anger drained away and weariness flooded in. *God, help me forgive.*

Todd knelt down beside him. "Barry, I am so sorry. What I did was wrong and caused so much pain. Will you please forgive me?"

Barry looked up at his new brother in the Lord. He struggled for the words then nodded. "Yes, I forgive you." He stood to give Todd a hug. The bitterness of unforgiveness left his heart and peace replaced it.

After lunch and a time of sharing and tears, Todd and his wife left. The healing God did in one afternoon amazed him. He hoped God would do the same for his marriage to Karen.

Robert walked over to him and placed a hand on his shoulder. "Quite a day."

"You can say that."

"Can I find a room to rest in? I should have listened to my doctors and taken a nap before now. I'm getting a headache."

Barry showed Robert to Chad's old room, then went downstairs and found his dad looking for something in the garage. He stopped when Barry walked in.

"Don't let me interrupt you, Dad."

He set down a box. "You've been gone for twenty years. There's nothing I won't put down to spend time with my son." He smiled and gave Barry a bear hug. "Let's go for a walk."

"Sure." Barry led the way down the drive to the edge of the sidewalk. "Which way?"

"Let's go this way." His dad turned to the left and matched Barry stride for stride. He held his back straight and walked with lightness in his step. "So how long will you get to stay?"

"Just a couple of days."

"Wish you could stay longer."

"Me too. But Robert has to get back."

"Do you mind if I ask about Karen? You said she left."

"For a good reason."

"Oh?"

The weight of his choices closed in on him and he slowed his steps. "Dad, I hit her." He slumped and dropped his head. His dad gave him a hug, then continued to walk and listen. Barry wiped his face.

"I drank a lot and…and got hooked on pornography." He looked away from the steady gaze of his father. "I got so angry with the direction of my life. I hated myself and my choices that got me there. I hated my debt. I felt like less of a man. I couldn't face it, and I blamed her. One day, I got so mad and so drunk, I hit her. I still remember the hurt look on her face. It tore me up."

"Have you tried to tell her all of this?"

"I don't know where she is, and she won't answer when I call."

"So it's wait and pray."

"And hope."

"What will you do while you wait?"

"I don't know. Find a job I guess."

His dad nodded. "You can come home. Robert and his wife will know where you are. It sounds like Karen talks to Megan, and she'll let her know you're here."

Barry liked the idea. He needed to renew his relationship with his parents and it would afford him time to grow in the Lord away from the distractions and temptations of the city. "You sure?"

"Absolutely." His dad put an arm around him. "You'll make your mom happy, too. You don't know how much she missed you ever since we woke up out of that fog. It'll give her a chance to catch up on lost time. Me, too."

"I'll have to go back to move my stuff out of the apartment and get out of my lease."

His dad stopped in the middle of the sidewalk and turned to face him. "Then go back and pack it up. Put whatever you need to in storage — we'll cover the cost until you get a job. We'll help you get out of your lease. Then you can come home. I like the idea of having you here." His dad's voice broke with emotion.

Barry put his arms around him. "That's what I'll do."

34

Karen strolled through Haley's garden while she waited for lunch with her brother and his wife. Since the near car crash two days ago, she was filled with a peace like never before. But today that peace eluded her.

The beautiful array of colors in the garden delighted her senses. Inscribed plaques graced each grouping of flowers with scriptures. Herbs filled a raised bed next to the house. She followed the brick path that meandered through the garden, past a fountain and disappeared into the woods.

Working in Margie's garden kept her mind off of David most of the time, but today she could only think about his marriage proposal. She didn't believe he could love her child, but could she shrug off her emotional attachment to him, despite her misgivings? She needed to decide once and for all what to do. The indecision tired her. She hoped visiting Haley's garden would help her find clarity, like it did Alita.

Karen found the pond Alita told her about and walked around it until she came to the bench located on the north side. She sat down and gazed out over the water before reading the plaque located next to the bench.

A bruised reed He will not break, and a dimly burning wick He will not extinguish; He will faithfully bring forth justice.
— *Isaiah 42:3*

Swaying in the winds
Life blows your way
Standing strong
As you trust and obey.
— Haley

God whispered the words of that Bible verse to her moments after she slid off the road — the day she learned to trust Him. What did God ask from her now? She sighed. She wanted the kind of relationship Margie and Megan had with God. They always knew the right thing to do.

She wanted to do the right thing, but when it came to her marriage all she knew was confusion. There was justification in the Bible for a wife to leave an unfaithful husband, and Barry cheated when he looked at those magazines. And that woman at the restaurant.

Wait. Trust. Obey.

Karen got up from the bench and hiked further into the woods. Barry humiliated her. He looked at those women and thought who knows what about them, then came home to her. She shuddered.

Was God really asking her to stay with Barry? The bruises of her heart and emotions threatened to break her already. And she feared this new tenderness she felt toward him would undo her if she stayed. *Why do I have to make the first step?* She wouldn't even be here, if not for Barry's choices.

"And I wouldn't know You, God." Karen slowed her pace, thinking of the cabbie who praised God for his prosthetic leg. Was it possible her bad situation could be turned around? She placed a hand on her stomach. *My baby.* There was already good coming out of her marriage.

She ran away from Barry based on his actions. *What about my own?* Leaning against a tree, she wrapped her arms around her waist and rested against the rough bark. She cried when she remembered how she had treated Barry over the last few years. Always pointing a finger at him and throwing her anger around like a weapon. Just because she didn't hit him didn't make her outbursts right. She broke her share of household items throwing them at Barry. She used hateful words and showed him disrespect. Shame filled her heart and the tears wracked her body. She fell to her knees, her head in her hands. "God, forgive me."

You are forgiven. Now wait on Me.

Karen looked toward the heavens. She lifted her hands in silent surrender and wept fresh tears when understanding of His mercy overcame her.

"Karen? Are you okay?" Haley knelt down and put her hand on Karen's shoulder.

Karen sat up. "I've been a fool. I blamed Barry for our troubles and expected him to make all the changes, but I didn't treat him right. We both need to change." She burst out with new tears. "This journey is not what I expected when I came home. It feels impossible."

"God never asks us to do it alone."

"I'm glad of that."

"What has He asked you to do?"

"To wait. To trust Him."

"To wait on what?"

"Barry." Karen shrugged. "To see whether he will make changes. To see what God will do."

"What about David?"

"I won't divorce Barry. At least for now. But God didn't say I couldn't have David for a friend." *What am I saying?* The words sounded lame even to her, but an emotional bungee cord yanked her heart back to David when she thought of final good-byes. She stood up and dusted off her jeans.

"Are you trusting God if you keep David around just in case?"

Karen avoided Haley's gaze.

"What does God want you to do?"

Karen sniffled. "I just want to be loved."

"God wants to be enough for each of us." Haley rubbed Karen's back.

"I know, but sometimes it feels nice to have an arm around you."

"That's what family is for. Not men you aren't married to."

Karen felt ashamed for hanging on to someone she knew deep inside was not a part of God's will. She held her face in her hands. Were her thoughts about David any better than Barry's fantasies? She didn't like the reprimand, but she needed it. *God, please forgive me.* "You're right. I'll… do my best to keep some space between us."

"I know it will be hard." Haley hugged her then backed up and looked her in the eye. "How are you doing working though issues with Barry?"

"His pornography makes me feel dirty and like I'm not good enough." Moisture gathered in Karen's eyes.

"It does that to women. That's why you need to talk to someone and work it out." Haley took Karen's hand and began to lead the way back to the house. "God can help you forgive and grow your love back, but you cannot bury your emotions over it. You'll end up resenting him. Albert knows a Christian counselor who can help."

"Thanks. I'd like to talk to someone.…I think. I'm not too sure how the forgiveness will work out. I mean, what if he doesn't change?" Karen kicked at the dirt. "That's why it's so hard to walk away from David. He seems the opposite of Barry in so many ways."

"I understand that. But as long as you're hanging onto David, you won't be able to fully engage in possibilities with Barry. I know forgiveness can be tough. I've walked through it myself. But it is possible even if the offender never changes." Haley wiped a stray tear from her face.

"But if Barry doesn't change, why should I forgive?" The idea of forgiving him if he never gave up those pictures filled her with disgust.

"Why don't we talk about it at lunch? Albert might be able to help you understand better."

"I don't know if I can eat right now. Even the thought of food makes me queasy. But I'll stick around awhile."

Haley raised her eyebrows.

Karen laughed. "I can't believe I haven't told you guys yet. On top of everything else, I'm carrying Barry's child."

"I'm so happy for you," Haley gave Karen a quick hug. "No matter what happens with your marriage, this child is a wonderful gift."

WHERE HOPE STARTS

Karen agreed then linking arms, they headed back to the house.

In the middle of lunch, Karen's phone rang. Glancing at the caller ID, she excused herself from the table. "Megan? It's good to hear from you. Sorry I haven't called in a while."

"I wondered if you went to visit Dorothy and the wicked witch. Oh, wait, that's Kansas. Got my states mixed up. Sorry. So, how are you?"

"Okay." Karen smiled at Megan's chatter. "Wow, I didn't get a chance to tell you the last time we talked, but I've made my life right with God." She held the phone away from her ear when Megan whooped in excitement. "Careful girl, you'll break my eardrums."

"I can't help it. That's incredible. Tell me all about it."

"I'll have to give you the whole story later; I'm at my brother's house for lunch."

"Sure. How's your mom? Any change?"

"No. The doctors don't expect her to wake up."

"So you haven't found out what the big secret is?"

"Not yet. My brothers and sisters don't know, and my dad refuses to tell me while there's any chance mom will wake up. He's so stubborn. I don't understand why he thinks he has to do that."

"Maybe you'll understand once you find out what happened." Karen shifted her weight from one foot to the other. "Maybe. Uh… how's Barry? And Robert?"

"I've been calling you, but it keeps going to voice mail. Robert's out of the hospital and Barry's out of jail. He's made some changes, too."

"I'm glad Robert is okay. But as for Barry's changes, I'll believe it when I see it. I know I wasn't a perfect wife, but he still hurt me, and it'll be hard to get past that. I want to trust God, though."

"I'll be praying for you both."

"Thanks. Oh. There's one more thing."

"Yes?"

"I'm pregnant." Karen held the phone away from her ear again.

"Congratulations. How far along are you?"

"Not sure exactly, still need to get to the doctor, but somewhere near the end of the first trimester."

"That is cool. I can't wait to tell Robert."

"Just don't tell Barry yet, okay?"

"Wouldn't dream of it. That is news for you to share. I'll be praying for you."

"Thanks. I'll talk to you later." Karen smiled and stuck the phone back in her pocket. She rejoined Albert and Haley at the table as the kids ran off to play. "Did I hear you guys talking about Dad?"

"He's concerned about Blake. No one's seen him since Alita got the restraining order." Albert set his fork down.

"Actually, he showed up at my place almost three weeks ago."

"Why didn't you say so?" Haley passed Karen the plate of chicken.

"It wasn't exactly a pleasant visit. He threatened me. I'm sure he would have done some damage if Margie hadn't seen his truck and called the police."

Albert huffed. "I can't believe he's my brother. Maybe you need to stay in Margie's house for a while. You'll be less vulnerable."

"I lived in New York City. Big bad guys aren't new to me. I'll be fine."

"If he comes around again, don't keep it to yourself, okay?"

"Okay." Karen rolled her eyes. Albert sounded like a gentler Barry. He used to yell at her when she walked home alone after a late shift at the restaurant. Looking back, he probably just wanted to protect her and she didn't let him. So much got lost in communication. How many other times did they misunderstood each other? *Forgiveness still sounds like climbing Mount Everest.*

If Barry didn't change, she saw no reason to forgive him. She pushed her food around on her plate. She carried her own guilt, but his offenses seemed so much bigger. Shouldn't he change first?

"Karen?" Albert reached over and stilled her hand. "What's on your mind?"

She glanced at Haley, who gave her an encouraging nod, then leaned over and whispered to her kids. They ran inside the house.

"You remember in the hospital when we talked about forgiveness?"

"Yes."

"Well…you said forgiveness benefitted the one hurt. That still doesn't make sense. How can it help me?"

"I think these are your favorite if I remember right." Albert took the jar of candy Charlie and Annie brought from the house before they ran off to play. He held out the jar to Karen.

She narrowed her eyes at her brother. What was he up to? "Okay, I'll play along." She examined the contents. "Mmmm. Chocolate covered almonds. I think I will." Karen reached into the jar and grabbed a handful of candy, but her hand got stuck in the skinny neck of the jar. She let the nuts fall back inside.

"Kind of hard to enjoy the candy if your fist is hanging onto it inside the jar. All you have to do is let go and pour it out." Albert poured some candy into her outstretched hand.

She knew her brother usually had a point to go with his illustrations. And this one concerned forgiveness. She looked at her hand full of nuts. Poured out of the jar, she could enjoy them. With her fist closed around them inside the jar, she was stuck. "So, holding on to the nuts, the nuts being the offense of course, is unforgiveness?"

"Give the girl an A," Albert said.

"And if I don't let go of the hurt I'll be stuck?"

"Make that an A-plus."

Karen ate the almonds in her hand. She didn't like the bitterness that seemed to fester inside her and color the world around her. Would letting go of her right to see justice change all of that?

Albert set the jar of almonds down. "God asks us to forgive because he knows what will happen to us if we don't. Our hands are closed to his blessings if our fists are tight around the hurt."

"I don't know how to forgive." Karen stood up.

"God doesn't ask us to do what He won't help us with." Haley walked over and put her arm around Karen. She allowed Haley to hold her in a brief hug. *God, help me.* Karen wiped her eyes, then laughed.

"I think I've cried enough in the last few weeks to water your garden."

"We've all been there," Haley picked up plates from the table.

"It doesn't feel like it." Karen gathered up the glasses and followed her sister-in-law into the kitchen.

Haley set her load down on the counter. "You aren't the only one hurting you know. Maybe, if you took the time to look around you could see that."

"I didn't mean to make it all about me. Albert told me you had a rough childhood. Will you forgive me?"

"It's not just me. Your dad hurt everyone in your family — even Albert and Elinor. They both witnessed your dad's treatment of you. "

"I know. But dad left them alone." Karen set the glasses in the sink.

"While you were home, but after you left…"

Karen gasped and grabbed the edge of the counter. "I thought it was just me."

"Most of the time after you left, your dad was just sad. If they stayed off his radar, they were fine. But kids will be kids. Albert took his own verbal lashings that went with the punishment. And Elinor's too, when your dad believed Albert's claim of guilt."

"When he talked about forgiveness…" Karen put a hand on her chest.

"From his own experience."

"But surely Elinor — "

"Watching Albert get torn apart with your dad's words has its own consequences. It—"

"Leaves bruises on the inside." Karen finished Haley's sentence.

"Exactly.

"I've been so selfish. Why didn't Albert tell me?"

"It only would have added fuel to your anger."

How did I miss it? Karen shook her head. She really had been self-absorbed. "If Albert can find a way to forgive, maybe I can, too. Someday."

"I'll be praying for you."

35

The pungent odor of the hospital assaulted Karen as she exited the elevator. She grimaced. She didn't remember such a strong smell the last time. She rubbed her belly with anticipation of getting past the morning sickness. Nearing her mother's room, she saw Margie exit the room. "How's Mom?"

"About the same. I've been sitting with her since I got off duty."

"Thank you, Margie." *I should have been here more often.* After all the years of ill will toward her family, she found it difficult to visit at all. *Is this the bitterness Albert talked about?* Her talk with Albert yesterday yielded more questions in her mind about forgiveness. How did someone just let go of so much hurt?

"I'm glad I had the time. Albert and your dad are with her now. Stop by for tea when you can."

Karen gave Margie a quick hug and watched her walk to the elevator. Karen's head began to spin and she propped herself against the wall for support. *I need to eat better.* She rested a moment and listened to the voices coming from her mom's room.

Her dad's deep, mellow voice touched a spot inside her she didn't realize was still alive. She caught her breath. *I loved you so much, Dad. You were my world. Why did you reject me? What did I do that was so bad?* Tears moistened her eyes.

"Did you know she's pregnant?" Albert's voice filtered into the hallway. She wished he had kept that bit of information to himself. She leaned her cheek against the door frame and continued listening.

"It would be a good time to make things right with her." Her brother voiced her own thoughts.

"How am I supposed to do that? She won't talk to me."

"Why don't you just tell her what it is she wants to know? Mom would understand." Her brother's voice carried a kind rebuke.

"It will just sound like I'm telling on her. Like I'm looking for an excuse for my actions." His voice lowered as he continued his explanation to Albert.

What did you do, Mom? She took several calming breaths. What had changed her family so much? She needed to know what happened all those years ago in order to understand and find some measure of peace. She leaned back against the wall and sighed.

Forgive.

I'm still not sure I want to. She pushed away from the wall. *Time to face them.* Stepping into her mother's room, she nodded at Albert. Her father's back was toward her. She cleared her throat.

"Karen." Her dad stood up and put his hat on.

"Dad."

"I'll come back later." He moved toward the door.

Karen watched him retreat. "Wait."

"Yes?"

"I want to ask you something." She moved closer to the bed and touched her mom's hand. It felt cool. She tucked it under the cover and turned to her dad. "Please, tell me what happened. I want to understand."

Charles lowered his gaze to the floor. "I told you already; I promised your mom."

"Dad, she's not going to wake up."

"Probably. But I owe her that possibility."

"Why?"

"Because you weren't the only one I rejected, and it's the only way I know to honor her right now."

Karen folded her arms and stared at her dad.

"I won't change my mind." He looked over at her mother.

"Fine." Karen stormed toward the door.

"Karen, I'm sorry. I can't go back and change my choices, and there's no way I can ever make it up to you. The only way this family will find its way back together is through forgiveness. Can't you find it in your heart to forgive?"

She paused at the doorway. "I don't know." She stepped into the hallway, then peeked back in.

Her dad reached for her mom's hand. "I'm trying sweetheart, I am."

Karen sped onto the ramp of the highway. Her family never practiced forgiveness before now. How does a person forgive? People probably heard of her father's rejection of her and expected it to be easy to forgive him. He didn't commit the atrocities other fathers did to their children. And she bore no physical signs of abuse. But inside she felt beaten up and unwanted.

She drummed her fingers on the steering wheel as she eased onto the highway. Albert's words on forgiveness bounced around in her mind. Hang on to the hurt and live in bitterness or let go of the right to demand punishment for her dad's actions and leave that up to God. Even if God let her dad off the hook.

I want to trust you, God, but really? Let dad off the hook? Everyone would expect things to be okay between them. Albert assured her forgiveness didn't always mean restoration. But still. And then there was Barry. Could she forgive him as well?

Trust me.

"I can't just shut these feelings off and on." Karen muttered to herself. Especially with these pregnancy hormones knocking them around.

Her stomach growled. She actually felt hungry for a change. She exited at Westfall, and headed to Applewood Hill. Eating there would give her a chance to check out the dining room and staff from a customer's viewpoint. She hoped her loan went through. Of course, life close to her family would have its drawbacks. She pulled into a full parking lot and found a spot on the end underneath some trees.

"Ah, the beautiful sister of Elinor." James greeted her at the front desk. She'd never tire of his British accent. "Did you stop by to see Ben and Sheryl? They are out at the moment."

"No, I'm only interested in eating. Do you have an open table for dinner?"

"You did not make a reservation? But never mind, we will find a spot for you. Wait right here." James disappeared to arrange for a table and returned with a smile on his face. "Follow me."

She followed him to an out of the way table in a corner. From her vantage point she saw the entire dining hall. "This is perfect. Thank you."

"My pleasure." He bowed slightly. "Your waiter will be with you shortly. If you need anything, please let me know."

Karen enjoyed a quiet meal while she scrutinized the dining room. The entire establishment exuded beauty. She imagined what it would be like if her marriage to Barry sparked like it did the first six years they were together. Her management experience and Barry's salesmanship were a great combination for operating a place like this. She smiled. Maybe a couple of kids running around in the mix. She blushed and looked down at her coffee cup. A part of her began to hope for the early love of their union. Could they do it?

She finished the last bite of her dessert just as James stopped at her table to check on her. She asked him a few questions about the inn and assured him she planned to keep him on as manager. Satisfied with her observations, she left a handsome tip for the waiter and made her way to the exit.

A smile played across her lips as she thought of the possibilities this place offered. With Barry. She had almost reached the door when she heard David's voice calling her.

"Karen. Wait up."

She tensed as if someone had thrown a bucket of cold water on her. She turned to wait, despite her urge to run. He pushed his chair back from the table where he sat with several other men in business suits. Whispering to one of them, he dropped some money on the table.

No. No. No. Just leave me alone, David. She headed for the exit and he followed. When she reached her car, she turned to face him.

"Checking out the Bed and Breakfast?" He stood there with a sheepish grin on his face, his hands stuck in his pants' pockets.

"I needed to eat." Karen leaned back against her car.

"Let me buy the place for you." David took a step closer.

"What?" Karen stood up straight.

"I keep telling you I love you. Let me prove it."

David, I'm married. You're engaged. I'm pregnant with my husband's child. We can't have this conversation." She reached behind her to open the car door.

"I broke it off with Mary." David reached around her waist to pull her close, and cupped her face in the palm of his hand. "We belong together." He leaned in to kiss her.

Too stunned to move at first, the brush of his lips against hers snapped her back to reality. She pushed him back, but he held her tight. "I can't lose you again, Karen."

"Let me go." She pushed until he released her. "Back off. You don't love me anymore than Barry did when he hit me. You just want what you want." Karen climbed into her car and slammed the door, then locked herself in. What got into him? She backed her car out and left him standing, gaping after her.

36

Karen poured a cup of chai tea and breathed in the spicy smell of cardamom as she nestled into the pillows on her couch. The David in the parking lot was not the David she loved in high school. This new version was selfish and pushy and… she sighed. She hadn't slept well since he offered to buy the bed and breakfast for her two days ago, and she realized how deep his intent ran. Shudders ran up her spine. She did not want him raising her child.

She sipped on her tea. God was pressing on her the need to forgive both Barry and her father. But she didn't know how. And she wasn't sure about the follow through. She knew that even if she forgave her dad, she didn't have to have a constant relationship with him. But whether she liked it or not, Barry was the father of her baby. How much would he remain a part of their lives? She vacillated between trusting God and fear of Barry.

Last night she dreamed about running the Applewood Hill with Barry. Their two kids played nearby while they worked in the dining room. Then Barry became angry and chased her until she dropped with exhaustion. He hit her over and over.

Their oldest yelled, "Daddy stop hurting Mommy!"

He turned and stalked toward the children as they backed away.

She got up and grabbed his arm. "Don't hurt the kids!"

She woke in a sweat. *It's a dream.* She had cried herself back to sleep, praying for God to save them.

She set down her teacup. He had hit her only once, but she believed he would have done it again. She shook her head. Even if he never raised his hand to her or their children, she dreaded living in a house full of anger. She did it as a kid and knew how much damage it could do. She didn't want to live through that again.

Karen pulled her new Bible off the coffee table and placed it in her lap. She had spent the last couple of days searching through it, trying to understand how to forgive. God asked her to, yet she didn't feel like it. How did she get around that? She opened to the Sermon on the Mount and read the phrase again… *"In prayer there is a connection between what God does and what you do. You can't get forgiveness from God, for instance, without also forgiving others. If you refuse to do your part, you cut yourself off from God's part."*

Chewing on her thumbnail, she got up and paced the apartment. Would He really refuse to forgive her if she didn't forgive her dad and Barry? She couldn't be without God. Maybe she didn't understand it. *I'll ask Margie.* She headed over to the garden.

"Margie." Karen hollered, waving at her friend when she looked up from her flowers.

"Did you come for tea?" Margie greeted her with a hug.

"No. A question. I read a verse in my Bible I'm confused about."

"Of course." Margie led the way toward the bench under the oak tree. "Tell me what's on your mind."

"It says in the Bible God will forgive me the same way I forgive others. So, if I can't forgive my dad and Barry, He won't forgive me?"

"That's what it says, and I try to take God at his word even when I don't understand it. I do know that refusing to forgive displeases God, and we only hurt ourselves."

Karen stopped a few steps from the bench and turned to Margie. "But I can't forgive them."

Margie looked at her with a sad smile. "You mean you won't?"

Karen sat down on the bench. How could she explain what she didn't understand? "I don't know how."

"Jesus talks more about forgiveness later in Matthew. He tells the story of a man who owed his master a lot of money." The older woman sat down next to Karen. "When the servant pleaded for mercy his master forgave him his debt. But then the forgiven servant went away and found another servant who owed him very little and actually threw him into prison for what he owed.

"Other servants in the house reported this to the master and it made him angry. He threw the first servant in prison, along with his family. When we don't forgive, we are locked into a sort of jail, too. One of bitterness. That servant chose not to forgive. It wasn't inability that drove him to unforgiveness."

"So you're saying I'm choosing to not forgive."

"Yes."

"But..." Karen's shoulders slumped. "I've asked God to help me, but I can't get out of my mind what they've done. I keep waiting for...for..."

"For a feeling of forgiveness?"

"Yeah. I guess that's it. Don't I need to feel good about it for forgiveness to be real?"

Margie chuckled. "You know, I've helped several moms through their labor and delivery. Most of them chose some sort of medication to lessen the pain. That's perfectly fine. But some of them wanted to give birth without drugs. And you know what?"

Karen shook her head.

"Medical necessity aside, out of the ones who thought of having a natural birth, only the ones who made a firm decision ahead of time made it through without drugs. The ones who waited to see how they felt ended up opting for the relief."

"Forgiveness is kind of like that. If you take the first step and choose to forgive, God will give you the faith to walk it out. The feelings come after the obedience. Sometimes those take awhile. Sometimes they never come. Trust God through the process. He's waiting on you to take the first step and choose."

The older woman put an arm around Karen and pulled her close while she cried. They sat under the tree until the tears subsided. Then Karen returned to her apartment. Could she let it go? *God, help me to let it go and learn to trust you. Help me to want to forgive.*

Two hours later, Karen pulled into the hospital parking garage. She climbed out of the car and headed inside. Margie made a lot of sense. *I just need to do it. Decide once and for all to forgive.* Her breath caught at the thought of letting it all go. She balled her hands into fists and pushed through the revolving doors. *Help me to be willing, God.*

Quiet permeated the hallway as she stepped off the elevator. She went straight to her mother's room and relieved the hospice nurse. Sitting in the chair closest to the bed, she warmed her mother's hand with her own. At one time in her life, her mom always had time for her.

The day Karen started second grade, she returned home in tears and covered in mud. Panicked, she stood in the doorway, looking around the room full of ladies, plastic containers spread out on the coffee table.

A nosy next door neighbor took one look at her and broke out in a cackle. "Why look at that child. She looks like a cat drug her through the mud."

Karen bawled and ran up the stairs.

The laughing increased until one voice rose above the rest. She stopped on the landing and listened.

"You should be ashamed of yourselves, laughing like that at a child. It's time you all leave." At that moment, her mom's voice was the sweetest sound on earth. Karen sat down on the top step.

"But the party," objected one lady.

"I have more important things to take care of than look at some silly plastic."

Karen found a clean patch of material on the sleeve of her muddy dress and wiped her eyes. She waited with her head buried in her arms while her mother cleared the house. In the silence that followed the exodus, her mother climbed the stairs and sat down, pulling Karen close to her.

She listened to Karen's tale of boyhood mischief that landed her in a muddy patch on the walk home from school. Muddy daughter and spic-and-span mother sat side by side until all the tears were cried out. Only then did her mother insist on removing the dirt.

Her mom threw their closeness away the night her dad rejected her.

I need to forgive Mom, too. Karen let loose of her mother's hand and stood up from the hospital bed. She had a lot to think about and she wanted to be in the quietness of her own apartment. As she turned to leave, she bumped into Alita.

"Oops. I didn't know you were here."

"I'm sorry if I intruded. I usually come around this time every day."

"I didn't know you came every day."

"I miss a few here and there. But your mother treated me so well. It's the least I can do."

Karen sat on the edge of the bed. "How are you doing without Blake around?"

"Pretty well, I guess. The house still feels empty, even with a dog in it." Alita smiled. "I've rediscovered some hobbies. I went to the craft store and picked up some stamping supplies."

"I'm glad. Do you know what you'll do about Blake?"

"We don't even know where he is. I just have to wait for now."

Karen looked down and rubbed the edge of the bed cover between her fingers. "Can I ask you something?"

"Sure." Alita sat in the chair.

"How did you do it? I mean, living with Blake all this time and not being bitter? You had so much more than just anger to live with."

"I was bitter for a long time."

"What changed?"

"I decided to forgive him. Every day."

Karen swallowed. There it was again. *Decide to do it.* "If you could go back, would you do anything different?"

Alita hesitated, leaned back in her chair, and blew out a breath. "I'd like to think I would have gotten help. But if I could change anything, it would be to forgive him sooner. My bitterness toward him only added fuel to the fire." She shrugged. "Maybe it would have made a difference."

Karen crossed her arms. "That deciding thing —"

"It's hard. But with God, you can do it." Alita gave Karen a hug. "I'll stay and sit with your mom awhile. You go on." She smiled and shooed Karen out of the room.

An hour later found Karen pulling into her drive. A car sat in front of her apartment with a woman leaning against it. Mary? Karen parked her car and climbed out.

Mary hurried over and stood toe to toe with Karen. "Who do you think you are waltzing in here and poisoning David's mind against me?"

Karen held up her hands. "David and I are old friends. That's all."

"Then why did he break up with me?"

"That surprised me, too."

"He says he plans to marry you."

"I'm already married."

"Lots of women cheat on their men."

I'm sure you would know. Karen glared at her, then turned to go.

Mary grabbed her arm. "Don't walk away from me."

Karen shrugged off Mary's hand. "What do you want?"

"For you to stop seeing David."

"I'm not seeing him. I've hung out with him a few times as friends. He's been the one to push the issue. I told him to back off, but I don't control the man, and you should stop trying. You might stop cheating on him, too."

Karen turned her back to Mary and crossed the remaining distance to the bottom of her stairs. She didn't even turn around when Mary got in the car and left. With that woman on the offense, Karen had even more reason to keep her distance from David. At least one decision was made.

She tossed her purse onto the couch and took off her shoes, then went to the kitchen for water. That's when she noticed the flowers. Margie must have brought them in. The clear vase was etched with delicate swirls. It looked like real crystal. Someone spent some money on her. The vase held at least a dozen orange roses. That was her favorite flower to get from…he wouldn't. She marched to the table and grabbed the card. Ripping open the envelope, she pulled out the note.

My Dearest Karen,

I still believe in us.

With all my love, David

Karen's breath caught in her throat. "Don't you get it? I don't love you. I don't want you to raise my child." She tossed the note on the table and paced back and forth across the apartment. Voices crowded for attention in her mind. David's. Barry's. Megan's. Margie's. Joanna's. Dad's. God's. She stomped her foot.

"I don't feel like forgiving anyone," she yelled to the empty room. Grabbing the vase, she threw it across the room. The glass shattered, water splashed and the roses fell in a heap.

Staring at the mess she let out a guttural cry, then grabbed a plate from the counter and threw it against the wall, adding ceramics to crystal. A glass from the sink followed.

She picked up another object and stopped. Elinor had given her this new snow globe after finding out Karen was pregnant. She watched the snow drift to a slow stop over the tiny image of a mother leaning over a baby nestled in a cradle. She set the globe down as sobs wracked her body. She dropped to her knees and then to the floor. "Oh, God, I need you. Please help me to want to forgive."

37

Barry taped another box together and stacked it next to the door. He spent three days catching up with his parents before he and Robert returned to New York Thursday afternoon.

Now with the help of Robert's friends from church, he was emptying out his apartment. He planned to donate most of the furniture and knickknacks to a charity. The sentimental items, books, and their personal records would go in storage. *And the computer is out of here.* It was just a trap.

He and Karen made a lot of memories in this place. He looked for their photo album but couldn't find it. *She must have taken it with her.* He smiled. If she held onto the good memories, maybe she would be willing to make more.

Robert arrived with Megan and a stack of pizzas. "I promised the guys food, so I figured I better deliver."

"Thanks for all your help. I couldn't have done it without you."

The rest of the muscle showed up and they took a few minutes for introductions before they dug into the pizza, then went to work. Megan helped Barry pack while Robert directed the guys taking furniture to the truck.

"Hey, Marino."

He looked up from the box he was working on. *The landlord.*

"What do you mean by this? I come in and you're emptying out your apartment without a word to me. Trying to run out on your lease?"

"Hold on, I've got money for you. Next month's rent plus one for breaking my lease. I came by this morning, but you were out."

The landlord took the envelope and counted the bills. "Okay. It's all here. Stop by when you're done and I'll give you a receipt. Don't leave the place a mess."

Barry went to the bedroom to pack up their closet. Not sure what to do about Karen's clothes, he packed them and labeled the boxes so they could easily find them later. He pulled some sweaters down from the top shelf of the closet and a letter fell to the floor. He set the sweaters on the bed and picked it up.

It was unopened, addressed to Karen's maiden name, postmarked several years ago, with a Westfall, Missouri address. He found his Atlas and looked up the town. It was just north of Kansas City.

She had never told him about her family, and since he didn't plan to reciprocate, he never asked. He put his thumb under the flap to open it then stopped. She should open it first.

He hurried to find Robert and Megan and handed them the letter. "What do you think?"

Megan looked at the address. "You've found her."

"I want to see her before I move to my folks." Barry ran his hand through his hair. "Am I crazy?"

"I think you better go. Now." Robert smiled and handed it back.

"Now?"

"Sure. We can see to the rest of this. You've told us what goes and what you're keeping. We'll clean up the apartment, too."

"Go ahead, give it to him." Megan beamed and winked at her husband.

Robert laughed. "Okay, who can argue with a smile like that? We want to give you this to help." He pulled an envelope out of his pocket and handed it to Barry.

"What's this?" He took the envelope, opened it, and stared at the bills inside. "You didn't need to do this."

"We want to. It'll help you with a plane ticket."

"I can't believe you guys. You've done so much for me already. Thank you." Barry gave his friends a hug, then called the airport and found a flight with one layover, arriving in Kansas City by early evening.

He stopped and explained to his landlord that his friends would clear out the apartment for him. The man grumbled about the situation until he met Robert and took a good look at his business card.

Barry packed a few more boxes and labeled some of the more personal items then added some clothes to his duffel bag. Before he left, he called his parents and explained his plans to find Karen. He promised to call when he knew more.

He tucked the letter into his pocket, then hailed a cab and headed to the airport. He needed to arrive early to purchase a ticket. *Lord, give me a seat on that plane.* So much had changed for him since Karen left. Did they have a second chance?

Barry watched out the window then looked over the shoulder of the cabbie to check the speed limit. It felt like they were crawling. What if she wasn't there?

I brought you this far. Trust me.

He pulled Karen's ring out of his pocket and took several deep breaths. God worked in his life, and He could work in her's, too. He squeezed the ring in his fist then put it back in his pocket. He would wait as long as it took for her to trust him again.

38

Barry entered the sanctuary and found a seat in the back. Anxious to see Karen, he chose a church close to the address on the letter. *Maybe someday she'll come to church with me.*

As the congregation began to sing, he looked around the room. His eyes landed on Karen engrossed in worship. *She's here?* Stunned, his throat constricted and he gripped the seat in front of him and strained to get a better look.

Karen radiated joy. She found God. He blinked back a tear. *Thank you, God, for leading me here!* Now at least he could apologize, ask for forgiveness.

He sat through the sermon without hearing it. His mind focused on his wife. He made himself look away so she didn't sense him watching her, though he longed to run to her and pour out his heart.

When the pastor invited the church to stand for the final song, Barry slipped out the back. As much as he wanted to talk to Karen, this wasn't the right place. Not here in front of so many people. If he couldn't find her at the address on the letter, he would talk to the pastor of the church. Before the day ended, he was determined to apologize to his wife.

Lord, let me talk to her and tell her how sorry I am and how You have changed me. Let her be open to a second chance. Peace filled his heart and determination guided him.

After a fitful night of sleep, Karen woke filled with a willingness to forgive, but she was a bit afraid of walking it out. She hurried to church, looking forward to worshipping God.

All her fears about forgiving her mom, dad, and Barry slipped away as she focused on God during worship. Tears moistened her cheeks. She would wait for her mom to wake up to discover the secret. She would also set aside the divorce, and see what God's plans held for her marriage. Peace filled her.

Wanting to see her dad before everyone arrived for the family picnic, she hurried to her car when church ended. Anticipation mixed with nervousness as she drove to her parent's home. She was ready to forgive, but could things ever be the same?

As she walked up the path to his door, she stopped short when her dad stepped outside onto the porch.

"Hi, Dad."

"Karen. What brings you out here before everyone else?"

Karen looked up at him from the bottom of the stairs. "I need to talk to you."

"I told you, I'm not changing my mind. I won't talk about it anymore." Her dad folded his arms.

"It's not that. I…it's just…" Karen threw up her hands. "This is hard." *God help me find the words.* "Dad…I forgive you." The burden of hurt lifted and an unexpected joy filled her heart. She cried and dropped to the stairs.

Her dad sat down beside her and put his arm around her. At first she stiffened at his touch, then she leaned into him and the years melted away. "Oh, Daddy. I've missed you so much." Karen's tears joined his.

"I wish I could take away all the hurt I caused." He pulled her closer. His body shook as he cried. She remained in his embrace for several minutes, surprised to find she still loved him. God was faithful.

"Here, I have something to show you." He opened up his wallet and pulled out a folded card and handed it to Karen.

"What's this?" She took the offered card.

"Open it."

She unfolded the card and gasped. It was the Valentine's Day card she'd made her dad all those years ago. "You kept it?"

"When you walked out of the barn that day, I picked it up and hid it. After you left home and I found the Lord, I dug it out and put it in my wallet to remind me to pray for your return." Her dad grinned. "Course, I didn't need to be reminded."

She nestled into the crook of his arm and they sat in silence together. They were still there when everyone arrived for the family picnic.

"Guess I better fire up the grill." He kissed the top of her head and got up. She waved to her siblings.

Her niece and nephew ran up and hugged her.

"Can you take us horseback riding?" Annie grabbed her hand.

"Mom and Dad said we could go, if we can talk someone into it." Charlie pleaded.

"We'll see." She laughed and tussled their hair, then grabbed the bowl of potato salad Haley held and headed out to the picnic tables.

Albert caught up to his sister and gave her a hug. "Does this mean you've made your peace with Dad?"

"Yeah."

"What brought you around?"

"I was here to talk..."

"Do you know that guy?" Elinor came up from behind.

Karen turned and looked back toward the cars. A man stood there, watching them. Could it be?

"He drove up right after we got here and he's just standing there like he's looking for someone," said Elinor.

"Yeah, I know him." Karen took a deep breath and walked toward him. *How did you find me?*

"Karen?" Her dad called from his station at the grill. "Where are you off to?"

She swallowed hard as nausea threatened to overwhelm her. She left her father's question unanswered and continued toward Barry, stopping a few feet away from him.

"Hi. You look well." Barry moved closer, then stopped.

Karen waited.

"I..." Barry took a deep breath. "I'm sorry. I was a fool and I pray someday you can forgive me. There's more I want to say when you're ready. I'm staying at the Applewood Hill Bed and Breakfast in Westfall if you want to talk." He pulled an envelope out of his pocket and walked toward her. She took a step back. He stopped. "I found this. It's how I knew where to look. If you want it." He held it out to her.

Opportunity to forgive stood in front of her, but the determination to follow through danced just out of her grasp. She stepped closer and took the letter. Their hands brushed and she sucked in a breath at the shock it sent through her. She looked at the envelope. *The missing letter!* She blew out a deep breath. "Thank you. I'll...I'll be in touch."

She watched him leave.

"Is that your mother's letter?" Her dad's voice startled her. She nodded and continued to stare at Barry's car driving slowly down the lane to the highway. Gripping the letter tight, she turned and faced her dad.

He met her gaze. "You'll have your answers." His shoulders slumped, then he turned and went to be with the rest of the family.

Do I open it? She already forgave her dad. Did she have to know anything more? She walked to the porch and sat on the swing.

After a few minutes, Albert joined her. "Need to talk?"

She looked at him. "I don't know what to do."

Albert took the letter from Karen, turned it over in his hands, and then gave it back to her. "Read it. You'll know everything and it won't come back later and pull you down. Mom thought it was important enough for you to know. Maybe it's what we need to get us back on track as a family."

"You're right, but I think I want to read it alone." Karen wiped her tears away.

He nodded. "If you need me, you know where I am."

She watched him walk around the side of the house, then looked down at the letter in her lap, still hesitant to open it. "Lord, I'm afraid."

WHERE HOPE STARTS

Trust me.
She took a deep breath, opened the letter and began to read.

Dear Karen,

I've waited for you to come, but for reasons I don't understand you've chosen to stay away. I would rather tell you everything in person, but you need to know regardless. First, be assured of my love for you. I have repented of my wrongs and asked the forgiveness of both God and your father. I hope you can forgive me, too. Charles was always a difficult man. Even though we went to church on Sundays, during the week he was different. As Blake and Joanna never tired of telling you, he was an angry father. The year before you were born, I quit trying. Our marriage fell apart. Some close friends of ours tried to help. They knew we struggled in our family and they often took me and your brother and sister out for the day.
Sometimes they took just me. And sometimes the husband stopped by and made sure Charles behaved. I could call on him day or night. He became my rescuer. We became intimate within months. We were careful, but not careful enough. That man is your biological father.

"What?" Karen put the letter down in her lap. *You had an affair? How could you?* An image of her dance in the field with David came to mind. A woman betrayed and hurt, her mom turned to the most likely source for comfort.

Karen squeezed her eyes to hold back the tears. Her thoughts turned to her dad, who wasn't her dad. Is that why he rejected her? For something she didn't have any control over? She started shaking when the anger rose up inside her. She closed her eyes, clenched her fists and took several calming breaths. "God, help me not to grab back the forgiveness. But I really do want to throw something right now."

She opened her hands and lifted them up to God. The peace from earlier that morning returned. Her eyes widened as realization flooded through her. "I didn't do anything wrong." She had not pushed her dad away after all. She picked up the letter and continued reading.

> *We intended to tell Charles... I planned to leave him and take you and the other kids with me. But after you were born, Charles changed and gave God the credit. He stopped being angry and abusive. I didn't tell him the truth about you. The affair ended, and I kept it secret for thirteen years.*
> *I tried to be a good wife, but Charles destroyed any love I might have had for him. I never forgave him and didn't trust him. My walk with God was almost nonexistent.*
> *One night at a church function I ran into your biological father and his wife. He and I ended up alone on the porch and he asked about you. The conversation stirred up old feelings, and I'm ashamed to say I let him kiss me. It should never have happened. Your father overheard. It was the night before Valentine's Day. After we got home, we fought. He said he couldn't look at either me or you without remembering what I did. He turned his back on God and all of us. I crawled into a shell, even refusing to come out and defend you.*
> *After you left home, I left. God forgive me, Elinor and Albert were still at home. But God was gracious and your dad turned back to Him within a few years. Ultimately, that's what brought me home and helped me to find my way back to God so I could forgive Charles. I pray, by the grace of God, you will be able to forgive us. I love you.*
>
> *Mom*

Karen was dumbfounded. She never would have guessed this was the big secret. Now, it burned on her mind to know who her biological father was. Her dad knew. She stood and paced on the porch. Did she want to know? *God, what should I do?*

Trust me.

"Trust you? Like trust you and don't ask, or trust you and ask?"

Karen marched down the steps and across the yard to Albert, pulling him away from the table where he sat eating. She led him to the side of the stable and handed him the letter. "I need to know what to do now."

"You want me to read it?"

Karen stopped her pacing. She asked a lot of her brother. It might change the way he viewed their parents. The way he viewed her. "It's up to you."

"Give me a few minutes." Albert read and reread the letter then pinched the bridge of his nose. "That explains a lot."

"Maybe, but now I have more questions."

"Do you need to know the answers?" Albert handed the letter back to her.

"I don't need to know it all for God to work, but… I don't know…"

Albert sat down on an old nearby log and leaned his elbows on his knees. "What do you feel toward the other man right now?"

Karen thought about it for a minute. "Curiosity and anger."

"And what do you think you need to say if you meet him?"

Karen shrugged. "I don't know."

"Can you forgive him? And Mom?"

"I will. I know that's what God wants. But the feelings aren't there yet. You know?"

"Maybe you ought to wait to get your answers. Give God time to show you what He wants you to do."

"There's not much more I can do." Karen folded the letter and put it in her pocket. "I think I'll go on home for now."

She walked around the corner of the stable to her dad's table. She laid a hand on his shoulder and whispered. "You are still my dad." She kissed him on the cheek and left.

39

Karen needed to think. She left her dad's place and drove. There was nothing she could do about the contents of the letter for now, but Barry was another matter. She never expected him to show up, much less apologize. *Do I dare believe him?*

An hour later, she pulled into a state park, found a place to park in the shade and called Megan.

Her friend picked up on the second ring. "Hey girlfriend. How was your surprise?"

"You knew? Why didn't you warn me?"

"What would you have done? Left the state?"

"Okay. Okay. You got me. We haven't talked yet, but he stopped by my dad's house today. He apologized. Is it real?"

"Yes. Absolutely. Give him a chance. You'll see. Have I ever steered you wrong? No, don't answer that."

Karen laughed. Megan's hope was contagious, but Karen wasn't quite ready to embrace it yet. She sobered. "I will forgive him. But another chance? I need to hear what he has to say and pray about it before I give him an answer."

"Wise woman."

"Thanks, Megan. Even if it doesn't work with Barry, thanks for praying. God has helped me to forgive and that's huge. I better go. Talk at you later."

Karen headed for the bed and breakfast to find Barry. James informed her he left to explore Westfall. She tried his cell phone, but he didn't pick up. She left a message for him with James then drove into town and stopped at a café to get a coffee and newspaper.

Sitting on the bench outside, she glanced up every few minutes to look for him. After an hour she gave up and headed to the antique store next door.

"Karen."

She turned. David was heading straight toward her. She crossed her arms and waited.

He ran across the street and stopped in front of her with a puzzled look on his face. "Did you get the roses?"

Karen nodded.

David wrinkled his brows together. "Care to join me for lunch?"

"No." Karen shifted on her feet. She needed an exit strategy. David wouldn't make it easy. "I need to go." She started to walk away.

He reached out and grabbed her arm. "What's wrong?"

"Nothing." She looked down at his hand gripping her arm.

He ran his free hand through his hair. "Right. Are you upset about my offer to buy you the bed and breakfast? Or this?" He pulled her close and kissed her.

She turned her face away and pushed against his chest. "Stop!"

"Come on…"

A hand grabbed David's shoulder, spun him around and planted a fist in his face. David staggered back against the wall, nursing his jaw.

Karen stepped back. "Barry?"

He turned to Karen. His nostrils flared. "Is this the guy you were with when I called that night? I guess I know what you were doing."

Karen glared at him. "Who are you to talk? You were the one who cheated on me with all your magazines and Internet sites. And what about the woman at the restaurant?" She hated the words she spewed out of her mouth. She had been ready to forgive, yet here she stood yelling accusations in public.

She covered her face and took a step away from him. "Just go away and leave me alone."

Barry let out a pent up breath. "You're right. I'm sorry. I'll pack my bags and leave tonight if you ask me to. You can reach me on my cell phone." He turned to go.

She stared at him. *He admitted he was wrong.* She watched him walk down the sidewalk then took a step to go after him.

David grabbed her arm. "That's your husband? Like I said, he's a jerk. Leave him and marry me."

She pried her arm loose from his grip. "Leave me alone, David." If she had any doubts about walking away from him, they had just been confirmed. She ran after her husband. "Barry, wait."

He paused and turned around.

She stopped in front of him. "Please, I'm ready to hear what you came to say."

Karen and Barry walked into the orchard behind the bed and breakfast. The setting bringing peace into the moment. She led the way to the swing and sat down. Barry sat opposite of her on the stump of a log. He leaned forward with his elbows on his knees and looked at her. "I'm sorry. I've made horrible choices, and I've hurt you. There is no way I can take back what I did..." He choked up.

She waited.

"I can't stand that I hurt you. I'm ashamed every time I remember hitting you." He looked away and wiped his eyes with his sleeves. "I've hurt you in ways no one can see, and I hope and pray by God's grace, you can find it in your heart to forgive me someday."

Karen never heard Barry talk about God this way or saw him cry before. His apology seemed sincere. Tears welled up, but she blinked them back. Until she heard the rest, she was going to keep the tears to herself. "Go on."

"I need to tell you about some things I did. I don't want any secrets to come back and bite us later. I'm not proud of any of it. If it were possible to spare you knowing, I would."

Karen scrunched back in the corner of the swing and closed her eyes. *I don't like the sound of this. God, help me hear him out.* "I'm listening."

"If you choose to forgive me, it has to be everything." Barry got back up and paced between the trees. "After you left, I went to Dennis."

"No." Karen sat up straight.

Barry nodded. "He asked me to take out one of his clients' daughters, the woman I'm sure Megan told you about." He raised his eyebrows. "She was actually an undercover cop. Running into Robert and Megan tipped her off that I didn't actually work for Dennis and saved me going down for him." He shook his head. "It was a stupid idea."

"Tell me the rest."

Barry scratched the back of his head. "Lots of drinking and lots of pornography."

Karen winced. She knew that part, but to hear the admission of guilt come out of his mouth was both hurtful and a relief that he took responsibility for his choices. "And…"

Barry walked away from her and stopped next to the gnarled branches of a nearby tree. "There was a woman."

"What?" Karen leaned forward. She clenched and unclenched her fists. She wanted to run.

Stay.

She shook her head. *Not an affair. Please.* "How can you…"

Listen.

She closed her mouth and leaned back in the swing. "Go on."

Barry came back and sat down across from her. She crossed her legs and looked away.

"We didn't sleep together. But only by the grace of God. I went looking for a way to pay you back when that guy picked up your phone. I thought you and him…that…" His shoulders slumped and he held his face in his hands. "It didn't make it right."

She held herself stiff, refusing to allow him to penetrate her defense. She had made her share of mistakes, but his loomed so big right now. He spent the next hour talking about his choices and mistakes while she was gone. She willed herself to listen without comment. "Is there more?"

"No." He shook his head. "Only the debt, but it's been paid off."
"How?"
"My parents. God did a miracle in me, Karen." Barry grinned.
Karen narrowed her eyes. *Is he for real, God?*
Trust me.
"I hated Robert at first, but he dogged me at every step, determined to see me find God. When my anger sent him to the hospital and I ended up in jail, I took a good hard look at myself and I didn't like what I saw. I realized I was trying to prove myself good enough. To you. To me. To my parents. None of it worked. After reading a Bible another detainee gave me, I understood only God can make me good enough."
"Words are easy, Barry. How can I believe you're for real?"
He sighed. "I deserve that." He leaned forward in his seat. "I threw all the magazines away. I threw out the alcohol and disconnected the Internet. I gave my life to Jesus and was baptized. I've started AA and plan to get counseling for my anger, the gambling, all of it. I'll be meeting with Robert for Bible study and to be accountable about the pornography. I know I have a sexual addiction, and I hate it. Karen, I'll do whatever it takes to make it right between us."
"I don't know if I want us to be us again."
"I hope someday you will. I'll wait as long as it takes." Barry's shoulders slumped. He closed his eyes and mumbled under his breath, then smiled and his posture straightened.
She nibbled on her lip. Was he praying? "Anything else you want to tell me?"
Barry took a deep breath. "I went to see my family. I hadn't seen them in twenty years and they forgave me for everything. I'll tell you about that part of the story another time." He stood up and leaned against a tree. "When I found your letter, I wanted to find you right away — to ask for your forgiveness. That's the short version of a long story."
Karen stared at her husband.
"I know it will take time for you to trust me, but with God as my strength, I will never betray that trust again. He knelt next her. "I'm not perfect, and I expect I'll disappoint you from time to time. Pornogra-

phy is a strong addiction, but I promise to fight the temptations and get the help I need. I love you more than ever and I promise, I will give God full access to my life. I will never, ever raise my hand against you again. Please forgive me."

Karen blinked back tears. She needed to make a choice. To be right with God, she needed to forgive Barry. And hope the trust followed.

Trust Me.

She got up from her swing and wrapped her arms around her waist, willing her body to stop trembling. She blew out a long breath and closed her eyes. *God how am I supposed to do this? I know you want me to forgive him, but it hurts.* Tears streamed down her face. She opened her eyes. "I know…" She choked on her words. "I…" She closed her eyes, but all she saw were images of the choices Barry shared with her. *God, I can't do this yet.* "I can't. I have to go."

She stumbled out of the orchard and around the house to her car. Barry followed. She leaned against the car and covered her face, then slid to the ground and cried. Barry sat down beside her. She stole a glance at him.

Tears ran down his face. "I'm so sorry, Karen."

"I need to think." She pushed up from the ground, unlocked her car door, and got in. She looked up at the man who used to hold her heart and she felt bile rise in her throat. She gunned the engine and backed out of her parking space. *God, I don't know if I can get past what he's done.*

Karen glanced in the rearview mirror. Barry stood rooted to the same spot in the parking lot, shoulders slumped, watching her. *How could you do those things, Barry?* She wiped her tears with the back of her hand, then pulled out onto the highway.

The road twisted through the countryside. A deer bounded in front of her car and she swerved to miss it. Her breath shuddered through her and she pulled off onto the shoulder. Leaning her head back against the headrest, she folded her arms tight against herself. "How am I supposed to do this, God?"

Forgiving her dad for something so far in the past seemed easy compared to this. "It hurts." She pressed the back of a fist to her mouth and took a deep breath. Megan and Robert made it through. Could she and Barry? Did she want to?

Forgive.

"But…" the sound of a siren whizzed by her car. She glanced out the window and caught her reflection in the side mirror.

You have been forgiven.

"David." Her hand flew to her lips. She wasn't innocent and she blamed her choices on the pain Barry and her dad inflicted on her. She groaned. *I will forgive him, but how do I trust again? How do I know he won't go out there and do it again?*

She picked up her phone and called Megan. When there was no answer she dropped the phone in the seat beside her. "What now?" She pulled back onto the road, turning back toward Westfall.

Driving through town, she passed the inn and David's parents' place. She slowed when her parents' orchard came into view. Pulling into the drive, she followed it up to the house. Her dad was waiting on the porch when she stepped out of the car. "Can we talk?"

He poured her a cup of coffee and they sat down at the table together. He cleared his throat. "You've been crying."

Karen nodded and took a sip of the coffee.

"Your husband?"

Karen's eyes widened. "How did you know?"

He leaned forward and took one of her hands in his own. "I know the pain of betrayal, too."

Karen tensed. *You were the betrayer, too.*

You forgave him.

Karen bit her lip. "How did you trust mom again?"

"First, I forgave her. That made room for trust. Then the rest came one day at a time. But I finally had to simply choose to stop being suspicious of her."

Karen snorted and shook her head. "Does it always come down to choice?"

Her dad chuckled. "Pretty much. But once you make that choice, God steps in and does the part we can't do on our own."

"Like when I forgave you?"

He nodded.

She looked down and placed a hand on her gently rounded belly. Did she want a future with Barry? Even if they didn't reconcile, she wanted their child to grow up with love, not bitterness. She needed to forgive even if the trust never came.

She had quite a bit to think about. "Thanks, Dad."

40

Karen tried on seven outfits before she decided on jeans and a royal blue button-down shirt. She planned to follow through on her decision to forgive Barry, and after thinking and praying about her marriage for a week, she came to a place of peace about trusting him. She knew it would take time to rebuild the trust, but she was open to the possibility. For now, trusting God with their relationship was the first step. Their future was in His hands. She smiled. *Maybe we can make it after all.*

Pausing in front of the mirror, she pressed her shirt against her abdomen and looked at her rounded belly. Tonight she was going to tell him he was going to be a daddy. Karen hummed as she chose earrings to compliment her outfit. She heard the door open. *He's here.* Warmth rose from her feet to her chest and she caught her breath.

"Be right out. Make yourself at home." She took one last look in the mirror, then opened her door. "Barry?" She stepped out into the kitchen and froze in her steps. "Blake!"

"I hid my car. No nosy neighbor will see it and come to your rescue this time." He swaggered right up to her.

Karen smelled liquor on his breath. There would be no pretense of talk this time. *God, help me.* She backed up against the wall. "You'll regret it, if you hurt me."

"I don't think I will. I need to teach you to mind your own business, and then I'll be out of here." He pulled his hand back and slapped her, knocking her head against the cupboard. She raised her arm to shield her face from another blow.

"Please. Stop." The punch to her stomach knocked her breath out. She folded her arms over her midsection, fearing for her baby. "Oh, God, save my baby."

"Now ain't that sweet." Blake slapped her again. She fell to the floor.

He aimed his foot at her. She tried to crawl away, cringing, waiting for a blow that never came. She looked back over her shoulder in time to see Barry attack Blake from behind. Keeping one eye on the men, she yanked her purse off the counter, pulled out her cell phone and dialed 911. They promised to send someone out and told her to stay on the line. She peeked around the counter and watched the fight.

"God, protect us. Let the police get here in time." She sobbed in fear. She laid the phone down, careful not to hang up and crept over to the table. Maybe she could grab a chair and hit Blake with it. Blake knocked Barry down, then looked over and saw her. He moved toward her, but Barry got back up and grabbed him around the neck from behind.

"Karen, get out of here," Barry struggled to hold Blake.

She edged around to the door, but Blake threw Barry off and grabbed her around the waist. "You're not going anywhere."

Barry punched Blake in the back, the force of Blake's reaction pushing her down against the wall. She looked up to see Blake pummeling Barry in the face. When he fell, Blake kicked him over and over. "Blake, stop it. You'll kill him. Is that what you want?"

Barry's stillness seemed to register in Blake's head, and he stood with his hands to his side. His body shook. Karen rushed to Barry's side. Blake backed toward the door, then ran, leaving her with the quietness of Barry's shallow breathing. "Oh, dear God, save Barry. Keep him alive and give us another chance." She grabbed her phone off the counter. "We need that ambulance, now!"

"It's on the way, ma'am. Stay on the line."

She prayed over Barry until she heard the sound of sirens and feet stomping up the stairs.

WHERE HOPE STARTS

The ICU nurse put her hand on Karen's shoulder. "You need to leave for a little while so the doctor can check your husband over."

Gathering her purse, she stepped into the hallway just outside Barry's cubicle and leaned against the wall to wait. Twenty-four hours had passed since the paramedics brought him to the hospital. The first several hours were spent in surgery while doctors worked to relieve the pressure on his brain.

If Barry hadn't arrived at her apartment when he did, she would probably be in there right now. She ran a hand over her stomach. An ER doctor examined her and did a sonogram. So far the baby was okay. She pulled out the picture they gave her and stared at it. She squeezed her eyes against the tears, but they came anyway. She slid to the floor and buried her head in her arms.

"Hey, could you use a friend?"

Karen looked up. "Megan!" Karen got up and gave her friend a hug. "When did you get in?"

"Just now. How are you holding up?"

Karen pulled out a tissue and blew her nose. "As best I can."

"Come on. There's someone here you need to meet."

Karen followed Megan to the waiting room. The older woman standing next to Albert looked vaguely familiar. The man next to her turned as Karen entered and she caught her breath. He looked just like Barry, only older.

"You must be Karen." The older woman reached out her hands to Karen. "I'm Belinda, Barry's mom. This is George, his dad. I sure wish we were meeting under different circumstances."

"I'm so glad you're here." Karen melted into her mother-in-law's arms. She imagined having had these arms to comfort her all those years she missed her own mother. She wept into the woman's shoulder.

"I know this is a lot to bear. But God will hear us. How's he doing?"

"About the same. The doctor's in with him right now. They said when you got here you could see him."

"Good, but it may be a while before the doctor is through. Albert told us you haven't eaten all day. No, don't argue. You need to be strong for Barry, so you need to eat. For the baby, too."

Karen offered a weak smile. She felt Belinda's strength lift her up. "How did you know?"

"Megan let it slip on the way from the airport." Belinda chuckled and hugged Karen. "Our first grandchild. Do you mind that we know?"

"Of course not."

"I better get a hug, too." Barry's dad wrapped his arms around Karen. "It's good to finally meet you. Don't look at me so funny, we knew about you long before Barry ever told us himself."

This big man's laugh warmed Karen. "How?"

"Why don't we go down to the cafeteria and we'll tell you the whole story. Albert can let us know if there are any changes. You need a break."

Karen turned to her friend. "You coming, Megan?"

"I think you need some time with Barry's folks. I'll be fine here."

"You actually forgave the boy who killed your son?"

"It was the only way out of the bitterness." George patted Karen's hand.

"I know all about that."

"God's answered our prayers in both of your lives." Belinda put her arm around Karen.

"We didn't have a chance with everyone praying for us." Karen offered a tired smile. "Let's check on Barry. Are you ready?"

"Right behind you."

They got off the elevator near the ICU. A gurney rushed past them, an oxygen mask covering Barry's face. George held Karen up as her knees buckled. "Barry." She gained her equilibrium and went in search of the ICU nurse. George and Belinda were close behind her.

The nurse was in Barry's cubicle. "What happened?" Karen put her hand on Barry's pillow. "I saw them rush out of here with my husband."

"There's more swelling. The surgeon is relieving the pressure. We'll let you know when he's out of surgery."

When they got back to the waiting room her dad folded her up in his arms. "My dear sweet Karen. You've been through so much." He kissed the top of her head. "I'm praying for him."

"Thank you. Barry's parents are here." After quick introductions, they joined together in prayer while they waited.

"There you are."

Karen looked up at the sound of Joanna's slurred speech and accepted a hug from her sister.

"So, your husband decided to show up?"

Karen winced at her sister's boisterous voice. "Joanna, this is Belinda and George, Barry's parents."

"Barry? Who's Barry?"

"My husband."

"Oh. That's who you're in here to see. What happened?"

"He's in surgery."

"Why?"

"Joanna, why do you have to make a scene? Get some help." Karen turned away from her sister.

"I don't need any help."

"Come on, Joanna. Let me take you home." Karen's dad put his arm around his older daughter and led her out of the room.

Megan got up and hugged Karen. "You okay?"

Karen nodded and brought her tears under control.

Karen squeezed Barry's hand. He made it through surgery and now they waited to see if the fluid would build back up or not. His parent's came in and prayed over him then left to give her privacy. She sat down on the chair and laid her head next to him. "God, I love this man. I don't know how or why, but I do. Please let him live and give us another chance." Sobs shook her body.

Later, the doctor found her in the same position. "Mrs. Marino..."

She stood up. "How is he?"

"He's in a coma."

Karen swallowed. The thought of never being able to talk to Barry again… She took a deep breath. "When will he wake up?"

"He is stable. His brain doesn't appear to be retaining fluid anymore. Other than that, there's no way to know when, or if, he'll wake up. Or if there will be any brain damage. If he remains stable for another day, we'll move him out of ICU."

After the doctor left, Karen went to the bathroom to splash water on her face before facing family with the news. Nausea rose up in her stomach. She gripped the bathroom counter and took several deep calming breaths. She rushed into a stall and emptied her stomach, then went back to the sink, rinsed her mouth out and splashed her face again.

She glanced in the mirror and grimaced. She touched the bruises on the side of her face, then turned away. *It's all Blake's fault.* Karen dropped to the floor as tears washed over her. "God help me. I can't do this."

An arm went around her shoulders. "Come on. We'll help you."

Karen looked up at Elinor and nodded. She would deal with her anger at Blake later. She needed all her energy for Barry. She leaned her head against her sister's shoulder on the way back to the waiting room. Barry's parents, Megan, Albert and his wife, along with Elinor gathered around her. She felt at peace as they each lifted her up in prayer.

She relayed the doctor's report and they all encouraged her to go home and rest.

Belinda rubbed Karen's back. "Margie stopped by earlier and insisted Megan, George and I stay with her. She also has a nice comfy bed for you when you're ready for a break. Let us take you back to her place."

"I'll stay here. I'll call you if there's any change." Elinor gave her a hug.

Karen sighed. God took care of Barry when she left him in The City. She could trust Him now.

41

Karen waited in the lobby of the bed and breakfast. This place would be home before too long. She hoped she and Barry had a shot at running it together. The bank had approved the loan and she had set up an appointment to sign the papers. With or without Barry, this was her future.

James walked up and took both of Karen's hands in his. "How is that husband of yours? I'm praying for him."

"Thank you. The doctor's don't know much. It's only been a couple of days, but at least he's stable and out of ICU now. I'm thankful for that."

"Yes. Let me show you to Barry's room. I am so sorry to ask you to pick up his belongings."

"I understand the need to rent the room out." She chuckled. "I don't own the place yet."

"I look forward to working for you." He joined in her laughter.

"Can I ask you a question?"

"Of course. I am an open book for Elinor's family."

"When are you going to marry her?"

James blushed. "Whenever she will have me."

"It's my turn to pray for you."

He chuckled. "Ah... here we are." He unlocked and opened the door. "If you need assistance, please let me know." He handed her the key.

"I will."

Karen closed the door behind her and breathed in the faint scent of Barry that lingered. Her heart ached for him. "God, heal him." She pulled out his suitcase and gathered his clothes from the dresser and toiletries from the bathroom, then took them to the car.

Her next stop was the state park. Grabbing her water bottle and a snack bar from her purse, she headed down the trail. About halfway around, she found a bench and sat down. She was winded and enjoyed the cool breeze across her face.

The first night at Margie's she slept twelve hours straight, then she ate an unladylike amount of food. Talking it over with Barry's parents, they decided it would be best if they all got plenty of rest each night. The hospital would call if there were any changes. During the day, they would take turns sitting with him. The best they could do was pray.

She finished her snack and bent down to tighten the laces on her tennis shoes when she heard someone call out her name.

Karen glanced up and saw Margie moving down the path toward her. "Hi. Enjoying your walk?"

"Oh yes. These paths are much easier for my old bones than hiking around our place. Remember when Sam took you hiking?"

Karen smiled and joined Margie on the path. "I always enjoyed my times with you."

"How's Barry?"

"Stable."

"I'm so glad to hear that. I'm sorry I haven't been much of a host. They've scheduled me for a lot of hours at the hospital. Are you and Barry's parents okay at the house?"

"It's been great. We're getting to know each other." She laughed under her breath. "I'm hearing all kinds of stories about Barry growing up." Karen grinned then took a swig from her water bottle.

"How are things in the forgiveness department?"

"I forgave Dad. I chose to forgive Barry, but didn't get a chance to tell him. Trust is another matter. But my love for him is growing." Karen blushed. "Blake is another story." She wished she could forgive once and have it done, but life didn't work that way.

"The trust comes with time, but forgiveness is worth the effort."

"Sounds like you speak from experience."

Margie nodded. "A lot of hurts in my life I haven't told you about." She paused and looked at Karen. "I gave my husband a second chance, and I've never been sorry."

Karen raised her eyebrows.

"Let's sit down and I'll tell you about it." They found a bench under a shade tree and Margie continued her story. "When Sam and I were young." Margie laughed. "Younger. We had our share of struggles."

She looked away as tears welled up in her eyes. "We were naïve. Didn't know how to guard our hearts. We tried to help some friends who were having trouble in their marriage. It brought troubles of our own. Sam had an affair. He hated himself for it."

Karen held her breath. Was God answering her questions?

"We got through it and were stronger for it. We found our way back to God. But his actions carried lasting consequences. The woman had a child."

Karen touched Margie's arm. "Sam was my father, wasn't he?"

"You know?" Margie looked at Karen.

"I didn't know who until just now."

"Your mom will be glad you finally know."

"That's why you welcomed me into your life." Her biological father had been there the whole time.

"I would have loved you regardless, you were so sweet. But you were Sam's girl." Margie smiled. "Of course, I had thirteen years to get used to the idea before you showed up at our doorstep needing our love and support. We hated what happened at your house, but Sam loved every minute you spent with us."

"And after what Mom did, you still sit with her at the hospital?"

"Forgiveness allows for a lot of love."

Karen thought about the new love she had for her dad and her husband once she obeyed God and forgave them. Would trusting Barry work the same way? Would God enable her to trust him to remain faithful? To trust that hitting would not be a part of their life together?

It was impossible on her own. But she had made the choice to forgive. And when Barry woke up from his coma, she would tell him. Then see what God did from there.

Karen rode the hospital elevator up to see her mom. She hadn't stopped by since Barry arrived with the missing letter. She rubbed her temples. The past week of constant vigilance blurred in her mind. Other than sleep and food, sitting with him had been her focus.

After the doctor's report yesterday, Belinda encouraged her to keep a realistic perspective, live her life and make plans for the future, so Karen had taken Megan on the tour of the bed and breakfast and orchards. She loved it.

What I would give to have her living nearby. She swiped a tear from her face. Taking a deep breath, she stepped off the elevator. She didn't want to face the uncertainty of her future alone.

Put your hope in Me.

Megan nodded. She didn't know if Barry would ever wake up, but she would cling to that hope.

Entering her mom's room, she sat in the chair closest to the bed. "A lot has happened these last few days, Mom. I forgave Dad. The missing letter showed up and I know he's not my biological father. I forgive Sam and you too." She felt a slight squeeze from her mother's hand and looked up at her face. Did her eyelids flutter? "Mom?"

She pulled out her phone and called Albert. "Are you coming this morning?"

"I'm on my way right now."

"Come straight to mom's room, okay?"

"Sure. What's up?"

"She moved a finger."

"I'll be there soon."

"Call the others." She stuck her phone back in her pocket. "Mom, it doesn't matter who my biological father is. Dad and I will be okay." Her mother's hand moved again. "I'm married now....to Barry. We've had some problems, but God is changing us." Karen smiled. "Yep, I've come back to God." Fingers moved against fingers. "Mom, you're going to be a grandma." She turned when she heard a sniffle at the door.

Karen's dad watched her.

"Come here, Dad." Karen put her dad's hand into her mom's. "She moved her hand. Talk to her."

God, let Mom wake up. We need to say goodbye. She stood by the head of the bed and watched her dad. Tears spilled down his cheeks. She stroked her mom's face. "Blake isn't here. He's…well, you know Blake. Alita will be here soon and Barry's upstairs in his own room. I know he would have liked meeting you."

"Everyone's on the way." Albert walked in with Haley and the twins.

"Mom, Albert's here." Karen moved aside for her brother.

He nodded at her and took his mom's hand. "Mom, I love you. I miss you." He choked back sobs and moved aside for Haley.

"Mom, the kids and I are here."

"Hi, Grandma." Charlie crowded in next to Haley. "Say hi to Jesus for me."

Karen swallowed the knot in her throat and bit her lip.

Anna squeezed in next to her brother. "Give Him a hug for me."

Charlie elbowed his sister. "Me too."

Albert motioned for them to make room for Alita.

She put an arm around Haley and leaned against her. "I love you, Mom. I'm sorry Blake's not here." She leaned over and kissed her mother-in-law.

Leaving James in the doorway, Elinor stepped closer to the bed. "Mom? Are you really awake?" Elinor's eyes widened and she looked up. "I felt her hand move! Mom, I love you so much. I wish…I wish…oh, I can't do this." She placed a brief kiss on her cheek and went to stand with James. He placed an arm around her and she leaned into him.

Albert stepped back up next to the bed. "Joanna isn't here yet. I called her, she should show up soon."

Karen joined him. "I'm sorry for waiting so long to come home." She kissed her mom on the cheek and pulled back when her mom's grip tightened on her hand. The barest sound interrupted the quiet.

"What?" Karen said, leaning closer.

A faint whisper left her mother's lips. "I love you."

Karen cried. "I love you, too, Mom."

Everyone crowded closer to the bed. "Charles?"

"I'm right here, sweetheart." He took her hand and brought it up to his lips.

"I love…you. All…of you." Her breathing stopped.

Their mom was gone. Her children said their last good-byes and slipped out of the room. Their father stayed behind to be with his wife a few more minutes.

While her siblings milled around outside her mom's room, Karen slipped off to the elevator. She wanted to see Barry. Even if he wasn't awake, she needed to share with him what just happened in her mom's room. She glanced back towards her mother's room. Albert and Haley were headed her way. She held the door for them and they went up together.

42

Two doctors talked outside Barry's room. *Two doctors?* She recognized the one, but the second, a woman, was new. *Maybe they called in a specialist.* From the elevator she could hear only part of their conversation. Something about the brain.

The new doctor turned to a passing nurse. "Get in touch with Mrs. Marino. She needs to be here."

Karen began to run. *God, please, he has to be okay.*

The new doctor left and the other one entered Barry's room.

She rushed in after him, then hesitated. Belinda and George stood to the side holding hands, staring at the bed. Blocking her view, two nurses worked around Barry. Machines chirped and beeped. The doctor typed something into his laptop then pulled out his stethoscope. Karen felt nauseous and light-headed. She placed a hand over her stomach.

Her mother-in-law slipped an arm around her. "Oh, sweetie."

Karen shook her head. She finally forgave and was ready to give her marriage another chance, her future looking hopeful. And now...

She covered her mouth and fled the room. *I can't lose Barry.*

Belinda followed her. "Karen."

She turned as the edge of her vision went black. She felt herself falling and hands catching her.

"Karen, Barry's okay." The voice reached inside and pulled her out of the darkness. She looked up and saw Albert's face.

"Barry?"

"He's okay." Albert touched her cheek.

"I have to see him." She sat up, tears streaming down her face.

Belinda put a hand on her shoulder. "Don't get up too fast, sweetie. You'll black out again."

Haley knelt next to her and offered a bottle of water. Karen sipped it, then stood with Albert's help. She waved her brother aside and walked to Barry's door. Taking a deep breath she stepped inside. The nurses smiled and left the room. The doctor stood next to the bed.

"Is he…?"

"He's coming out of the coma." The doctor grinned. "He woke up for a bit, but was very confused and didn't remember what happened or who he was. Don't be surprised if it takes a while for him to get his bearings, that's normal when someone wakes up from a coma. He might not even know who you are at first."

Karen placed a hand on Barry's forehead. She should have been here, but her mom needed her this morning.

"He's not out of the woods yet. We won't know if there is any permanent brain damage until we can run some tests, but his vitals are good." The doctor grabbed his laptop. "Be patient. There's no way to tell how long this will take. I'll be back first thing in the morning."

"Thank you." Karen took her husband's hand. "Barry, come back to me." His hand twitched. "I forgive you. Oh God, bring him back." Her tears fell freely as she pulled up a chair and rested her head on the bed.

Megan and her family stopped by throughout the evening. They wanted to stay at the hospital and wait with her, but she urged them to go home. She would call if anything changed.

Several times through the night, Barry stirred. Once he opened his eyes and gazed at her. Wrinkling his brow, he looked around the room.

"Barry?" She leaned in. The dim lights cast shadows across his face.

He pulled his hand out of hers. Touching the IV tubing in his hand, he looked back at her. "Who are you?" He closed his eyes and turned his head away from her. "I need…what…" He sounded out of breath.

Karen hit the call button, then placed a hand on his to still his frantic flailing. "Shh. It's going to be okay. I'm right here, and I won't leave you."

His movements calmed and he turned toward her. "Why?"

"I'm your wife."

"Wife?" Confusion clouded his face. "I don't know..." He sighed. "I just don't...know." Moisture gathered in his eyes and he turned away.

She rubbed his shoulder as a nurse came in. "Shh...I'm right here." Quiet breathing indicated he had fallen back asleep. The nurse checked his vitals while Karen described what happened.

"You're doing a great job with him, Mrs. Marino. This is all normal." She smiled. "Be patient. He'll come out of it." She started to leave, then stopped. "We're all praying for him at the nurse's station. There's lots of tweets flying around about him under the hashtag PrayingForBarry."

Karen pulled out her phone and signed into her account. There they were — a long list of them. Many of them were retweets from James Abbott. She clicked on his profile and smiled. He would make a great addition to the family someday, if Elinor ever gave him a chance.

Updates from Megan and Barry's family were littered throughout the conversation. She added her own. "Thanks for your prayers. He's waking up. Keep #PrayingForBarry!"

She set her phone on the night stand, rested her head next to his, one hand on his chest, and dozed off.

A hand touched her head and she jumped. Barry watched her with a grin on his face.

"Oh, Barry." She hugged him.

He touched her face. "I love you, Karen Marino. How long have I been here?"

"You've been in a coma about a week. Do you remember anything?"

"The last thing I remember is the fear in your eyes and knowing I couldn't protect you." Tears streaked his face. "Who was that guy?"

"My brother." Karen sat on the edge of the bed.

"Your brother?" Barry's eyes widened.

"Welcome to my family. They have an APB out on him right now, but I'll fill you in on that later."

"We didn't get to have our talk."

Karen took a deep breath. "Right now, all I can think to tell you is that I forgive you. We can talk about the rest later."

"I've been asleep for a week. I want to talk now."

"If you're up to it." Karen smiled.

"Talking to you? I'm up to it anytime." He took her hands. "I didn't know if you could ever forgive me."

"To be honest, I didn't either." She squeezed his hand and smiled.

"I want another shot to make our marriage work. I'm liable to mess up, but I'm ready to work on it. And I promise to find a job, no matter what it is. I will never lift a hand against you. And I don't want to ever look at that trash again." Barry reached up and touched her face. "You are enough for me."

Karen started to cry.

"Don't cry." Barry wiped her tears. "It's going to be okay."

"But I need to ask you to forgive me. That guy on the phone…"

Barry drew in a breath. "Go on."

"He was my high school sweetheart. There were days I wanted to walk away from you and pick up where he and I left off." Karen nibbled on her lip.

"I'm listening."

"I let him kiss me. I realize it could have led to regrets. Can you forgive me?"

"Of course." Barry cupped her face in his hands. "You've forgiven me so much."

"I couldn't get you out of my mind." She smiled. "I guess you're stuck with me."

"So does that mean we can try again?"

"I know it will be hard work — for both of us. And trust won't come overnight. But I want to give this another try. There's something you need to see first, though."

Barry tilted his head. "What's that?"

"I was going to tell you the night Blake barged in." She reached into her purse and held the sonogram picture out to him.

"What's this?" Barry examined the picture.

"Well, this is the head. You can see the little heart right here."

He looked at her and his eyes widened. "This is…"

"…our baby."

He grinned. "I'm really going to be a daddy?

Karen nodded.

"I can't believe I'm going to be a dad."

"Believe it."

"There's a lot we need to talk about." He grinned and squeezed her hand. "But there's something I want to be sure you know up front."

"What?" She tensed.

"I want to leave our kids a different legacy than our parents left us."

She caught her breath and covered her mouth with her hand. "That sounds… perfect." She scooted her chair closer. "There's just one thing."

"What's that?"

"Let's not go back to New York."

"Is that all?" Barry laughed.

"What do you think about running a bed and breakfast?"

"A what?"

"That one you're staying in, is for sale. I've already been approved for a loan." Karen offered an apologetic smile. "It's a good investment. They have a steady clientele. What do you think?" Karen held her breath while Barry puzzled over it.

"I like it. Hey, do you know where they put the stuff I had in my pockets when they brought me in?"

"I think in this drawer. Hold on." She pulled out a manila envelope and handed it to him.

He peaked inside and grinned. "Close your eyes."

"What's this?"

"A gift. I planned to give it to you that night. Give me your hand."

She reached out and he slid her ring onto her finger. Her eyes flew open and she stared at her wedding band.

"I brought it with me, hoping you would be willing to wear it again."

"I am." Karen touched his face. "Thank you for coming home to me."

He grinned. "It was a good day to come home, Mrs. Marino."

Discussion Questions

1. Did Karen make the right decision to leave Barry? When, if ever, should someone leave? What should be the goal?

2. Do you think a wife contributes to the atmosphere in the home that either encourages faithfulness, or not? How does she do this?

3. Was it wrong for Karen to go out with David? When is spending time with the opposite sex, other than a spouse, too much/wrong?

4. How does a man's sexual addictions affect his wife?

5. Karen and her siblings all experienced their dad's anger. They each responded differently. Which affects who we are today the most - what happened to us, or how we react to what happened?

6. Is there ever a time when parents should keep secrets from their kids?

7. Did Karen's story help you understand forgiveness differently? How?

8. Discuss the difference between forgiveness and trust. Does one need to come before the other? Can one happen and not the other?

9. What did Karen and Barry each have to surrender in order for there to be healing? What types of things are helpful/necessary to surrender?

10. What role did hope play in restoring Karen and Barry's relationship?

For additional discussion questions visit www.angeladmeyer.com.

MORE GREAT BOOKS FROM CROSSRIVERMEDIA.COM

THIRTY DAYS TO GLORY
Kathy Nickerson

Catherine Benson longs to do one great thing before she dies while Elmer Grigsby hopes to stay drunk until he slips out of the world unnoticed. Against a Christmas backdrop, Catherine searches for purpose while fighting the best intentions of her children. She gains the support of her faithful housekeeper and quirky friends. Elmer isn't supported by anyone, except maybe his cat. When their destinies intersect one Tuesday in December, they both discover it is only *Thirty Days to Glory*.

GENERATIONS
Sharon Garlock Spiegel

When Edward Garlock was sober, he was a kind, generous, hardworking farmer, providing for his wife and growing family. But when he drank, he transformed into a unpredictable bully, capable of absolute cruelty. When he stepped into a revival tent in the early 1900s the Holy Spirit got ahold of him, changing not only his life, but the future of thousands of others through Edward.

THE UNRAVELING OF REVEREND G
RJ Thesman

When Reverend G hears her diagnosis — dementia with the possibility of early-onset Alzheimer's — she struggles with the fear of forgetting those she loves and losing her connection with God. But she soon discovers there's humor to be found in forgetting part of the Lord's Prayer and losing a half-gallon of ice cream. And she finds while the question she wants to ask is, 'Why,' the answer really is, 'Who.'

CONFESSIONS OF A LIP READING MOM
Shanna Groves

As she held her newborn son, Shanna Groves should have reveled in the joys of motherhood. Instead, she was plagued by questions and fear. Something was terribly wrong. The sounds she once took for granted were gone, replaced by silence. Then the buzzing started. In *Confessions of a Lip Reading Mom*, Shanna shares her struggle to find God's grace during her roller coaster ride of unexplained deafness.

CPSIA information can be obtained at www.ICGtesting.com
Printed in the USA
LVOW12s1441311213

367619LV00016B/807/P

9 781936 501151